THE DUDE

Also by Max Brand
in Thorndike Large Print

MAX BRAND

1892-1944

The Dude

Thorndike Press • Thorndike, Maine

A-1

Library of Congress Cataloging in Publication Data:

Brand, Max, 1892-1944.
  The dude.

  1. Large type books. I. Title.
  [PS3511.A87D8 1987]   813'.52   87-18115
  ISBN 0-89621-849-X (lg. print : alk. paper)

Large Print edition available in North America by
arrangement with Dodd, Mead & Company, New York.

Large Print edition available in the British Commonwealth by
arrangement with A. M. Heath & Company, Ltd., London.

Cover design by Abby Trudeau.
Cover illustration by Debbie Pompano.

THE DUDE

CHAPTER 1

When the Naylors arrived at Cumshaw station and dismounted from the train, they were received with a good deal of awe, touched by amusement. The amusement did not spring from the appearance of Mrs. Naylor, nor from that of her son and daughter, for they were dressed in the height of fashion; when men wore padded shoulders, and when the ladies still laced. Mrs. Naylor was armored in heavy whalebone at the dictate of fashion, and her daughter was pinched away to a chest tone, as it were.

But the smiles of Cumshaw were directed toward the form of Mr. Joseph Naylor, who had come to meet his family. He was too important in the community for these smiles to be other than covert, but the youngest eye in the town could not fail to notice that Joseph Naylor was half Sunday and half Monday. That is to say, he was dressed in a good black coat, a bit shiny at the elbows, and now dusty on the shoulders from his drive in from the ranch. His brown, wrinkled neck was tormented by a stiff white collar. He wore a black vest, with a golden watch chain draped across the front of it; and his white cuffs, which hung down over the backs of his hands, had both been smeared by the black stain of the harness, as though he had hitched up the team with his own hands.

Joseph Naylor's splendor stopped at the waist. From that point down he appeared in blue overalls, which work and washing had faded at the knees, and these overalls, in turn, were stuffed into the tops of heavy boots, not the delicate creations which a young cattle man loves, but blunt nosed, heavy cowhide, ignorant forever of attention other than a good greasing at the beginning of the rainy season.

When Joseph Naylor went forward to greet his family, an old black hound, whose lines of body and soul drooped toward the earth, rose and followed; and with the joy of the familiar scents and the familiar voices, all his body was one great waggle of greeting.

"Now, Moses," said his master. "Don't you go spoilin' all those fine clothes. Hello, Sally, doggone my eyes, if you ain't a picture!"

His wife, his son, and his daughter halted as they saw the picture of the head of the family advancing toward them. Then, one after the other, they submitted to his embraces.

He said to his daughter: "Hullo, honey. Do I dare to hug you, Rosie? You're tied up so small in the middle that you look like you might break!"

And to his son: "Alf, you look plumb petered out and pale. It's time you come back onto the ranch."

There was very little answer to these remarks, and the family went to a handsome surrey at the hitching rack.

"You wanta drive, Alf?"

"Not these poor, down-headed skates," said Alfred Naylor, better known as The Angel because of the blueness of his eye and the blondness of his hair.

"Oh, they can jog along right smart," said his father, with a reproachful glance. "Want to set up here with your pa, Rosie?" he went on.

"Perhaps I'd better stay back with mother," said Rosamund.

"I wish," said Mrs. Naylor, "that you'd remember your daughter is grown up! Her name is Rosamund, Joseph!"

The rancher pointed the handle of his whip at the black hound.

"Did I ever tell you the name of the father of Moses, there?"

"I don't suppose you ever did."

"His name was Champeen Ballynock Heatherford Criscross Dunally."

"I don't see what that has to do with the name of your own child, Joseph," said Mrs. Naylor stiffly. Her daughter touched her arm, to make peace.

But Joseph Naylor drawled on: "Only this: they called him Bally, for short, and he sure knowed that name. If you was to stand out and holler for Champeen Ballynock Heatherford Criscross Dunally till you was black in the face, he wouldn't of stirred an ear nor a foot, even if he was just around the corner of the house. But just say 'Bally!' and he clomb right over your shoulders and tried to wash your face for you."

"Joseph," said his wife, "is there the least mite of point to that story?"

"Sure they is," said the rancher. "It goes to show that names is just handles, and they're only worth what they lift."

"I never heard of such an idea in my life!" said Mrs. Naylor.

Her son turned in the front seat with a laugh.

"He had you there, mother," said he.

"Alfred, don't be vulgar," his mother reproved him.

This stopped interregional conversation for the time being, and they drove on through the streets of Cumshaw. Naylor pointed right and left with his whip.

"I got a fifteen hundred dollar offer for that corner lot, Alf. Over yonder, I'm gunna put up a bowlin' alley and poolroom, without no tobacco shop hitched on. That'll keep the boys from takin' on with tobacco too young. Have a chaw?"

Young Alfred looked down to the ragged plug of Star chewing tobacco with disgust.

"Here's a fresh side," said his father, turning the plug and brushing it clean on the knee of his overalls. "Have a chaw, Alf?"

Alfred shuddered.

"I don't chew," he said shortly.

Joseph Naylor fastened his teeth in the solid stuff and gradually worked off a large bite.

"Come to think of it," he mumbled, fitting the chew home in the pouch of his cheek, "you never *did* chew. Never took on with the idea of it, did you?"

"Never!" said his son.

His father did not appear to notice the emphasis, but reaching his foot back under the seat, raked forward an old Winchester.

"Is there still danger on the valley road?" asked Alfred Naylor.

"Danger? I dunno that there is. But sometimes there's rabbits. And I've even seen a deer come streakin' down the slope, not longer ago than last week."

"Did you get it?" asked the boy, with a greater show of interest.

"It was in the evening," said his father. "It was gettin' pretty smoky, and I was below him. I misjudged him pretty bad and he went slidin' away. He turned himself into a grey streak, that deer did! Look at them two houses, Alf. Both new since you seen the town last."

"Are they?" said the boy, with a yawn.

At this his father looked at him in quiet thought, and said no more.

They turned out onto the valley road. Cumshaw was the town, Cumshaw the river, Cumshaw the mountains from which it flowed, but all of this lower stretch where the river left its gorge and flowed through the widening level was known as Naylor Valley.

Naylor had made it what it was. The time had been when the valley was like any other of a thousand sunburned Western hollows, but now a fresh tide of green washed up to the very doors of Cumshaw town. And in the distance, where the walls of the valley drew together at the mouth of the ravine, could be seen the lofty face of the Naylor dam.

For twenty years he had labored, gambled, taken long chances and made them good, kept his family in poverty, lived on nothing himself, until, at last, he had saved enough money to build the Naylor dam. And the dam had changed the face of the valley; made money run out of the soil almost as fast as the river waters poured. Far below Cumshaw, the ranchers and the farmers felt the benefits of the dam. There were no longer wild floods in the spring when the snows melted, and in the summer there could be no bitter droughts. Farmers could build on the very edge of the stream if they chose, and the ranchers knew that their cattle would not die like flies in the periodical dry spells. The result was that all of the lower valley, even where the irrigation ditches did not extend, was booming. Cumshaw had doubled its size, quadrupled its wealth, through Joseph Naylor.

The road went straight up the valley for a distance, then dropped in beside the river and followed the windings of the water.

"Gunna plant trees here in the fall," Naylor said. "Gunna turn this into a mighty pretty drive, in about twenty years, or less, maybe!"

"Are you?" said his weary son.

The rancher looked again at Alfred, who sat slumped forward on the seat, his eyes blankly fixed upon the trees, the alfalfa fields, the cattle which spotted the pastures. And Joseph Naylor sighed.

Now they drove to the left, and away from the water, until, coming to the top of a little hill, Naylor stopped the sweating team and pointed to the left.

"There you are!" he cried.

They saw a naked little shack with sagging roof and bulging walls, a fig tree on one side, a stunted oak on the other.

"The old prison!" cried Mrs. Naylor.

"What did you say, Sally?" asked her husband, turning suddenly in his seat.

"I wish the old house were torn down — I wish it were turned to dust and blown away!" she cried in a real passion. "I hate it! I hate it! It just makes me think of the years and the years!"

Naylor looked blankly at her.

"Oh, but we had happy days there, too!" said Rosmund softly. "I can remember lots and lots of them!"

"Ay, Rosie, can you remember?" said her father. "Can you remember, honey?"

"Rosamund, you talk like a little idiot!" said her mother. "He'll keep the wretched old thing forever, now!"

"Oh, ay," said Naylor. "As long as I got a sight in my eyes and a voice in the roots of my tongue, I'll keep it. They's a rabbit over yonder, Alf!"

14

Young Alfred, his languor forgotten, leaped to his feet and snatched up the rifle, as the jack rabbit scurried across the road and darted beneath the fence.

"Alfred, don't you dare to shoot — you'll frighten the horses — they'll run away!" screamed Mrs. Naylor.

Alfred, unheeding, fired; the rabbit spyhopped high into the air and bounded on.

"High to the right, Alf!" said his father.

The surrey lurched as the startled horses jumped, but Alfred, retaining his feet, with gleaming eye and set teeth fired again. Again the rabbit leaped, but this time it fell and stirred no more.

"If there's going to be any more foolishness," said Mrs. Naylor, "I'm going to get out and walk to the house!"

"Sally," said her husband, "a rabbit in the hand is worth a lot more than ten rabbits on foot, in this neck of the woods, and don't you forget it! Hop out and get the rabbit, Alf."

Alfred shrugged his shoulders.

"I don't want the thing," he said. "What's it to me? We won't be eating rabbit, I hope."

"Hold the reins," said his father without further comment; he passed them to his son and climbing down, squeezed through the fence.

"Look at that man!" said his wife. "If it's not enough to break a woman's heart! It's not enough to slave for twenty years with him, but now that God and our own work have given us a chance to be decent folks, look at him! He looks like something from the Sunday comic section. Oh, Rosamund, suppose that the count had come with us, as he wanted to — *what* would he have thought?"

"Don't!" said Rosamund, and held up one slender, gloved hand in protest against this horrible thought.

Naylor came back carrying the rabbit.

"It's a fat young jack," said he. "He'll make me a supper, if you don't want him, Alf."

"*I* don't want him," said the son. "I detest that meat!"

"I seen the time," said his father, "when you was glad to eat what you could kill; and so was I!"

"If that's not like you, Joseph," said his wife. "If that's not *like* you! Always harking back to the past. Because we were miserable once, do we always have to be miserable?"

Joseph Naylor looked at his wife from the corner of his eye and climbed silently back to the driver's place. He jogged the horses up the road.

CHAPTER 2

They spent the day seeing the place.

If in details Joseph Naylor had rashly made arrangements other than those his wife had prescribed, on the whole he had let her have her way. There was no sign of cattle corral nor haystack near the house; the barn had all the dignity of another dwelling; and all that Mrs. Naylor could find to object to was the smell of fresh paint, which made her dizzy.

"It's the newness, Joseph," she said. "It's the dreadful newness that upsets me!"

"Ma," said Naylor, "seems to me like you can't boil a year into a minute. If you wanted things to look old, what's the matter with the shack we had before?"

She gave him a withering glance and said no more.

It was a depressed quartet that sat down for dinner. Mrs. Naylor, rallying, led the conversation, but finally talked on alone. Then they went into the library.

It was a spacious room with tall, narrow windows filled with leaded panes. The library had a Gothic touch; but the bookshelves were nearly empty. Naylor had tossed old newspapers here and there, and there were a few battered text books, out of the school days of the children. There was a Bible and a one volume Shakespeare. There was a *Pilgrim's Progress*, and a Ridpath, *History of the World.* Young Alfred looked upon these books with exactly the same sudden heartache which he had felt when he faced the old house and dared not enter it.

It was as though the contents of the books were dead, also, Christian and David and Jonathan and Moses, and all the great men of the past, and Lear and Falstaff and even gay Mercutio.

The boy shrugged his shoulders and told himself that he had become a sentimental fool; just then he heard his mother exclaim: "Rosamund, Rosamund, *why* didn't you remind me about the books? What will Lord Ponting think when he sees these empty shelves?"

"Rather have empty bookshelves than empty heads," said Naylor.

"Joseph, do be still," said his wife. "I don't know what to do. I'm half mad. Rosamund, I might wire to a New York bookseller and tell him to send on a library—"

Alfred Tennyson Naylor looked earnestly at his father, and it seemed to him that the tanned face of the old man was the only living thing in the room; the rest were shadows. He himself was without reality, and the true Alfred Naylor was to be found somewhere in the past, a ragged boy, turning the pictures and the pages of Ridpath, with the heat of the lamp close to his face.

"Who might Lord Ponting be?" Naylor asked.

"A friend of ours," said his wife bluntly. "Joseph, you go to the tailor tomorrow."

"Yes, honey," said he. "What for?"

"For clothes!" she shouted, furious. "You're worse than naked!"

He gaped at her and began to pack his pipe in silence.

Mrs. Naylor had insisted upon a fire, but though they opened all of the windows, the room was much too hot for it. The new chimney smoked, as new chimneys will; the heat brought out strongly the odor of paint; and Alfred grew hot and began to sweat as the paint was sweating. His hand, resting on the back of a chair, grew sticky.

"Well, folks," said Joseph Naylor, "it takes you a mighty time to tell me all the news!"

"There's no news," said his wife grumpily. "I've written to you every week, anyway."

The father of the family cleared his throat.

"Ain't you kept something back from me, honey?"

Mrs. Naylor started and looked askance, almost in fear, toward her son. Alfred's face looked hot but he said nothing.

"I don't know what you mean," declared Mrs. Naylor, aggressively. "What's in your mind, Joseph?"

"Why, Sally, ain't it true that every last one of you has been opening up a business in New York?"

"Opening up a business!" said all three in one amazed breath.

Joseph Naylor frowned behind the smoke cloud that steamed up from his lips.

"Well, I kind of thought so," said he.

"What sort of business, if you please?" asked his wife.

"Why," said Joseph Naylor, "I'll tell you how it is. When I seen the cancelled checks come in, I kind of thought that maybe Alf, here, had opened up a gents' furnishin' shop and livery stable."

"Joseph!"

"And Rosie I figgered had gone in for a jewelry place and a clothing store. And I sort

20

of was sure that you was runnin' a small hotel or a big boardin' house, Sally!"

His wife stared, speechless. Her passion actually made her face swell.

"*This* is worth hearing," said she.

"I don't mean no harm, Sally. But I thought maybe."

"You thought! You thought!" gasped his wife. "Boarding house! Great heavens above us! As if we didn't have enough to live down, as it is!"

"Live down? What you gotta live down, Sally? What you done wrong since I last seen you?"

"Ah, well," said Sarah Naylor, "there ain't any use — isn't any use, I mean — talkin' to you, Joseph. You wouldn't understand if I was to say that we'd spent the whole year and a half working hard to do enough right to undo the wrong that's been done right here in Cumshaw Valley."

"Naylor Valley, Sally," said he, gently. "And what wrong has been done here, if you please?"

"You see?" said she. "He won't understand. He doesn't *want* to understand!"

"You tell me, Rosie. What's been done wrong, here? Is it my fault about something?"

"Dear dad, no — of course not!" said the girl.

"It is!" said Sarah Naylor. "You might as well speak out now as ever. This is as good a

21

time as any for opening his eyes, if they *can* be opened!"

"Well, mother," said Joseph Naylor. "Suppose that you start in and try to open my eyes. I'm willin'. I never had to put on glasses yet, but maybe I ain't seen the facts about myself. I never spent much time in front of a mirror, as far as that goes!"

"I *will* tell you," said Sarah Naylor. "Joseph, we grew up here as blind and as stupid as the animals of the field. We grew up here without manners, without social contacts—"

"Which?" said Joseph Naylor.

"Without meeting any worth-while people—"

"Hold on. Ain't the Gregorys worth while? Ain't the Saul Sniths worth while? Ain't Lew Callahan and Montana Carter worth while?"

"You see?" said Mrs. Naylor in despair.

"I'd like to know who's worth while if they ain't!" said Joseph Naylor. "Maybe you've forgot, but I can't forget, the way that we was shut in with snow and misery, that winter when Rosie and Alf was both sick, and how Lew and Montana come down and seen the fix we was in, and pitched in to help. You recollect how Lew marched every day to town? And how Montana worked around like a trained nurse takin' care of the kids and even milkin' the cows?"

Sarah Naylor bit her lip.

"I don't forget anything," she said stiffly. "I expect to reward Callahan and Carter."

"Reward 'em? How?" asked her husband.

"They're old enough to be pensioned, I suppose?"

Her husband allowed a little interval of silence to come between him and his next words.

"Would you give 'em money?" he asked.

"And why not?" asked Sarah Naylor, in a passion again. "I'd like to know how else a person *could* reward a pair of rough, ignorant, uncultivated, uneducated mountain men? How else, Joseph! Pray tell me!"

He puffed once, twice, on his pipe, and then he said gently: "With the blood of your heart, Sally — and with the love of your heart, too!"

CHAPTER 3

Young Alfred stood up, dropped his hands in his coat pockets and spread his legs a little. He was not very tall; his face was pink and white — more white than pink since his stay in the eastern city — and he felt that there was a need for a few postures and attitudes of dignity if he were to be able to hold his head as high as the next man. Perhaps there was timidity and self-consciousness behind his bravado. There generally is in rather overbearing young men.

Now young Alfred said:

"And what was all of this about the gents' furnishing business, father?"

His father replied: "Why, it was just an idea of mine."

"A rather odd idea!" said Alfred, and looked at his mother with a laugh and a shrug of his shoulders.

"What ideas you may have about us, Joseph," said Mrs. Naylor, "I can only vaguely guess, but the fact is that you seem to have been more than twenty-five hundred miles away from us, this past year and a half. What *do* you think that we've been doing with most of our time?"

"Writin', I should say," said he.

"Writing? Writing what?" she snapped.

"Checks," said he.

She stared at him.

"Are you complaining of the amount we've had to spend to live decently — according to our class — in New York?"

"Oh, no, Sally," said he, "I ain't complaining a bit. The fact is that I ain't got an *idea* of complaining. I was just curious. If you put old Moses on a trail, you can't blame him for follerin' it. Can you? When you went away, you said that you was gunna send me back the cancelled checks and the explanation of the items every month."

"I hope that I did so," said she, coldly.

He endured the frost in her eye with squirming difficulty.

"You done so," he agreed. "I got no complaint about that, at all. You done so, perfectly regular."

"And you thought — gentlemen's furnishing — boarding house — great heavens!" said Sarah Naylor.

He drew from his pocket an old envelope,

covered with smudged figurings in pencil.

"Well, listen to this: Here's the items for one year for Alf."

"Very well. If you've been spying on us—"

"I ain't! No, no, Sally! Addin' ain't spyin'. But listen to this: Clothes, four thousand, eight hundred dollars — I leave off the odd. Four thousand eight hundred dollars — why, doggone me, Alf, you must of filled a couple of rooms with that many clothes!"

The voice of Alfred squeaked a little as he laughed.

"You wouldn't understand, of course," said he. "But of course one has to dress the way other people do."

"Does everybody in New York spend five thousand bucks a year on clothes, Alf?" asked his father.

"The child had to have a fur driving coat, of course!" said Mrs. Naylor fiercely. "You can't buy Russian furs for nothing, either. Then there are dinner jackets, morning coats, riding clothes, lounging suits, and a thousand details of scarfs and gloves and shoes to go with everything. *I* think that Alfred has managed it very well, considering that this was the first year, when he had to outfit himself thoroughly. Of course, that's an expense that won't come again every year!"

"Now, gettin' back to the livery stable idea," said the father, "I can pick up good enough hosses to please anybody, round about here, for a hundred or a hundred and fifty a head. And I see that checks for hosses run up around fifteen thousand dollars. That'd be a sizable herd to drive out onto the range, Alf! What you need with so many?"

"A hundred and fifty a head!" said Alfred in despair of ever making his father see. "You know what a thoroughbred is, father?"

"A high-headed blankety-blank," said Mr. Naylor. "That's what I know about a thoroughbred."

"Nobody would have anything — nobody that is anybody in New York. You see how it is, dad? Everybody drives a four-in-hand, at least. Lots of the people have two or three turnouts. Drive them different days, you know. Some of 'em have eights! All clean bred ones! I had only five hacks, and then there were four good ones for riding. You ought to have seen those four, though. I picked the right stuff, dad."

"Good for you, Alf," said his father. "I'll bet you did. Well, so it ain't a livery stable, after all. It's only eight or nine ponies? But, I'll tell you, Alf, you had to pay for some other things, too, along the livery stable line—"

"You mean the turnouts — the saddles,

bridles, blankets, surreys, etcetera?"

"That got up to thirty-two hundred."

"Did I keep it as low as that?" asked Alfred, with a smile of pleasure.

"Sure you kept it that low," said his father.

"I'll tell you how. Young Van Aydler was going to the Near East, and he sold out most of his stuff. I picked up things for almost nothing, at that sale."

"You got the makin's of a business man in you, son," said his father. "Now, turnin' back to this here list, it appears to me like you got through another twenty-eight or thirty thousand dollars that goes down under incidentals!"

Alfred bit his lip.

"That's going to be hard to explain!" said he.

"I shouldn't be surprised if it was," nodded his father easily.

"The fact is, dad, that—"

"Oh, don't try, Alfred," said his mother. "Joseph, you ought to know that every well bred young man plays cards!"

"Does every well bred young man drop thirty thousand a year on that sort of card playin'?" asked Naylor.

"Of course," said his wife, "if you're just deliberately going to be misunderstanding and ridiculous from the beginning—"

"Why, Sally, I don't want to be anything like

that, of course. I was just askin' a few questions. But if Alf dropped thirty thousand at cards — maybe he'd better take a few lessons from old Montana before he goes back East agin!"

"You see," said young Alfred to his mother, in a polite despair, "I knew that he wouldn't understand."

"Ay, but I do," said the father. "A gent that don't pay his gamblin' debts is a hound dawg in any part of the country, east or west."

He turned the envelope to another side.

"It cost Alf fifty-five or sixty thousand dollars to live a year in New York. I'm glad to see that little Rosie didn't spend that much. Didn't hardly cost her more'n fifty thousand. She kept under twenty thousand on clothes, I see!"

"Yes," said his wife, glad of this apparent change of attitude on the part of her husband. "And think of a real sable coat out of that, Joseph."

"Well, well," said Naylor. "Think of that, will you? That makes it pretty near nothin' that she spent on herself."

"Dear Rosamund is such a careful girl," said her mother fondly.

"A couple of jewels — lemme see — they run up to about thirty-two thousand?"

"Of course they're just an investment," said the mother. "In a couple of years, they'll be worth more than she paid for them!"

"Of course they will," said Joseph Naylor. "I ain't doubtin' that. And when I think what it cost the two youngsters to run themselves, you got on for pretty near nothin', Sally, takin' care of a whole house!"

"I did my best," said Mrs. Naylor proudly, but with a slight air of suspicion. "I don't throw the pennies away."

"Only fourteen thousand on clothes," said her husband. "That's a lot less than Rosie, ain't it?"

"I didn't have to have so many things," said Mrs. Naylor. "A woman of my age has to dress with dignity, but not with such variety, you know."

"Oh," said Joseph Naylor, "is that it?"

"Yes, of course."

"Less for jewelry, too. Twenty-four thousand. And the house was plumb cheap at eight thousand, I'd say."

"Yes, that was a bargain. Lord Mountberry had to give up the place for the year. We just moved in and found everything lovely."

"Food and servants and such things didn't come to more than thirty thousand," said Joseph Naylor. "You sure must of cut some of the corners mighty close!"

"Liberality, not prodigality was my motto in

CHAPTER 4

They rode up the valley together – Montana Charlie Carter, Joseph Naylor and his son Alfred. That is to say, they rode forth at the same time and in the same direction, but while the two veterans kept side by side, jogging their well-broken mustangs, Alfred was up on a pony like a wing of fire. It was a wild-caught black mare, much larger than the ordinary run of mustangs, with the beauty and the terror of the wilderness still in her eye. She seemed to know all manners of going, except straight ahead. She reared and walked upon her hind legs. She bucked viciously to the side and passaged in a professional manner; she backed into a clump of trees and then bolted across a meadow.

"And the kid likes it!" said Montana Charlie, as the cheerful laughter of the boy floated back to them.

The father looked after the boy with a melancholy eye of pride.

"Could use that on the range," said he.

"Could," assented Montana.

He was a dreary looking fellow, this Montana. At forty, he looked sixty, and even sixty years would have seemed a short space into which to compact the events of his lifetime. From faded blue eyes he looked forth upon the world; past his mouth drooped sickle-shaped moustaches which were his pride, though they were thickly streaked with grey. He wore a felt hat which was a shapeless rag, and battered leather chaps, though there was no need for those hot and heavy garments in this sort of riding. There was no touch of grace in his outfit, with the exception of the shop-made boots, and the long, spoon-handled spurs which projected at his heels. These were the sole proof that he was a cavalier of the mountain desert; once a knight of the frontier, always a knight! His head was bald, just fringed with sandy hair, and his sun-reddened neck was a mass of sharp-edged wrinkles.

He said to his compeer: "Yep, you could use a kid like that, but the crop that you'd raise out of him would mostly be weeds and cactus, for a spell of time, I reckon."

"How come?" said Joseph Naylor.

"I'll tell you how come, Joe. There's this

thing about it. Them that won't learn have gotta be taught with the whip."

Joe Naylor looked askance at his companion, but he waited patiently, respecting the wisdom of his friend. And the other continued in his grave way: "Look at the mare, there. She don't know nothin'. She don't want to know nothin'. She never will know nothin' except buckin' and pitchin' and hell-raising in general, except that the kid that's ridin' her can win her over. Now, you ask me why he's ridin' her at all?"

"Why shouldn't he ride her?" asked the father, a little irritated and showing it in his voice.

"Why should he?" asked the other, unperturbed. "Is she good and steady and got the makin's of a cuttin' hoss, say? Does she show sense? No more sense'n a column of fire. And so if that there youngster had his wits about him, he'd of picked out a hoss that wouldn't cause him to waste all of that muscle for nothing. He's done a day's work on her, and yet he ain't hardly been able to keep up with us on these old down-headed ponies!"

"Maybe you're right," agreed the father, "but can't you remember the time that you was young, old timer, and picked out a hoss with hell-fire in its eyes, for the sake of the fire, and not for the sake of any sense that it had?"

"Sure," agreed the other. "And that's why I'm twenty year older than my age. And that's why I got no wife, no children, no money in the bank, nothin' by way of a home but the boots I walk in for a floor and the hat on my head for a roof!"

"You gotta home while I got one," said Naylor staunchly.

"And who in hell would use a borrowed house?" asked the frontiersman fiercely. "What's a home but the thing that's yours? I'd rather ride on a borrowed hoss or live on borrowed money, which I ain't never done and I never will!"

The point of this was so apparent to Joe Naylor that he did not argue about it. He merely said: "You aim to say that Alf, yonder, has got a long ways ahead of him?"

"He has."

"He's got the chance of blowin' off a little steam, without the takin' of scalps," suggested Naylor.

"Ay, God help him. He's a rich man's son," said Montana Charlie, "which my heart bleeds for the poor kid, and I'm here to tell you so."

"Why, Montana?"

"The takin' of scalps is a man's game. It's a man's job to take the top off of an Injun; it's a waiter's job to take the top off of a champagne bottle. It's a man's job to tame a wild hoss; it's a fool's job to tame a wild woman. They's many a good man been found inside of silver conchos and golden braided Mexican jackets, wearin' gold spurs and bells, and an altar cloth tied around his belly by way of a scarf. But they ain't no men among the dudes that're fixed up in the big towns. If they start as men, they get weakened with too much play, and too much grub, and nothin' to live for; whereas the meanest and lowest desperado that ever buckled on a brace of Colts has sure earned his livin' while he lasted. How come? Because he's worked for his three squares, or made his Colts work for him. And he's learned to go like a wolf in the lean times with one feed a week. And he's a man, old timer, and you know it as well as I do! But the kids that are the sons of the rich men, they got no chance to blow off steam that way. All they got is booze and fool girls and hoss races and such, to take up their time. What kind of a man is gunna be turned out on that kind of pasturage, I ask you?"

Joseph Naylor was gloomily silent. His son had disappeared into the woods, but now he broke into the open again in arrowy flight, his body slung along the side of the black mare, as in that position he had best avoided the branches of the trees that swept about him. He was hardly half way into his saddle when the black mare soared into the air and landed on forelegs as stiff as iron rods. The shock nearly flung the boy to the ground, but he seemed to cling by a single hand, as a spider clings to its web by a thread, and for half a dozen jumps, he was dangling more in the air than the hook on the line of a fly-fisher.

The next instant, however, he was back in the saddle, and his yell tingled across the open, instantly muffled as the frantic mare dashed into another copse for the purpose of brushing off the persistent weight that clung to her as though with the claws of a cat.

From the distance, breaking through the crowding trees, they faintly heard the warwhoop of the delighted boy in the midst of his battle.

"And that's what you're gunna throw loose into the streets of New York? Every yelp like that'll be free, out in these here hills," said Montana Charlie, "but back yonder it's gunna cost him about five thousand bucks a throw!"

The father sighed.

"I hear you talk, Montana," he said, "and I cotton to pretty nigh everything that you say, I gotta admit! The kid is wild, and maybe the town ain't good for him. But what am I gunna do? How you gunna make a gent a forty-dollar-a-month cowpuncher when he's got five thousand a month comin' in of its own free will? It's like askin' the bull to pay the price of admission to the bull fight, ain't it? It don't sound nacheral, Montana!"

Montana scratched his head.

"Cut him off. Leave him flat broke," he suggested.

"That kind of a piece of meanness," said the father, "would nacherally make him hate me all the rest of his born days. He's got too much spirit in him to stand for a thing like that!"

"Ay," said Montana soberly, "and perhaps that's right, too. It's a bad thing for a young gent to figger that the world owes him more than he's gettin' out of it!"

Said Joseph Naylor: "Look here!"

They were on a low hilltop. Over the heads of the trees they looked up and down the sparkling greenness of the valley floor.

"What you see, Montana?"

"Couple a million feet of timber, and a pile of good grass, down yonder."

"You're wrong, Montana. This here valley don't raise trees nor grass no more."

"Ain't you feelin' a mite dizzy, or funny, or somethin', old son?" inquired Montana.

"If you was to crowd all of the trees in the world into one park, and spill grass over twenty million acres and make it grow wild and strong all the time like an alfalfa field, there wouldn't no harm be done. You can't do harm with trees and grass."

Montana waited almost anxiously, for he saw that a point of importance was coming.

"That was what I wanted to do with this here valley," said the rancher. "I wanted to turn the brown face of it so green that it'd break the heart of the sun to look at it long. I wanted to choke all of the crackin' ground in the valley with water, y'understand? I done it. I raised alfalfa. I fed it into cows. They was more than I could use. I filled corrals, and pitched the hay into 'em. Still there was hundreds and hundreds of tons left over that I had to ship out and sell on the market. That brought me in a fine piece of money on the side, y'understand?"

"I understand," said Montana, knitting his brows in order to follow the drift of his old friend.

"And the cows that I bought thin and sold fat, they brought me a lot of money, too."

"That's nacheral and right."

"And as the valley boomed, Cumshaw town begun to boom, too, and I'd bought up most of the land there, so that Cumshaw's boom was my boom!"

"I've often heard that said."

"And they's other things that I can do. I can

get enough electricity out of that there dam to run factories. I can cover Cumshaw with the face of big plants, all workin' hard, night and day."

"Ay, and likely that you will."

"Now d'you see what I mean, old timer? God give us the ground for the sake of growin' hosses and cows and trees and houses and grain, and such like things that come nacheral out of it, and all of them things is good for the ground and good for me and you, too. But this here is different. What I'm raisin' from this here valley is gold. You can't eat gold, you can't wear it for winter or summer, you can't feed it to cows or hosses or make barns or houses out of it. It ain't nacheral and it ain't right, and the result is that I've poisoned my wife and my two kids, and finally, I'm gunna have enough weight of gold to smash my own heart flat!"

CHAPTER 5

They came out at last by the side of the dam, which arose like the side of an inverted pyramid, the apex wedged into the foot of the gorge, and the base stretched across from the flank of one mountain to the shoulder of another. This ponderous fist of masonry thrust back the water of the Cumshaw until the lower gorge was filled, and the flood pushed on up the two branches of the fork above it.

It was a natural dam-site. Here at the lips of the gorge, mountains of hard rock stood close in on either side; behind it the narrow way widened rapidly until a capacious lake was held in the arms of the upper valleys.

"Hey!" said Montana Charlie. "It makes me dizzy to see all of this here tonnage of water. Suppose that it was to break loose, Joe—!"

"Don't suppose that!" said the other. "It gives me chills to have you suppose that. Know what would happen to the valley, there?"

"I dunno," said Montana Charlie. "What would?"

"Wipe it out as smooth as the flat of your hand."

"Those trees would stop it, Joe. Those pines would sure enough stop anything."

"Them? If they was made of iron, this here water would cut 'em down."

"They ain't enough hardness in water to do that. They ain't edge enough!"

"By the time this here water had traveled a thousand feet down the valley, what you think? You get a few million tons of feathers, even, traveling all together at the rate of a fast train on a down grade, and something has gotta happen when it hits a wall. Am I right?"

"Ay, sure you are," said Montana Charlie. "And if it *did* cut loose — why, it's wipe your house out, maybe!"

"I don't guess so. It'd wash up right around our feet, but I guess that it wouldn't reach to the house, though."

Montana's mind seemed filled with the great idea.

"Look at that dynamite house, you got over yonder, Joe. You ought not to keep it that close. One of these days somebody that's got a grudge agin you will bust the dam loose with your own dynamite. And then where will you be?"

"Where will I be? Nowhere," said the rancher.

"Nowhere at all. I'd be wiped out, that's where I'd be. All the good rich surface ground would be whipped away, and the alfalfa along with it by the roots. And where you see grass and cows now, Montana, doggone me if you'd see anything more than the cheek of rocks, or the toes and the fingers of the mountains stickin' up there where it's all velvet now."

"Is the soil as shaller as all of that?" asked Montana, shaking his head.

"This here coverin' of earth," said the rancher, "ain't no more'n a quilt throwed over the knees and the shins of the mountains. It ain't no more'n that, and it sure would be peeled off by this here water as easy as the skin slips from a ripe peach. It'd turn Naylor Valley into a junk heap in about five minutes!"

He shrugged his shoulders.

"But it ain't gunna," said Montana. "It don't look so very thick, this dam, but I guess that it's built pretty strong."

"You guess right," said the builder. "It's built so doggone strong that all of the dynamite in that there dynamite house wouldn't faze it unless it was touched off at just the right spots. They's places here that are sort of keystones, Montana, and if those right stones was knocked out, the dam it would come down like nothin' at all!"

Montana looked at the slender top of the dam again, and at the vast mass of the water which it restrained.

"Seems to me like it's bowin' out," said he. "Seems to me like those rocks, there, is flattenin' and gettin' thinner, and like that old dam is stretchin' and givin'."

"She ain't, though," said Joe Naylor. "She'll hold. She'll swaller all of the water that'll stack up in this here valley. She'll hold it all, no matter how long it rains!"

He pointed to the dusky atmosphere which covered the heights to the north and west, sweeping down into the valley with intangible skirts of shadow.

But Montana shook his head.

"You never could tell, Joe. They's such a mighty lot of weight in this here water. It ain't like hay. It's always sneakin' and workin' and encroachin' like anything!"

"Ay," cried out Joe Naylor with a sudden jubilance that shattered his usually quiet manner, "ay, and that's why I value it. I'm gunna chain it up and make it work. Sure, I've seen water ragin' and plungin' and batterin' and raisin' hell in general, but I'm gunna tame it down! I'm gunna use its wild hosses for the ploughin' of ground, and the thrashin' of wheat, and the lightin' of houses. I'm gunna run this here water down for irrigation, y'understand, but on the way, I'm gunna shoot it through a flume. Look here, Charlie. Look down there!"

"It fair makes ya dizzy," agreed Charlie. "What about it?"

"Look here!"

Naylor chucked a five-pound stone into the void. Far down the face of the dam it shot. It struck there on the face of a rock and puffed into white; a moment later they heard the report like the sound of a rifle fired in a well, and then the softer echoes climbed to their ears.

"Doggone me if that there rock didn't just explode sort of into dust!" said Charlie in mild comment.

"Shoot water down there in a flume, old son, so's the air won't have a chance to catch at it and hold it back, and I'll tell you what, that water will explode into enough electricity to haul a million freight cars up a ten per cent grade!"

"Electricity!" cried Montana Charlie. "Hey, Joe, where you goin'?"

"I dunno exactly how it's done. But they put in dynamos. I had a real smart young gent out here that looked everything over and he said as how he would eat all the hats in the valley if he couldn't make a water plant here that would make the eyes of everybody open. He said he'd run out a thousand wires, and every wire would deliver an eight hoss team at the end of it!"

"Think of that, Joe. Think of a thousand eight hoss teams snakin' bench ploughs along in the fall of the year!"

"I've thought about it. I've thought all about it. It'll fill up Cumshaw with factories and workin' engines. It'll fill 'em all up, because I'll sell 'em the power cheap. Then they'll have to build houses for themselves and their families. And — I own the good land, all round the town. I own it. They'd have to buy from me!"

"You got a strangle hold on the place, all right," commented Montana Charlie. "You and the dam, they're what have the strangle hold on Cumshaw!"

"Never be loosed," said the owner with a shake of the head, "until the water busts loose and makes those there big rocks in the dam wall bounce and dance along in the flood like bubbles in a wind! Well, partner, you see how it is. I'm just at the beginnin' of things!"

"Where's the kid?" asked Montana Charlie. "He'd oughta be interested in all of this here talk!"

"I been a-watchin' him for a spell," answered the father. "He's talkin' to something a whole pile more interestin' than dams and electricity."

"I don't hardly see how that could be," said Montana.

"Come here."

He drew Montana closer to him. Then, looking down the steep slope of the hill through a gap in the pines, as at the end of a glass, in a narrowed field of vision, he saw the edge of the Cumshaw River as it gathered again in peace at the foot of the dam, and on a stone at the side of the water was a girl with a fishing rod; and beside the stone, up to his knees in the river, stood young Alfred Tennyson Naylor, and behind Alfred was the lovely black mare.

"Look there!" exclaimed Montana Charlie. "Why, he's got that mare standin' without so much as a hand on her rein."

"He has," said the father, musing.

"But what's he standin' there for, up to his knees in the water, I'd like to know?"

"Waitin' to be asked to step out, I suppose."

"What you mean, Joe? Ain't he got sense enough to step out of the wet without bein' asked?"

"I dunno," said Joe Naylor. "Depends on the way that you look at it. Maybe he'll get asked, too."

"You got good eyes," said Montana. "And who might that girl be?"

"That's Molly Loftus."

"Pretty Molly Loftus? How could you tell that, at this distance, partner?"

"By the way of the turnin' of her head, and the raisin' of her hand, I'd say," said the other.

48

"And by the jump of the heart that you get when you look at her!"

Montana nodded without a smile.

"It's a true thing," said he. "They's an electric line laid between the girl and every gent that looks at her. But her, she ain't bothered by them at all."

"Looks like she was gunna be bothered now, a mite," said the boy's father. "Looks like maybe she was invitin' trouble."

For suddenly, at this point, young Alfred Tennyson Naylor stepped from the water onto the rock beside the girl, and the dripping from his boots made a silver etching of brightness under his feet.

"He's settin' down beside her, pretty comfortable," said Montana. "That's a surprisin' thing to me. Most usual, she don't let no young gents near to her."

"They's a trap for every bird that flies in the air," said Joe Naylor.

"Hey!" exclaimed Montana. "Doggone my eyes!"

He rubbed them.

"Did he kiss her then, Joe?"

"He did," said Joe, "or rubbed noses, or something. They was that close!"

"But look at here, Joe. She don't hardly know him!"

"Used to. When she was a kid in the valley, and him a kid, too."

"By God, Joe, you look pretty happy."

"Why wouldn't I be?" cried the father suddenly, rejoicing. "Because if he takes and marries Molly Loftus, won't she knock the foolishness right out of his head? I'd rather have it than two dams like this, and a half dozen of Naylor Valleys!"

CHAPTER 6

At dinner, Montana sat silent and stiff in his chair, hardly tasting the food before him. He excused himself immediately afterward and went up to his room.

"Poor fellow," said Mrs. Naylor. "He doesn't seem at ease, any longer."

Said her husband: "The finest gent in the world, is old Montana!"

"He has sense," she answered instantly. "He knows when he's out of place."

The eye of Joe Naylor grew blank, but he did not answer. Instead, he said to his son: "What about the black mare?"

"Oh, she?" said Alfred indifferently. "She quieted down, after a while."

"She's the best hoss I got," said his father.

"She doesn't stand over enough ground," said the boy, and put the matter beyond further discussion.

They sat in the library again. The smell of

the new paint and varnish was not now so op-
pressive, and the pure spirit of the pines drifted
in through the open windows. An owl hooted
in the woods.

"Joseph," said his wife, "I want to talk to you
about two things."

She held up two fingers.

"I'm listenin', Sally."

"Don't you think that Sarah's a more dignified name?"

"All right — Sarah. If you like that better.
Is that one of the two things?"

"That's only by the way. I want to talk to
you about the marriages of our two children."

"All right," said the father. "But talking
won't get 'em married, will it?"

"They're both engaged at the present moment," she said. "Though the engagements
haven't been announced!"

"Say, Rosie," said the father. "Are you gunna
step out and leave us so soon?"

Rosie looked at her mother, worried, and
Mrs. Naylor answered for her.

"A daughter's a daughter for all her life," she
quoted. "But when I tell you the wonderful
news, you'll hardly believe your ears, Joseph!
Lord Ponting has asked her to marry him!"

"Well, well, well!" said he.

"Is that all you have to say?" asked Mrs. Naylor.

"Well, but what sort of a feller is he?"

At that Alfred broke out: "Why, great Scott! He's *the* Lord Ponting!"

"Oh, is he?"

"He is," said Mrs. Naylor.

"What's his line?" asked Joseph Naylor.

"His line?"

"Sure. What does he work at?"

"Good heaven," said the wife, "what a question! He's a gentleman, of course!"

"Don't gentlemen work?"

"Why, Lord Ponting is one of the oldest families in England, Joseph!"

"That's interesting," answered the rancher.

"And just to think, Joseph, that our grandson will be the next Lord Ponting — and be raised in Ponting Hall! Just to think of that!"

"It sounds fine," said he. "Rosie, come here."

She went to him.

"D'you love this here Ponting?"

Rosie looked away, baffled, and her glance naturally sought her mother.

"You simply don't understand," said Mrs. Naylor, angrily. "In cases like this, of course it isn't simply a silly boy and girl love affair. It's — it's an alliance."

"Oh," said Joseph Naylor. "I thought it was a marriage."

His wife stamped.

"Will you listen to me?"

"As hard as I can, honey."

"When his lordship came to me with his proposal—"

"Did he propose to you, too, Sally? Sarah, I mean to say."

"Joseph! He proposed to me for the hand of Rosamund. I was dreadfully excited, but I pretended not to be. I told him I would need some time to think it over—"

"Did you do all of the thinkin', Sarah?"

"I don't know what you mean?"

"Why, I would of thought that Rosie would of wanted to do some of it for herself!"

"I thank God," said the wife, "that my daughter trusts in her mother's decisions!"

Alfred rose.

"Look here, dad," said he, with decision, "this'll be the match of the season. It'll put us all on our feet!"

"Well, well," said the rancher. "Maybe it will. But I never found a time when I couldn't stand up by myself."

"You see, he refuses to understand," said Mrs. Naylor. "You won't see that we have a chance to step into the very best circles of the oldest society in the world, Joseph!"

"It kind of baffles me," said the rancher. "What does it all mean?"

"Simply a common sense contract. Lord Ponting gives his great name; we give a little money, naturally. What else have we to give?"

"Ain't Rosie something?"

His wife gasped with rage and excitement.

"Yes, she's something! And so is our low past and our new name and our lack of position and everything low and obscure and shadowy that sticks to us! He's taking all of that when he takes Rosie!"

Joseph Naylor closed his eyes for a moment and folded his hands.

"How much does he want?" he asked.

"Oh, he's not one of the money grabbers," said Mrs. Naylor. "It's a love match, on his part, thank Heaven. He's perfectly contented with a hundred thousand pounds."

"Pounds?"

"Yes. That's less than half a million."

"Well — I ain't got it."

"You could raise it, though. You could raise three times that amount, and you know it. If you wanted to put a mortgage on the valley!"

"Half a million? Well — perhaps."

"Joseph, are you just going to sit there? Aren't you going to say a thing? Are you going to make it as hard as possible for your daughter?"

"Ma," said the rancher, "I've never balked

when Rosie wanted anything. I've bought her a new dress when the money was harder to come by than blood. And now that she wants a husband, I suppose that I'll buy her one, even if it costs a half a million—"

"Joseph Naylor!" shouted his wife.

"I don't see what else to call it," said he.

"Very well!" she snapped, as Rosamund retired to a corner in miserable confusion. "You can call it what you please. Only that you agree?"

She did not wait for an answer, but rushed on: "And then there's Alfred. My darling boy has done almost as well. Of course you've heard of the old Huntingdon-Wright family?"

"I never did."

"Well, there's not a finer family in the country. And Lydia Huntingdon-Wright is practically engaged to our boy now!"

"What's the price of her?" asked the rancher.

"Joseph, what are you thinking of?"

"You might as well talk to him in his own way," said Alfred tartly. "We have to help a little with the Huntingdon-Wrights," he explained to his father, "considering what they'll be giving us—"

"What will they be giving us?"

"Practically as much in our own country as Lord Ponting can give us in England!"

"Position, eh?"

"Open every door to us, dad! By Jove, they can't keep out a Huntingdon-Wright!"

"Would they want to keep you out, lad?"

"Why, who am I, dad? Great guns, I'm nobody! Out of the wild West. Nobody ever heard of us. Great deal better that they shouldn't. What? Ranching! That's a great social boost!"

"Boy, ain't you brave, honest, and able to pay your bills? Ain't that enough to get you into the houses of other gents that are men like you? What more d'you want?"

He was met by a triple silence, and at last his wife said slowly: "Joseph, you simply can't understand. You'd better not try! You — you'd actually want to have our only son married to some nameless girl around here like — like—"

"Why not?" said he. "Like Molly, for instance?"

"Molly what?"

"Molly Loftus, of course."

"The daughter of old Hugh Loftus? Joseph, are you really in earnest? The daughter of a worthless old—"

"Leave old Hugh be," said the father. "I've knowed him well all of these years and I never found him anything but right! Why you gotta jump on old Hugh? And even if he was a leper, would that make any difference about his girl? Is there anything wrong with his daughter, son?"

Young Alfred Tennyson Naylor shrugged his shoulders. The mention of Molly Loftus had not altered his color or his expression in the least.

"You don't seem to understand at all, dad," said he, "that some girls are impossible — no matter how pretty they may be. Molly's a nice youngster, and she'll make a good wife — for some cowpuncher on the range! That's about all there is to say for her, it seems to me!"

"Darling Alfred," said his mother, "you couldn't have put it better! *We* want something more than a cowpuncher's honest wife, I'm sure."

"All right," said Mr. Naylor. "And in the open market what's the price of a society girl — that stands over a lot of ground?"

"Discussion of a delicate nature like this," said his wife, "is simply impossible with you, Joseph. You'll have to get into a different frame of mind. In the meantime, I take it for granted that you don't oppose our wishes?"

"Sure I don't. It's beyond me," said the father. "Tell me one thing, Alf. Are you terrible fond of this Miss Huntingdon-Whatnot?"

"Fond?" said Alfred, raising his brows. "One doesn't approach that sort of a marriage in that way!"

CHAPTER 7

Joe Naylor went to bed, and the other three remained up for a long time, discussing their plans with the greatest excitement; for they all agreed that they had won their cause. It might well be that Joseph Naylor did not exactly approve of what they had done, but they felt that they had drawn a tacit assent from him and the plan of campaign was to push ahead as soon as possible.

It was impossible for them to stay in the West. On that they agreed at once, with young Alfred pointing the inevitable way. For, as he said, no matter whether Miss Huntingdon-Wright or Lord Ponting came to visit them, the result would be inevitable disaster. Given even another year and the house might be whipped into proper order, the garden made to look older, the furniture settled into place, so to speak, and above all, the father of the family might be polished a bit as to grammar, etc.

"He could talk a lot better," said his wife fiercely. "Look how I had to pitch in and work, and take lessons, just like I was learnin' a foreign language, you might say. And now I mostly never make a slip! He could do the same thing, just as easy!"

"He hasn't any will power," said his son, "except to please himself. He'd never make any sacrifices for us!"

"You mustn't say that," said his sister. "*I* can remember when dad and mother were simply fighting for us!"

"There never was any reason for it!" said Mrs. Naylor. "We might always have lived like gentlefolk, but your father wouldn't have it that way! He had his great idea, always. We had to live in hell for twenty years while he was saving enough money to build his miserable dam, and now that the thing is done, it's only right that he should pay us back for the hard time we've had!"

"Of course it is!" said Alfred.

His sister said not a thing, but looked from one to the other with her forehead puckered by pain.

"First of all, we've got to get out of this place," said the mother. "We've got to go back to the East. We've got to settle ourselves among the society which we've chosen for our own!

You both agree to that, of course!"

"Oh, yes, of course," said Alfred.

"Dear Alfred, how like me you are!"

"Of course I am, mother. It's the only thing to do. Out here, we'll turn into rustics, again! We have to get out. We have to trek back to civilization."

"Yes," said Mrs. Naylor. "And you agree perfectly with us, child, of course?"

She looked fixedly at the girl, and Rosamund said slowly: "I'd better stay here for a while. You two go back. I'll stay here and try to keep dad company for a while. He might not be very happy, if we were to all go away — you know, he leads a pretty lonely life!"

"Lonely foot!" said Mrs. Naylor unelegantly. "He has his work and his cows and his miserable dam, and that's all that he cares about! I don't see why we should consider him every minute of our lives, when he doesn't consider us, and hasn't considered us for twenty years and more!"

"You're absolutely right," said Alfred.

"Perhaps," said Rosamund, but she looked guiltily about her.

Alfred, rising from his chair, slipped to the door and jerked it suddenly open.

"Great heavens — Alfred!" breathed his frightened mother.

The boy stood against the blackness of the hallway, looking up and down it.

Then he closed the door again and turned irresolutely back into the room.

"What was it?" asked Rosamund, running to him in fear.

He bit his lip in anxiety as he looked at her.

"I don't know. I heard something go down the hall like a whisper."

"Oh, Alfred, it was the wind, of course," said his mother.

He shook his head.

"I'm not one of the kind who makes mistakes of that sort," said he. "You ought to know that. I'm no empty head to hear ghosts. And besides, I'll tell you what — the wind makes a whisper, but it doesn't make a sound like a ticking clock!"

The three looked at one another.

"Was it — did it — could it —"

"The noise started outside that door!" said Alfred calmly.

Mrs. Naylor said: "Suppose that Joseph —"

"My God," said Alfred. "Yes, suppose that he heard!"

Rosamund, white and still, sat in a corner and said not a word, but her frightened eyes went continually to the window or to the door.

Mrs. Naylor stood up, dressed in courage.

"Things have to be faced," said she. "I'm

going up now to see if he's just in bed or simply undressing. That would mean a good deal!"

"Besides, we might as well have it out now as ever!" said Alfred. "There's no use dodging the fact that we've got to have a showdown with father, sooner or later."

His mother raised a firm hand. All the cold creams, the massages, the lotions, could not alter the red stain of labor on that hand, or the hard squareness of the finger tips.

"You'd better let me handle your father, young man," said she. "I know him and you don't. Under that mild surface way of his, he's as hard as a rock. I know. I watched him trudge for twenty years straight toward that dam!"

"Oh, mother," said the girl, breaking in, "how can you speak so about it! Doesn't the dam mean anything to you? Aren't you proud of it?"

Mrs. Naylor looked at her daughter with nostrils that suddenly pinched in, and white spots appeared in either cheek.

"Rosamund," she said slowly, "there ain't a stone of that dam that ain't stained with my blood. Blood of my heart that kept a-bleedin' for nigh onto twenty years. You ask me what the dam means to me? I wouldn't be tellin' you, child. There is things that ain't talked about. *I* ain't gunna talk about it now."

The language of Mrs. Naylor had slipped back into the carelessness of a bygone year, and for a long moment her children looked at her, frightened by their ignorance of this woman who was their mother. The whole process of those twenty years of pain was unrolled before their eyes; and in that grimness of mental seeing, they stared at her.

The room was still hushed when the noise of a siren hooted faintly down the valley, joined presently by other whistles. It sounded like the close of a factory day. After that, those sounds died, and began again, with a strange wail.

"What on earth is it?" asked Alfred, frowning. "Is Cumshaw celebrating at this hour of the night?"

His mother made a brief gesture for silence.

She rose from her chair and stood with staring eyes as though she saw a horror.

The second wail of noise died, and in the interim of silence she whispered, so that both her children heard her: "Oh, my God! Oh, my God! —"

And then the third cry of the sirens hooted like far-off owls through a wood.

At this, voices broke out suddenly at the rear of the house, where the servants' quarters were situated, voices that shouted and clamored together, and seemed wrangling in a life and death battle.

Other voices sounded from the barn; footfalls trampled above their heads.

Then that third blast of whistling ended, and with it every voice was stilled for an instant.

Mrs. Naylor beckoned her son to her. He ran to her side and she leaned heavily on him. She could barely murmur: "The dam, the dam, Alfred! It's gone! It's the signal to warn the valley – the dam is broken! Oh, God, what have I done to deserve this?"

At that, all the voices broke out again, and Mrs. Naylor recovered herself and started for the door. Her children went with her. They raced up the stairs, and climbed the winding ladder which went to the roof.

As they did so, the master of the house came running down the hall after them in stockinged feet, huddling into a coat as he ran.

He clambered up the ladder after them, and all together they stepped out onto the roof. From that height they could see above the trees to the lights of Cumshaw, down the valley, and turning in the other direction, they could look to the dam-site. The moon shone full upon it, and the wall of the dam arose in a flat face of shadow, unbroken, as durable as ever.

The Naylors looked at one another.

"It's only a joke — it's a joke!" said Mrs. Naylor. "Alfred, get me downstairs. I feel pretty sick!"

"You'd better let me help, ma," said Joseph Naylor. "You're all broke up. No wonder. That was the danger signal. D'you hear it? I was woke up by the tail end of the first siren, and I waited and heard the other two. Listen to 'em!"

All over the house, the servants and the hired hands were raising hubbub. Mr. Naylor cupped his hands and called loudly: "Hey, Sam! Hey!"

"Yes, sir! Yes, Mr. Naylor!" wailed a voice from the ground. "Is it comin'? Is it comin'?"

"The dam's standin' as strong and as safe and as sure as ever, thank God," said Joseph Naylor. "Some fool has been havin' a joke down in the town, that's all that it means!"

And at that moment, the sirens began again in their weird, blood-chilling chorus, far away. The noise drew to them more clearly, in their new position.

"They'll be mannin' the dykes around Cumshaw, by this time," said Joseph Naylor. "Well, they's gunna be a good deal of cussin' around that town when they find out it's only a joke! And if—"

"Look! Look!" cried Rosamund, and staring

ahead of her pointing arm, they saw the face of the dam cracked upward from the bottom by a jagged streak of fire!

CHAPTER 8

"Montana knew it," said Joseph Naylor. "He knowed that they'd blow the dam on me, one of these days."

The whole central portion of the dam had been stripped away like paper and behind it they saw the solid wall of water glistening like rigid ice beneath the moon. Only gradually, as it seemed, did the mass gather headway, and then burst outward, as though a vast pitcher had been tilted up in the higher valley. The last of the dam wall peeled away to the right and to the left as the lunging mass burst through; and now the roar of the explosion boomed in their ears, followed by dimly pounding echoes. And after that a sound of crashing, as the roar of the loosed cataract flowed to them across the trembling air.

From the ground, wild cries of fear and lament rose up to them, and grew still; footfalls scampered through the house, sounding faint as the pattering of rats.

But those upon the roof were hushed.

They saw the glittering spout leap outwards. It struck the noble pines, and these went down like brittle stalks of grain before a scythe. The dark cloud of the forest thinned; a mere fringe of silhouettes stood black against the water, then these, too, were gone and the whole upper, narrow end of the valley was sheeted over with glimmering silver.

Sarah Naylor dropped upon her knees. She was at the very edge of the roof and her arms were flung up to the sky.

"Joe! Joe!" she screamed. "Stop it! It's gone! It's gone! Push it back! Joe, for God's sake! It's twenty years. It's torn away. Oh, God! oh, God! Alfred! Rosie! Joe! It can't be right. It can't happen! God wouldn't do it!"

She leaped up, tottering on the very verge of the roof. Alfred sprang toward her, but an arm of iron put him aside, and he saw his father take his mother and draw her gently back.

The flood was spreading fast, but the distance made its progress appear slow. At first it was like a pyramid, with spreading base, and upon this the upper strata of water heaped as though it were a solid material, or metal. And still, as the forward edge of the water cut down the valley, the vast spout drove out the hoarded weight of the water in an endless stream.

The roar and the crashing drew nearer to them, as though the noise had found its way clearly through the air, and now trampled about their ears.

Sarah Naylor screamed like a child under the knife, and fainted. And as her husband supported her, his two children came closer to him. So they stood in a solid group, and looked at the bright face of destruction as it poured down the valley toward them.

From this height they could see the buildings at the upper end of the valley, not far from the foot of the dam, and the furious front of the water lifted a head higher than the top of the barns. These were storehouses for grain, alfalfa, ploughs, harrows, and for all of the tools which were needed in working the land. It was a separate center, from which the labor at the head of the valley was carried on. And now this whole unit was struck, crushed together like paper walls, and tossed for a moment, then swallowed. A roof ridge reappeared a moment later like a boat in a wild sea.

The speed of that water was an incredible thing. As it came closer, they could see the front of the mass, which reached out a thousand arms, like the arms of devilfish. And sometimes a column of water would arise as the sweeping front reached a hill, and then it was like the brandished arm of a silver giant.

So the flood washed on, and Sarah Naylor, recovering, got unsteadily to her feet.

She began to laugh, and all that had happened and that was happening seemed as nothing compared with the dreadful sound of that laughter. And she reeled with it, drunkenly, and still laughed, and her husband, with a face of stone turned toward the water, held her, and said not a word.

The thundering of the water was now unbelievable. And it seemed to defy the power of gravity. There was a pleasant little hill just north, covered with poplars and other second growth timber, and this hill, and all of its trees, was wiped out by a single gesture of the flood.

Now, with a cry of terror, Rosamund pointed toward the rear of the house, and Alfred saw what seemed to him a promise of the end for them all.

Vast as was the mass of water that poured from the mouth of the dam, and which still leaped through the gap in a mighty cataract, yet its way was impeded by the hills and the woods it had encountered, and its advance down the valley had been irregular. But, following an open way to the rear of the house, one vast arm of the flood was thrusting out behind the Naylor house, and Alfred saw the white of its first bursting through the woods.

Then all around the place, like bright devils leaping from the earth, the water rose up, thundering. The noble woods were beaten to bits in a moment, and as the converging walls of water rushed against one another, and against the sides of the hill upon which the house stood, the strong building trembled and shook and made a deep groaning sound like a living thing in pain and in fear; and hurtling so high that the moon was dimmed by the flying arms of spray, the water cast up its hands; and a shower like rain fell on the four who stood on the roof, clutching each other, only hoping now that they might be able to die together; and they heard such an uproar, and such a bursting of cannonading water masses that their ears rang, and their brains swam on the pouring sound.

The forests were gone.

Those great woods near the dam had gone down hardly more easily before the first wild rush of water than did the lower groves, and even those which climbed the hill beside the house. Alfred, looking down, saw the earth licked away from about the roots of the great trees of the woods, and the next instant they were caught in shapeless hands and ripped easily from the places in which they had stood for generations, perhaps.

Sometimes the flood drew them back into its boiling maw. And sometimes those liquid hands caught up a six-foot trunk and cast the long shaft of it like a javelin into the air.

But the flood was passing.

The dreadful front of water was now trampling down the lower valley, and growing less furious as it spread its arms over a larger territory. Behind it, the water still spouted from the throat of the gorge, but in lessening volume and with a slighter speed.

The watchers from the top of the roof could see the gleaming ridge of the flood advancing, but when they looked up the valley the spout at the broken dam was about all that they could distinguish through a strange mist which lay dark as smoke from one side of the valley to the other. It was not thick enough to shut out the moon, but it dimmed the light, and after the wild thundering of the water, this mist seemed like a veritable breath of death which was hanging in the rear of the disaster.

It was partly water spray, as the force of the meeting currents played the part of the sun's heat and converted part of the charging forces into sheerest vapor; but in greater part it was the dust of the vanquished and beaten forests which had floated up into the air and hung there, slowly adhering to the water vapor, forming in muddy drops, and gradually falling back again to the earth from which it had come.

They waited until they could hear the thunder of the flood dissolving into a wide, dim murmur.

And then, distinctly above all other sounds, there was the shrill of the sirens of the town.

They seemed to be rejoicing, like horns after a battle, and in that manner Joe Naylor accepted them, for he said:

"Ay, they'll be a lot of 'em happy when they hear what's happened. "They'll be a lot of 'em that will crow a good deal and rub their hands when they know that I'm wiped out!"

He turned to his wife.

"You'd better go down to bed."

"To bed! To bed!" she cried hysterically. "How can you speak such a thing? How can you say such a thing? To bed? Oh, I'll never sleep again and I'll—"

"Sally!" He broke in on her rudely.

"Yes, Joe?"

"You better be goin' down to bed!"

She did not answer.

"Rosie," said the father of the family, "maybe you'd better go along with your ma. She'll be cryin' a good deal before long, I reckon. So will you, poor girl! Go along, the pair of you!"

And there was no talking back, no further arguing. They went away together without a word.

Their footfalls could be heard going down the steps, for now there was literally no sound at all about the house; only from down the valley the wild sirens of Cumshaw were wailing and yelling through the air, but dim as the singing of a wasp down the wind.

Alfred, his mind still fumbling at the vastness of this thing which had happened, closed his eyes, and raising his head a little, he breathed of the wetness of the air, and he inhaled the last fragrance of the pines. Under those trees he had spent most of the years of his life. They had given him shade. They had sheltered the animals he hunted. They had been written into his mind. Now they were brushed away and he understood, dizzily, that he never would see anything of them more, and that they were banished to this last thin ghost of perfume.

CHAPTER 9

He opened his eyes and saw his father standing with gripped hands, and the moon gleamed on the bristles of his unshaven beard, and on the bulge of muscle at the base of his jaw. He could not find any words, but suddenly he forgot everything except the disaster which had poured through the soul of this simple man; he stepped up beside his father, and was silent for a moment.

Then he was able to say: "It's to be built all over again, father."

He waited, hardening himself for the shock of wild curses and the gritting of teeth; but when Joe Naylor spoke, his voice was as gently drawling as ever.

"What for, son?"

"To irrigate the valley and make it greener than ever," said the boy.

"Ah, d'you think that?"

"Of course."

"Then look at that!"

He pointed to a glimmering flat, the floor of the valley.

"The standing water, you mean?" asked Alfred.

"Water? It ain't water!" said the father.

And the boy looked again, staring. He could see now that it was not an even, flat surface such as water would have made. There were low ridges and hollows, and all alike gave back the light of the moon, although dimly.

"It's the bedrock," said Joe Naylor. "If we was to want to make this here valley green again, we'd have to carry the soil back in on our backs, load by load. A year of work to make an acre. I reckon that it wouldn't be worth while, eh?"

The boy was stunned.

"It couldn't be possible!" said he at last.

"Seems like it is. It ain't water alone that's gone, and the wall of the dam. Other things has washed away. The earth from the floor of the valley, son. And other things, too, have gone down with the water."

Alfred waited.

"Rosie's young lord, he's gone down like one of the pine trees, bobbin' in the currents!" said the father. "I don't suspect that he'll want much to do with her now!"

"If he jilts her," said the boy, "I'll kill him!"

"Would you, now?" asked Joe Naylor. "No, I wouldn't want you to do that!"

"I'll kill him!" said Alfred, his voice trembling.

"Now look you here, son. If it was right for him to have her and the money with her, would it be right for him to be held to the bargain when he only gets her, without the money?"

Alfred did not find a word with which to answer. And his father went on:

"And what would she be doin', sittin' in Ponting Hall, as they call it, with her hands folded in her lap, bein' poor and noble, or darnin' of his lordship's socks, maybe?"

The boy groaned. He saw the truth in that homely picture.

"It ain't her alone," the father continued. "There's your ma, too. Poor girl — poor Sally! The flood has washed her down the valley, too. It's taken along the fine house she rented, and the work she done all of the last year, too! That's all gone. Her life, son, is as bare as the rocks of Naylor Valley!"

He added: "You, too, Alf! Doggone me if it don't hurt to think that you've missed out with that fine girl you was gunna marry!"

"Hold on!" said Alfred. "She wasn't so very fine, either!"

"No?"

"No, she wasn't. She won't miss me any more than I'll miss her!"

"You wasn't so plumb wrapped up in her, then?"

"I? My God, let's not even talk about it. Let's not talk about me, or about mother and Rosamund. It's you, dad. It's you!"

He put his hand on the arm of his father and gripped him hard.

"I'm going to show you something!" said he.

"Are you, Alf?"

"I'm going to show you that I'm not a spendthrift, only. I'm going to work. I'm going to do something."

"Are you, Alf?"

"You bet I am. I'm going to make life easy for you!"

"Well, now, think of that!"

"You'll never have to worry again."

"Are you gunna pitch right in?"

"You'll see me showing up on the first of the month!"

"Will I? Why, son, that's what I call mighty big-hearted. But I reckon that I'll get along, some way."

"Of course!"

"What would you do, Alf?"

"I'd light into that Cumshaw real estate that you have. I'll start managing that. I'll open a real estate office. I'm not a bit too proud to buy and sell!"

"Ay, lad, but Cumshaw is washed away by this here flood!"

"You don't mean that the town is gone, too? Why, you still can hear the sirens blowing!"

"No, the town is standin', all right. There ain't any doubt of that. That's not what I mean, but I mean that the prosperity of Cumshaw has been washed on down the valley. What's that town without the dam? Why, it's no more worth than the old place was before. It's no good at all. It's flat as a paper bag, blowed up, and smashed. It's gone. It's gone on down to the sea, with this here water, and all of the ground that I own there is no more worth while than — than this here fine house, Alf!"

Alfred fumbled in his mind, and then he nodded.

"Everything is gone, then," said he.

"Except the debts," said the father.

"Debts?"

"Ay, they'll be plenty of them! They was a mortgage, too."

"My God!" said the boy. "A mortgage, dad?"

"Ay, a mortgage. The money come in pretty fast, but what with makin' the improvements and the money I spent on the town — and then it cost your ma a tidy penny in the East—"

"Great God, how we threw money away!"

"Don't you go sorrowin' for that. Your ma did everything for the best."

"But how much mortgage?"

"Comin' around close to forty thousand dollars, Alf!"

"Forty – thousand – dollars!" said Alfred.

"But we'll manage – the two of us working together!"

"Ay, father. Of course we will. My God, I'll work day and night! I'll show you! You've worked for all of us! I'll work now for you! I'll show you what I can do!"

"Will you, Alf? What could we do? We might get a job on a ranch, somewheres, if I ain't considered too old to run cows again!"

"Forty dollars a month – forty thousand to make. Why, if we saved every penny, that way, there'd still be a thousand months to work – before we were even! We could work for forty years, just to pay off the mortgage!"

"Now you come to think about it, I suppose that we could. But then, we could go through bankruptcy, Alf. That would give us an even start."

"My God!" cried the boy. "Bankruptcy? I wouldn't stand for that. The disgrace!"

"Why, a lot of good men have gone through bankruptcy, Alf!"

"I suppose that they have," said the boy. "But *we* won't!"

"What else could we do?"

"I'll find a way. I'll coin my blood. I'll find a way, somehow, of paying off the thing!"

"It does me good to hear you talk. It does me a pile of good."

"I'll show you, dad!"

"Good boy, Alfred! Now, maybe we better go and turn in. A fellow can work better if he's slept the night before, you know!"

"You go on down to bed, father. I want to stay up here. I want to think things over!"

"Well, I'll go along. You know best what to do, Alf. I guess they ain't much left in my brain. It's sort of used up, and my thoughts are all washed on down the valley!"

He disappeared down the steps, going slowly, slowly, and tears stood in the eyes of his son as he listened, and as he heard the dragging step go up the hall.

Then he turned back and clutched the low parapet with both of his hands and breathed deeply.

From below, he heard a stifled sound of a man weeping, so different from the sobbing of a woman or of a child. It chilled the heart of the boy to listen, and he thought for a moment that it might be his father.

But then he saw the negro going slowly down the path beside the house — that path which once had been shadowed by the tall pines, now naked to the eye of the moon.

As he went, the man sobbed and wrung his hands; and now he paused, holding up his arms, and he groaned out, so that the boy could hear:

"Oh, Gawd of mercy! Oh, Gawd of mercy!"

He went on, mumbling and weeping, and presently Alfred was aware of tears streaming down from his own eyes. Tears of self-pity, because of that noble resolve he had taken to sacrifice himself for the sake of the others!

Recognizing his weakness, he was instantly filled with self-scorn. He dashed the tears away and began to stride up and down the roof top, shaking his head to keep despair away.

After a moment, the sadness left him. He saw his way into the future, cleaving like a bird through the cloud masses of gloom, and he came out into the bright sun and the blue sky of success!

Alfred laughed to himself, softly and fiercely, and with his hands gripped hard, so that the nails dug into his palms, he vowed again that he would do such things as few other men had done.

But always it was not pity for his mother

or for his sister that stirred in him, but a consuming passion to give strength to his father once more, and take away the sting of this dreadful defeat which was no fault of his.

He had another thought which he would confide to no one. Somehow he would find the destroyer of the dam and kill that man, with a pleasant slowness, choking the breath from his throat!

CHAPTER 10

Alfred determined to remain up all of that night, but when he lay down on his bed after a time, for a moment of rest, his eyes closed in spite of his resolution. When he wakened, the sky already was grey in the east, and he found that a quilt had been carefully drawn over him.

He snatched it off, and throwing it into a corner he leaped to his feet, thoroughly alarmed and fierce with shame.

He who was to save the entire family, in the very first instance, had been cared for by the others!

He would show them!

He went straight down to the stable and there the black dog, Moses, came out and mourned at his feet, with lowered ears and wagging tail. Other hands had cared for Moses since Alfred was last with him, but it was Alfred who had raised him through his days of puppyhood, and Alfred, for that reason, would always be his master.

Alfred gave him not a word, and the dog followed humbly into the stable.

At the stable door sat the negro, Sam, on an upturned box, smoking a cigarette and staring blankly before him. He looked at the boy with an unseeing eye and continued, again, to stare out over the waste of the valley.

But Alfred gave this desolation never a look until he had saddled the black mare and ridden her out.

Before the door of the stable she humped her back and threatened to pitch, but a stinging cut of the quirt made her change her mind. She tossed her head up, looked back askance at him, as though to say that she recognized this masterful hand, and immediately settled down to her work in the most peaceful manner in the world.

So she brought Alfred straight down through the garden before the house and at once he was in the midst of devastation.

Far across the edge of the hill the hand of the water had reached, cutting like a saw. Only a few broken stumps showed what had once been the flourishing grove of trees, and his father's alfalfa patch, which took the place of a lawn, was rent squarely across, where the swirl of the fast traveling water had touched it.

The house itself, perched upon the crest of the hill without any background, without any approaches, was as if loosely balanced and about to fall. The black mare fumbled in a depth of mud where the road once had climbed the hill, and an instant later she was skidding over a smooth surface of rock.

When they came down to the bottom of the valley, the picture of ruin was more complete. That fair valley which had bloomed so the day before, now looked for all the world like an arroyo, newly adrip with a rush of rain water, which does not come to nourish, but to destroy. Only here and there appeared a tuft of scraggly trees, in the lee of a strong hill. But even some of the low hills themselves had been carved away, and were represented now by low mounds of stone.

Alfred Naylor regarded these things with a grim face, and went on like a man in a new world.

The sound of other hoofs came toward him, and suddenly he saw Molly Loftus riding up, with the pink of the morning framing her face.

"Who did it, Alf?" she called to him.

"If I have any luck, I may find out," said he.

He rode straight on, but her voice checked him.

"Haven't you got half a word for me?" she said.

He turned the black mare toward her for an instant.

"Talking won't help me just now, Molly. I've got to get on!"

"Oh, Alfred," said the girl, "I'd like it a lot if I could help. Do you think that your mother would let me come up to the house and do whatever I could?"

He rode the mare close to her and looked earnestly into her eyes.

"You go ahead and do that," said he. "Mother is a wreck, of course. And I don't know how much good Rosamund will be at a time like this. You go ahead, Molly. You're a fine sort of a girl. By Jove, you're a friend!"

She flushed and jerked a nod at him, and then she was away up the valley, riding rapidly. He waited for a moment, looking after the rider, and noting the grace with which she gave in to the motion of the horse.

"She's a beauty," said Alfred Naylor to his heart of hearts. "But what does that mean to me?"

He had other interests that drew his mind away on a road paved with iron. And so he went on down the valley to the town of Cumshaw, and found the whole population gathered in the streets.

They came around him like flies around

honey. They were as full of questions as birds in May are filled with notes.

But he pushed through them. They showered on him demands to know who it was that had done the thing? And who first had telephoned the warning that set the sirens blowing? And who was it that had a poisonous grudge against his father? And what would his father do now? And would the dam ever be rebuilt? And what would happen to Cumshaw without the dam?

He paid no attention to these remarks and questions, until he came to the house of the president of the Cumshaw National Bank, who ran out of his front door and down the steps in a flannel bathrobe and a pair of carpet slippers that flapped and flopped like foolish wings on his feet.

He looked like a man running from a fire as he hurried to Alfred and fairly dragged him from his horse. The reins he gave to the first bystander. Then he fairly carried Alfred into his house. He was in a dreadful panic; and also he was filled with fury.

They would catch the man who had done this thing. Killing would not be nearly enough in the way of punishment for him! They would catch him and apply Indian torments—!

"Mr. Grierson," said the boy, "I want you to forget about the dam for a moment. I want to ask you about another thing. I have a proposal to make to you."

"Did your father send you in to make a proposal?" asked Grierson.

"I came to tell you that I'd like to enter your bank, Mr. Grierson."

"You would? You would?" muttered the other absently.

Then his eye fixed hungrily on Alfred again.

"Did your father send you?"

"No. I had the idea myself."

"Your father doesn't know that you've come?"

"No. Why should he?"

"Because — I beg your pardon if I'm rough, young man — but what in hell would I do with you in my bank? No, sit down. Don't get into a fury. I'm not insulting you. But what could I do with an extra man in the bank? What can I do with the bank itself, unless your father has some ideas!"

He reached over and clutched the boy by the sleeve.

"You're sure, Alfred? You're sure that your father didn't give you some message for me?"

"I came by myself — of my own accord," said Alfred. "The fact is that I'm going to pitch in now and do my part for my family, now that dad is down and out!"

"Down and out!" said Grierson, aghast.

He stood over Alfred and clasped his hands, almost like a man in prayer.

"Down and out?" he echoed.

"Didn't you know? You're his banker, aren't you? You should know how he stands, I should think!"

"I'm his banker? I've always thought that he only put a corner of his affairs through my hands! I'm his banker? But, my God, from what I know of his affairs, he's a ruined man!"

"I suppose that he is," said Alfred with a sad dignity. "And that's why I've come into your house asking for a job."

"You come asking for a job!" cried Grierson, breaking out into wild laughter. "*You* come asking for a job! Why don't you beg from a beggar, then? I tell you, if your father's ruined, if he's bankrupt —"

"He's not bankrupt," said the boy sternly. "He's a gentleman — he never will be bankrupt!"

"Oh, damn pride and foolishness," said the banker. "I tell you that with the dam gone, I've got my hands loaded down with loans that ain't worth the paper they're wrote on. What's the price of lots in Cumshaw the minute the dam is ruined? Not a cent where it used to be a dollar."

"If the dam is down, it doesn't mean that it's

down forever," said the boy. "We're not the people to cry after a fall. We'll get up again and—"

"Hell," said Grierson, "you talk like a Sunday-school! You'll get up and raise the dam again on your shoulders, I suppose?"

He held up both his hands.

"I don't want to insult you, lad. But leave me alone, now. I'm more than half mad. My life's ruined. Cumshaw's ruined. Everything's gone. God forgive your father for not keeping guards posted on the dam. God forgive him for that, I say!"

Alfred stood up and went toward the door, disgusted; but Grierson followed him, trembling with grief and with emotion.

"Look here — he used to make us feel that Cumshaw was based on iron. He used to come in here and buy up lots and things. He wouldn't sell 'em again except for a terrible price. Looks like he's cleaned up half a million on real estate. Look here, boy. Look here, Alfred! He can't have spent all of that — and all the money that he made out of the crops in the valley. He's got hundreds of thousands left, some-where, and he can build the dam again. My God, for that matter, we'll all put in to help. We know what it means to us. I know, for one. I'll work in the bank all day, and work all night carrying stones. So would every other man in Cumshaw. Go back to your father. Tell him that we've got to see him. Tell him that we're desperate! Why, he's got this town in the hollow of his hand! Alfred, Alfred, for God's sake ride hard, and get him back here again!"

Alfred left the house. He found that the street was black with people, and above the black, a white flash of faces turned toward him as he appeared, and what was almost a groan of expectation broke from many throats.

The screen door slammed as the banker stepped out beside him. And Grierson shouted in a high, thin voice:

"It's going to be all right! Fellow citizens and neighbors, it's going to be all right. We've heard from Joe Naylor. He made Cumshaw, and he won't see it fall. Wait and see what Joe Naylor is going to do—"

Alfred turned to contradict him, but Grierson caught him by the lapels of his coat, and his face was like a mad man's.

"Get out of here — don't say a word. Let us live on hope, anyway, for a day or two!"

CHAPTER 11

It was a strange progress that young Alfred Naylor made through the town of Cumshaw. The people pressed around him. He was continually having some grave-faced man catch hold of his stirrup leather and walk a few paces beside him, giving him some serious message.

There was Brandon, the blacksmith, for instance, who trudged beside him and said:

"You tell your pa that Brandon ain't lost heart. Brandon will work like hell. If the dam can be put up agin, I'll go and clench every damn stone of it together with iron clamps so that dynamite can't bust 'em loose. Y'understand?"

There were other messages of the same import. The town of Cumshaw, staggered and distressed, had not given up. With true Western spirit, they wanted to fight the battle out to a later stage, and every man he talked to was willing to work with heart and hand.

By the time that Alfred Naylor shook himself loose from the last of these clinging hands and calling voices and entered the valley, he was beginning to see several things with new eyes — that, first of all, he himself was perfectly insignificant in the opinion of all men, and that his one claim to honor was that he was a sort of special messenger who would convey tidings to his father; that his father was a great man, in the estimation of all of these fellows of the town; and that something had to be done!

Something would have to be done for these dependents! They were to that slangy old rancher like the serfs and the subservient barons to some overlord of the feudal system. They looked to Joe Naylor, and they looked up with confidence and with infinite distress!

Alfred was moved more than ever he had been before. Even the onrush of the flood itself had not seemed to him so significant. And as the water seemed to have torn away the old valley, so now it seemed to Alfred that his old life had been brushed to one side. Lydia Huntingdon-Wright and all the hopes and the aspirations which had clustered around her now became thin as a spider webbing, something dreamed rather than something real!

But the reality, for him, lay in the work he

saw falling to his hand. He hardly knew what he should do. But a vast and vague labor rose before him, and his heart leaped up to it as a boy's heart will toward any great thing.

He came out into the valley – Naylor Valley, all men called it – and almost for the first time he was proud of the title and swore to himself that the title must be made good!

There were others before him. Here, there, and far off, he saw riders and men on foot. They did not seem to be stirring; each was rooted like a plant in some spot, looking at the devastation around him, and young Alfred Naylor looked in turn, but only as the black mare carried him forward at a gallop.

The sun was rising high and hot; steam now wavered up from the mud and the drenched wreckage of the valley, and through that changing curtain of fog he pushed his way and looked right and left, not overwhelmed but taking note of what might be repaired.

What struck him first of all, now that he was regarding things intelligently, was that he had been in error about the greatness of the catastrophe. Toward the upper end of the valley, where the force of the loosened waters from the dam had burst down as through a narrow flume, it was true that the very soil itself had been ripped away and the naked rock laid bare, but here where the mouth of the valley widened, the rush of the waters had lost much of their force. The very burden which the flood had picked up, carrying whole groves of trees as it did, had lessened and checked it.

Those mighty arm-loads of trees had been dropped, here and there, in indescribable tangles. He saw trunks broken, bent, twisted, shattered to matchwood. But they had served a purpose in slackening the force of the water, and the other load which the flood carried — the mud it had stripped away from the rock, had been in large part dropped also. The lower valley was floored with a new deposit of soil, and its thickness he himself could test, and did involuntarily do so when the black mare floundered belly deep in a drift of mud.

But he nodded to himself, even as he extricated the good mare from that which held her. This was rich soil, richer than ever. If part of the valley was stripped and naked as a leper in olden days, the lower portions were, on the other hand, reinforced.

Yes, something could be done with the valley. Perhaps more than ever, if only the dam could be rebuilt!

Toward that goal his whole heart was leaning now, like a greyhound upon the leash. The greatness of the task did not appall him. The singleness of the goal, rather, increased his pride and his sense of strength. There was only one thing that had to be done, and he would do it! He and his father together! He would pay forth his blood, if need were!

Others of those spectators of the destruction, recognizing him from afar, came hurrying toward him, but he gave a willing rein to the mare and rushed on by them. He knew what questions would be asked. He knew they would pour their words on him to demand what his father was going to do!

And then, as he drove on toward the house itself, standing white and still on the top of the naked rock, like a funeral monument, he came upon a man on a weedy mustang, which jogged along with a patient dogtrot, a man who puffed at a short-stemmed pipe, and who was spattered from head to heel with mud. He did not recognize that man, but as he came up behind him, he heard the rider singing.

"Dad!" cried Alfred Naylor.

His father drew rein and nodded as the boy rushed up beside him.

"Hello, Alf," said he. "Old place looks kind of wet, don't it?"

"I've been in town," said Alfred. He did not wish, suddenly, to explain that he had gone into the town looking for a job. He was almost ashamed of that determination he had had to labor as a bank clerk, until he had learned to strike some Napoleonic blow. "I've been in town, and they're wild with excitement. They say that everything is ruined for them unless the dam is rebuilt!"

"Well, well!" said his father.

"They say that Cumshaw is no better than a junk heap, unless something is done about it."

"Do they say that?"

"You know Grierson?"

"Of course."

"I went to see him. Afterwards, he came out and talked to the crowd that had gathered — to hear a word about what you planned to do. Grierson told 'em a lie. He told 'em that you planned to put up the dam again, that you *would* do it! And I wish you could have seen that crowd. I saw tears on the faces of a lot of those men, and a rough, hard looking lot they are, as you know!"

"We raise 'em sort of rough in the West," said the father.

"But don't you see what it means?" cried the boy.

"Well, Alf?"

"They all depend upon you! You made Cumshaw. You made it, and you have to save it!"

"I do?"

Joe Naylor rubbed his knuckles across his forehead. "Well, well," said he, "you gotta remember, Alf, that it took me more'n twenty years to build the old dam. And I'm gettin' along in years. I'm pretty old!"

"You?" cried the boy. "You're not old a bit. You're not more than fifty!"

"Fifty-two. But it ain't the years that you count on your fingers; it's the years that you count in your head and your muscles and your bones. Them are the ones to take the token of, Alf! I'm an old man. I've done my work, and my work's been washed out!"

Alfred stared at him as though he had heard words in some strange tongue.

"You mean that you'd give up?"

"Why, Alf, it's common sense. When a man's beat, he might as well say so!"

"Do you mean that?" asked Alfred, his own voice sounding hollow upon his ear.

"I mean that, Alf. Besides, what good would it do for me to fool the people there in Cumshaw and to make 'em feel good with promises? Inside of a week I've got nigh onto fifty thousand dollars comin' due. Well, that's a good deal, and not a penny in the bank to meet it, as you might say. Suppose that I make 'em a promise right now. Well, they's only a week to wait before they'll know that I'm a liar!"

Alfred Naylor strained back his head, and his whole body trembled. He was like a bit of flame, shaken by the wind, straining fiercely up, able to melt steel at a touch.

"By God!" said Alfred.

"Well, son?"

"That's it," said Alfred. "I'm going to show you that I *am* your son. You and me, dad, against the world."

"Why, that sounds fine," said the other.

"I'll tell you what I'm going to do. I'm going to tell people with my own mouth that you're going to rebuild that dam!"

"Hey? Hold on, son!"

"I'm going to tell them. So are you. You say that you're – tired. Well, I'm not tired. I could work for fifty years, day and night. I shall, too! *I'll* build up that dam!"

"And the fifty thousand, boy?"

Alfred stared hotly into the face of his father.

"I'll have fifty thousand dollars in your hands inside of a week! You have a week?"

"Ay, but how would you do it, Alf? Can you borrow that much from your friends in the East?"

Sudden light burst upon the brain of the boy.

"I haven't any friends in the East," said he. "I was a fool, and they were a lot of spongers and rotters. I see them now. I haven't any friends except mother and you and Rosamund. You're what I have, and I'm going to work for you. You and I, we'll put up the dam. We'll make this valley into a garden. You wait and see. You wait—"

The words died away. A haze of fire seemed dancing before his eyes, and his glance was lost in the distance. He was like a fire himself, ready to melt hard metal, but no metal was at hand!

CHAPTER 12

Molly Loftus found plenty to do at the house of the stricken Naylor family. They did not need consolation, so much as they needed work done. Every servant had disappeared from the house, as rats are said to flee from a doomed ship while she still lies at the wharf-side. Only old Sam, the negro, remained at hand, and he was so utterly confused with terror, so unnerved by what he felt had been the stroke of the hand of God, that he was worse than useless, and wandered about with a haunted eye. Mrs. Naylor, white and silent, had gone into the kitchen; Rosamund moved helplessly about with a broom and a dustpan; and Molly Loftus straightway marched to the corral and milked the cows, and then carried the milk into the creamery behind the house.

She was busy there, presently, and so occupied with the skimming of cream and the putting away of the new milk in pans that she began to sing softly to herself, unaware of what she did. She turned with a start when a voice said quietly: "Hello, Beautiful!"

At the rear window appeared the head and the broad shoulders of a handsome fellow who had taken off his sombrero so as to look in upon her. The eyes of Molly opened, and the skimmer trembled a little in her hand; yet she answered, unmoved: "Hello, Dude. How long have you been out?"

The Dude smiled upon her. He had a lazy, misty eye, and his smile possessed the naïve charm of a lazy child a little too fond of sun and open air, a little too pampered by its parents.

"Three days, Beautiful," said he. "You see I came right home."

She overlooked the last part of his speech, and remarked: "Keepers go to sleep?"

"Not to sleep," he corrected her. "But they got a shade careless. So I asked one of 'em into my room and borrowed his keys."

He began to make a cigarette, as though the story lacked all interest from that point.

"And then?" she demanded impatiently.

He looked at her as though in surprise at this excitement.

"Why, then I walked out."

"You're jus' too lazy to talk, even!" she complained.

"How could you walk right out, through about twenty guards, and what-not?"

"Them guards are mostly what-nots," he said as though in agreement. "The fact is that it was night, Molly, and there was a guard looking so lonely up there on the wall that I went up to keep him company."

"Did you kill him?"

"Me?" asked the soft-voiced bandit, amazed. "Kill? Why, honey, what an idea! I jus' borrowed his Colt, and his rifle, which he was all tired out with carryin' up and down that wall. And he didn't mind loanin' me his coat and trousers, so's I could tear 'em up and tie 'em into a rope, d'you see?"

"Had you knocked him over the head?"

"They's a little sleep producer that rocks a gent into dreamland, Molly. It's called Mr. Right Cross. I introduced him to that guard, and he dropped right off to sleep."

He lighted the cigarette.

"And then you let yourself down from the wall?"

"That's what I done."

"And walked here?"

"Well, you wouldn't want to walk in a country that's so full of hosses. I borrowed a hoss and saddle and come right along."

"And not a word said about your escape!"

"Oh, yes. It's in the mornin' papers. I borrowed one down the line and read about myself while I was havin' breakfast. I'm a 'celebrated desperado' now, Molly."

He laughed in his gentle way, and looked at her in a fresh appreciation.

"You ain't aged much since I started the rest cure, Beautiful," said he.

"D'you know that they're apt to look for you here?" she said.

"They'll try your house first," said the criminal. "And before they spot me up here, it'll take 'em five or six hours. Chances for a smoke and a talk, Molly dear. Shall I come in, ma'am?"

She looked him over coldly.

"I like you fine, Dude," said she, "but you're a shade too friendly, if you don't mind my sayin' so."

He took a breath of smoke in his hand to cast it gracefully towards her.

"Remember, Molly. They's no friends like old friends."

"Even a safe-cracker?" she asked him.

"What's a safe or two between friends?" said he.

"Why, anything from seven to fourteen years, Dude," said she.

"But you see how it is," said he. "I boil down the sentences. Turning the months into days, that's my motto."

At this, she laughed, and Dude Harley, half closing his eyes, dropped his head to one side in enjoyment.

"Do that again, Molly."

"Do what?"

"Laugh at me. I like it."

"H-m-m," said Molly, not as dangerously as she could have wished.

"At me, or with me, I don't care. I like whatever you do, Beautiful."

Molly tried to frown, but a smile trembled through. And he nodded encouragement.

"Let yourself go, honey," said he. "You'll like me fine, once you give yourself a chance. The girls won't take me serious, Molly, but you have a longer head than the rest."

"If I took you serious, Dude, wouldn't I send for the police?"

"You'd send for the minister, Molly," he assured her, unabashed.

"Am I to marry you?"

"Why, of course, Beautiful. After you've looked the rest of the field over, you'll put your money on me. I ain't afraid of that!"

She did not dispute with him; she merely laughed again; and he nodded, as though he agreed that there was plenty of absurdity in his last remark.

"Havin' a long head," he explained, "you'll see that I'm due to give a girl a comfortable life."

"Because the state prison don't send out its darning, you mean?"

He looked at the ash of his cigarette, blew it off, and then examined the burning coal.

After that, he regarded her with the same lazy, appreciative smile.

"You ought to see farther ahead than that."

"I wouldn't hurt your feelings, Dude, but how could I guess that you'll make a girl comfortable?"

"Because I like comfort myself," said he.

"Too much to work. Yes, I know that."

"Too much to be a hired man. That's all. And I haven't had to; and yet I've lived pretty fat, Molly."

"You've put the fat in the fire, too," said she.

"Well, not all of it. Look at this deal, Beautiful."

He slipped five bills from his wallet and fanned them out like a hand of cards.

"Straight flush of thousands, Molly!" said he.

She was sufficiently amazed to draw a little closer; she looked so startled and beautiful that a single flash burned in the eyes of the man, and instantly faded again. "Take a look."

"I don't want to touch it," said she. "I guess

it isn't stage money, after all."

"No, you could hire a show with this here."

"Where did you get it?"

"Aw, it's just one of the cornerstones that I've buried, Molly. Going to put up a big building in the same style, one of these days. And then you'll come and live with me."

"Thanks," said she, "but I'd hate to live alone."

"Oh, I'll be there," said he. "Once I know that I can put you under my wing, Beautiful, I'll fly so far that the sheriff will lose sight of me agin the sun."

"You mean New York, I suppose?"

She did not love him; she was not even seriously interested in what he had to say; but it fascinated her strangely to see the drama of his hopes and of his emotions; she was even delighted by the perverse fear that she might be drawn onto the same stage!

"I don't mean New York," said he. "I'm gunna blow so far that my accent won't mean a thing to the natives. I've seen places, Molly. I could show you a little blue bay on the Adriatic with white houses climbin' down to the sea, and orange-colored sails leanin' away in the wind. I could show you a white beach in the South Sea, and let you hear the niggers singin', and see the palm trees, and listen to the water comin' down to the ocean. I know some places."

"You've been a pretty active bird, all right," agreed Molly. "A regular hawk!"

"A pigeon, Molly," said the Dude, "that would sit in your hand and never budge a wing. A homin' pigeon, Molly, that always comes back to you, as you gotta agree!"

She looked at him with eyes that suddenly misted. And then she went closer to him, murmuring: "Poor Dude! I'm sorry about you! I'd like to help you to be happy—"

The cigarette dropped from his fingers and he gripped her suddenly by the wrists.

"Molly," he said through his teeth. "Laugh at me, will you? But never talk serious to me, till you're willing to be my wife!"

She was too frightened, too stunned by this quick change from pleasant idler to tiger, to stir or to protest, when a door banged, and a quick step came down the hall.

Big Dude Harley vanished, and she, with her wrists aching, glided back to the milk pans as young Naylor came into the doorway, and then took a milk pail off a hook—

He saw her. He saw the pans of fresh milk, and the skimming in progress.

"Hello!" said Alfred Naylor. "You're here before me!"

"Yards," said she. "Were you going to tackle the cows?"

He bit his lip with absent-mindedness, and looked past her, out the window.

"Hello!" said he. "Hello, Molly! Who dropped that cigarette on the floor?"

And he started toward the window.

CHAPTER 13

She looked incredulously down at the floor where the cigarette butt fumed faintly. And then she realized the danger. If young Alfred Naylor reached that window and looked out, there were two chances out of three that he would get a bullet through the head.

Dude Harley was too newly out of prison to risk a speedy return to a striped suit; besides, he was famous for the readiness with which he used his guns, and the deadliness of their effect. In fact, he had been jailed for robbery merely because that was the crime for which the state had the most copious evidence. While they held him safely upon that charge, they would afterwards slowly work up their testimony for more serious charges.

Young Alfred Naylor was two steps from the window, two short steps from death.

"It's one of mine, if you have to know!" said she.

Alfred turned sharply about.

"One of yours?" he repeated, amazed.

It was well before the day when women smoked, so the boy turned back upon her sharply.

"You – Molly – pretty Molly Loftus – lovely Molly–"

He began to laugh, his eyes dancing.

Pink leaped into her throat, into her very forehead.

"Dad wouldn't like it," she explained.

She went quickly past him, picked up the cigarette, and stood in the window, resting her hands on the sill. In that way she blocked him from advancing to a discovery.

But he stood before her, still laughing a little, still studying her with eyes brightened by a new amusement.

"I never thought–" he began.

"You'd better run along," said Molly.

She was angry with him, because he had forced her to this lie.

"You wish I hadn't come in?" he suggested.

She was sullenly silent.

"Why, Molly, I wouldn't tell!"

He came lightly to her.

"I wouldn't tell a word to a soul!"

He laughed again and slipped his arms around her.

Terror and shame and joy flooded through the heart of Molly. Fear because she dreaded lest the outlaw outside of the house should see or guess this thing and put his hand upon the boy; and shame because she did not have the strength to push young Naylor away from her though she knew well enough that she was no more than a careless amusement to him; and a great joy at his touch!

Her head went back helplessly. But as he kissed her, he saw something so sombre and vital in her eyes that he drew back hastily.

"Molly—" he began.

Then he caught his breath. The seriousness was out of her eyes, because she had put it out; and she was smiling at him cheerfully.

"Are you going to be able to come over, once in a while?" he asked.

She paused before she answered; her face turned hot. And even that cool young man blushed a little as he explained: "I mean to say that mother and Rosamund are in a fever. They hardly know what to do. Dad — the heart's knocked pretty well out of him. It would be great to know that you're around, now and then, while I'm away."

"You're going away?" she asked, and her heart sank suddenly.

He looked down at her feet, troubled; for he

could not mistake the quality that was in her voice, and he liked and respected her well enough to be embarrassed.

"You see how it is," he explained rapidly. "Nothing much that I can do here to help. You understand, Molly, because you're an understanding sort of a girl. I have to do something, now. The burden's on me—"

"But what, Alfred? What can you do? Go to work on a ranch?"

"I would, by the Lord," said he. "I wouldn't let work stop me, no matter what. But that's not fast enough — that's not fast enough—"

He spoke rapidly and softly, talking out his own thoughts.

"Then what?"

"I don't know. I try to think. God knows! I've got to make money. I've got to make it fast. I've got to make money, lots of it, fast, fast! And I can't do that by hanging around the house. I'm — I'm going to leave today — now! I'm going off—"

"But where?"

"I don't know, really. Wherever the black mare takes me, once I put her on the road! I'll follow my nose, and see if it leads me to a wishing gate. Wish me luck, Molly, will you?"

She stared searchingly at him for a moment. Not for nothing had she been raised among the rough men of that undying frontier. And then she said briskly: "I'll tell you what — I'll wish that you keep out of jail!"

"What? Oh, well, I hope so, too. Goodbye for a week! Goodbye, Molly! God bless you for anything you do for the old folks—"

He went out quickly, laughing and nodding back to her; but she was not deceived. There is nothing in the world so gullible as a young girl when she is placed with youngsters of her own age; but when she sees at all, she sees deep, and now Molly was able to pierce the carelessness and the laughter of the boy and get at his heart for a grim instant.

What she saw was the truth, and the truth was enough to have made an older and far more callous woman than Molly grave indeed. She even made one step in pursuit, but then she checked herself and remained for a moment with her head bent, breathing deeply.

"Well, Beautiful," said a voice immediately behind her, "are you all busted up because Handsome has left you?"

She did not turn immediately toward Dude Harley, but she answered with a shrug of her shoulders:

"You think it's a joke, don't you? But suppose that he'd come to the window and looked out at you?"

"Look here, Molly," said he, "d'you think that I'd shoot your best young man for you? Not me! Not the Dude, honey!"

She was able to face him now and see distinctly that he was only a mask of his former smiling self. She wondered if he only had heard, or if he only had seen. If it were hearing only, then she might pull the wool over his eyes. But if it were that he had seen young Naylor hold her in his arms, then she shrewdly guessed that the trail of the Dude would lie at the heels of Naylor in his journeys, as truly as the trail of the wolf lies in that of the elk calf in winter. So, through the mist of the Dude's good-natured smile, she could see the danger glimmering.

"I shouldn't of taken so much trouble about it, though," said she.

"Because he'll spread the word around that Molly Loftus smokes and carries on, eh?"

"He won't do that. He's sort of a fool, I suppose, but he's decent."

"Is he a fool, too?" asked the Dude, carelessly in tone, but with much attention in his eye.

"He's had too much of a good time in the East. He's learned how to appreciate himself too much. It don't take long for a boy to get all starched up with pride, does it? Not unless he

117

has to work for wages and have a straw boss or somebody stepping in his face all day long. By the way, Dude, did *you* ever work for your living?"

The Dude grinned at her.

"I was always sort of weakly, Beautiful," said he in explanation. "Work never seemed to agree with me none. I never had no back for it, and it sure made my heart ache something terrible."

She could not help laughing, partly in amusement, and partly in triumph, for she was sure, now, that the big Dude had seen nothing of importance.

"Although," said the Dude, "there's something to be said for my line as a job, but you'd call it a profession more than you'd call it hired work by the day."

"You like it, Dude, don't you?"

"It's a good, clean line," said the Dude. "No office hours. Mostly everything got to be done with forethought. Regular job for a brainy man, as you might say, Molly. It's gunna bring me in so much coin that I'll be able to give you a mighty fine present, when you step out and get married to your beau."

Molly yawned widely.

"All right," said she, her voice still apparently stifled with weariness. "All right, and

make it a house and lot, with a vegetable garden good and big in back, because that kid
never will make enough to support himself and
a cat!"

The Dude looked earnestly, gravely at her.

"Why, he was always considered a bright
young chap, Beautiful. What's wrong with
him?"

"Are you a friend of his?" she asked.

"Sure I am," said the Dude hastily. "You can
talk right out to me, Molly. I'm real sorry to
hear that he don't get on with folks very good."

"I'll tell you what you do, then. Tell him
that he's out of place around here, because we
don't know how to appreciate mixed-up styles.
Will you tell him so? If he's got a ticket back
East, he'd better use it. There's no place for
him to go in reach of a hoss and a saddle!"

She waited, more anxiously than she would
have cared to show, and suddenly she saw a
glint of satisfaction cross the face of the Dude,
and she knew that his suspicions were at last
disarmed.

"It's fathead, that's what's the real matter
with him," she explained further.

"Him going to step out to do so much for
his family, eh?" asked the Dude.

"That's it. He didn't know where he was
goin'. And he'll come back before his week is

up, all right. He'll come back with the skin off of his nose, most likely."

"You sure got it in for him, Beautiful. How come?"

"No, I ain't got it in for him, but I'm sort of tired of his airs, if you know what I mean, Dude?"

"Sure I know. I could sort of tell, listening, just now."

"And he'll got out now, and get into trouble, and he'll just come back and bust the hearts of his ma and his pa, and they're the best people in the world, Dude. Why — I could cry when I think about it!"

Tears, in fact, sprang into her eyes!

CHAPTER 14

The Dude was a man of penetration, and not one given to hasty impulses of any great strength, except those which vitally concerned his own comfort; but now it appeared to him that he might have a chance to put up a peg for his hat, as people say. He lounged upon the window-sill.

"Look here, Beautiful," said he.

She saw that she had won even more than she had played for. The result was that she pretended to throw everything away.

"I've got to get this work done," she said. "Otherwise they'll think that I just came over to get the latest gossip about 'em, and to gloat because they're stony broke."

"Are they broke? Has this busted the old man?"

"I don't know. Anyway, I've gotta finish taking care of this milk, and then do the churning. Clear out, Dude."

"That's a kind goodbye," he suggested.

"It's not goodbye. You'll come again."

"Ay," said the Dude, with a certain ring in his voice. "And again and again after that. Only I was just saying — how tied up are you to this family?"

"Pretty much. Dad has always lived in the hills, here, you know."

"Didn't they high-hat you, pretty much, after old Naylor struck it rich?"

"Mrs. Naylor got money in the head. Well, you can't blame her much. She put in twenty years carryin' the hod, and when she got the weight off her shoulder, she turned a bit dizzy and didn't know whether to drop or to fly off the ladder! But Rosie was always friendly, and Mr. Naylor is as thick as thieves with dad. He always was."

"Sure," said the criminal. "Naylor ain't got the kind of a coat that changes in fair weather. But what about Alfred?"

"The kid? He's in short trousers and don't count — except by the bushel."

The Dude laughed, deeply, richly contented.

"You're all right, Molly," he said. "You sure can read a man. I'd hate to have you turn over the page to me!"

She paused, and tapped the skimmer on the edge of the earthen crock in which the cream was kept for the churn.

"You're all right, Dude," said she, "but your eyes are too good."

"Whacha mean by that, Beautiful?"

"I mean, you always could see the short cuts and never wanted to stick to the road."

"Where you get to, that counts more than the trail to it."

"Sure, unless you get hung up in a bunch of cactus thorns on the way."

He nodded at her, convinced and even pleased by her diagnosis. She had not said so in so many words, but any sensible man could infer, he thought, that if the goal actually were reached, she would not take the place of a man's conscience. He did not feel that it was wise to press her, to try to extract a promise. There were two main objects before him, at that moment. One was to flatter her to the depths of her heart. And the other was to come to her the next time with enough money to turn her head. Truly he was not one who bothered about the means if he achieved the ends, and since a long and faithful courtship had not brought him a great distance on his way, he was prepared to try short cuts, now — many of them! He wanted Molly Loftus. He wanted her as much as he wanted money and an easy life!

"This kid bothers you a little, don't he?" he

asked in a brisker manner.

"He does, all right. He's starting out to do something grand, and he don't know how to keep from catching cold. He'll come home with pleurisy, as you might say, and then the whole household will have to take turns at his bed. Well, it's a bad time for the poor Naylors to be hung up, that way!"

"Well, then," said the Dude, "I'll tell you what I'll do for you, Molly. I'll go after that soft head and take care of him for you!"

She started; and then she shook her head.

"Don't you do it, Dude."

"Why not?"

"I don't know what sort he is. He might get you into trouble."

"I can take care of myself."

"Suppose that he took a fancy to the reward on your head?"

The Dude laughed easily.

"I'd guarantee that he wouldn't collect it."

"You think so. But he could call in help, maybe."

"Is he as bad as that?"

"I don't know how bad he is. But you better forget about him and take care of yourself. They'll be hot after you, before long."

"Sure they will. But I can handle them. It's a hard game, but I'd like to do it for you, and the Naylors."

"Would you, Dude?"

"I would."

She turned dreamy, worried eyes upon him.

An axe, at that moment, began to ring cheerfully upon the firewood at a nearby shed.

"Why, Dude, you *are* a white man!"

"Thanks," said he, and grinned.

"Will you, really? Just for that kid?"

"Just for you, and the Naylors — if they're your friends!"

She went deliberately to the window and took one of his hands in both of hers, and she let her eyes rest tenderly upon him.

"It's like meeting you for the first time, Dude," said she.

And she saw his color change, and his eyes gleam; but then he stepped back with a wave of his hat.

"I'll report with the kid in tow," said Dude Harley, and disappeared.

As for the girl, she leaned for a moment against the wall and listened to the blows of the axe, as loud and with as metallic a ring as the explosions of a rifle.

And tears came slowly up into her eyes. For if young Alfred Naylor were of the stuff that goes wrong, she could guess that even a master craftsman like the Dude could not save him; and in the meantime, she knew what hopes and what payment the Dude was looking forward to if he did his work smoothly and well!

However, she was not a girl of a very inward mind. She went resolutely back to the skimming of the cream, and then, having poured the sour milk into the big five gallon pails, she started with the pile of soiled milk tins for the kitchen.

Joe Naylor came past her, as she reached the porch. He was carrying a large armful of wood, freshly cut and therefore fragrant.

"Hello, honey," said he. "Bless my soul, you've turned in to help like a good one, ain't you?"

At that moment, Mrs. Naylor appeared, shadowy behind the screen door of the kitchen. This she thrust open and revealed herself with a face stricken with emotion.

"Joseph!" said she.

"Hello!" said he. "What's wrong?"

"Joseph, we've got Sam, at least, for that sort of work!"

"Why, what's the difference whether Sam does this or something else? Sam ain't much good, today. He won't be, neither, till he's got to church and said a prayer or two for us all."

He pushed past his wife, and she, with a sad glance at young Molly Loftus, turned after him. He dropped the wood into the wood-bin with a temendous crashing.

"That's the way with some sorts of folks," said Joe Naylor. "They gotta get into God's confidence, after something has gone wrong, or they don't feel very good about it! Good old Sam, he'll come back all perked up. You wait and see! He'll be chipper enough to make a hoss trade, old Sam will!"

Said his wife slowly:

"You know that there are five of the most important men from Cumshaw waiting for you in the front room?"

"Hello!"

"And Mr. Grierson, the banker, is one of them!"

"Well, well!" said the rancher, and pushing back his hat, he scratched his head in thought.

"What might they want of me, Sally?"

"They want to know what you're going to do! They want to know if the dam will be built again—"

"And I gotta go talk to em? Well, I suppose now's as good as any time."

He went sauntering out of the room and down the hall. And his wife looked after him with the tears running down her face.

"What's it to any of us," said she, "compared to what it is to my Joe? And, oh, Molly darling, how brave he is! He never says a word! He never says a word!"

She dropped into a chair, not crying, because there was iron in her, and Molly did not attempt the role of a comforter. Instead, she went to work washing the pans and making a good deal of rattling and other noise. She kept it up briskly, because her own heart was full, until Mrs. Naylor put a hand on her arm. "Listen, Molly!" she whispered.

A door had blown open. A voice sounded down the hallway, a monotonous and rather nasal voice, which belonged to Joseph Naylor, but what he was saying made it seem to Molly the sounding of a clarion for a battle onset.

He was saying: "...a man won't always stay down, even if he's knocked down. I been knocked down, friends. Sort of by a foul blow, too, as you might say. But I don't intend to stay down. I'm going to start in again where I left off. I can't do it in one minute. But just the same I'm going to build the dam again and—"

The rest of this sentence was lost in a veritable outburst of applause; and in the kitchen, Mrs. Naylor and Molly listened, agape.

"Has he lost his wits?" breathed his wife.

He came back to them.

"You might bring in some coffee for those gents," said he.

His wife fell upon him, aghast.

"Joe, Joe," she whispered. "What d'you mean by it? You know that we can't build the dam again—"

"Are you pretty sure?" he asked her. "I dunno. Not by myself, I know, but with all of your helping, all of us pulling together—"

"I'd work my hands to the raw bones!" said Mrs. Naylor fiercely.

"Ay, honey, I knew that you would. And then there's Alf. He's turning out a great boy. He's got plans for raising a whole pile of money. If the dam's built, it'll be more Alf's work than it will be mine, I'm afraid!"

He pretended not to see the face of Molly, as he spoke, but she was ever in his eye!

CHAPTER 15

"Hot?" said the miner. "Hot *as* hell!"

"Sure it is," agreed big Dude Harley, and he stroked his long reddish moustaches.

His reputation for finery in costume, his very nickname was the saving of the Dude. It created a mist behind which he could retire at any moment, for those who hunted for him were sure to have at least his name in their minds.

"Dude" Harley, with accent on the "Dude." That was the man they hunted. They all had their minds filled with stories of his extravagance, of the fifteen-hundred-dollar saddle which he had bought in Mexico City; of his five-hundred-mile ride to bid in at an auction in which a famous Mexican decorated sombrero was for sale. They expected to see him tall, handsome, gaily clad; and, therefore, this rusty, moustached, grimy, overalled fellow, who apparently was just down from the mines, never would draw their attention. He had worked in exactly this manner more than once. He felt that he could work in the same way another thousand times. This was his touch of magic. In this manner he vanished into thin air from the scene of his crimes, and actually had ridden more than once in the posse which was rushing out in pursuit of himself!

So he stroked those long, saber-shaped moustaches now and nodded at the man who sat at the table with him in this large saloon.

"It's a good night for beer," said the Dude.

The other grunted.

"The right weather for beer is when you ain't got the price of old Red-eye," he declared.

"Why, maybe you're right," chuckled the Dude.

"How you come to grow them long moustaches at your time of life?" asked the miner, whose irritation at the thought of beer had made him unwontedly sharp of eye.

"Come out of a hairy family," said the Dude.

"That so?"

"Sure it's so. I had a brother that was born with hair two inches long, and he started shavin' when he was twelve. Me, I'm the least hairy of the bunch. They used to call me Baldy at home."

The miner blinked at him, and then grinned.

"Well, have a drink."

"Thanks," said the cheerful Dude. "I don't mind if I do. I'll take one long and cold."

"Whiskey!" barked the miner at the waiter. "And a long soft one."

The waiter grinned, and went on.

Someone said, in a swirl of people coming in and heading for the gaming tables: "There's Sheriff Axon."

"Where?" said the miner to the Dude.

"Why, there he is," said the Dude.

He turned full about in his chair and pointed with his thumb straight at the face of the passing sheriff.

"That's Axon," said Harley. "They say that he's out after Dude Harley!"

He enjoyed that speech almost more than words could tell. To sit quietly under the very eye of the sheriff and point him out, and announce at the same instant his own name, as the goal of the search of the man of law — that was a consummate pleasure to the Dude.

And he laughed inwardly as he saw the sheriff stiffen a little, and color with pride at this public recognition. The sheriff pretended not to have heard. He barely flicked the admiring face of the Dude with a passing glance and hurried on, self-conscious. The Dude smiled to himself.

A worthy man and a wise man was Sheriff Axon. But, after all, he was not in the same category with himself. The sheriff was brave, experienced, patient, expert in his craft, and he wanted above all things in the world to put his hands a second time upon the Dude. But still the latter smiled. He was confident in his superior brain. He felt a foxlike richness of resource.

"By jiminy," said the miner, "seems like I've seen his picture. That was after he captured the Dude, I guess."

"Maybe. He got a lot of notice for that."

"You'd of thought there was never any sheriff before."

"Well," said Harley, "the Dude is a slippery guy."

"Sure he is. But slipperier ones than him has been nabbed. Kind of slick the way that he got out of the pen, though."

"It *was* a slick job," said the Dude, with relish. "Left no dead ones behind him, either."

"He left a couple of dead reputations behind him, though," grinned the miner. "They're makin' a fuss at the faro table agin. Has that kid won some more?"

"Or lost, maybe," said the Dude.

"Nope. When a winner begins to lose, the crowd groans. You can hear 'em mourn. But these here are yelpin' like a pack of puppies whinin' to be fed. Listen to 'em!"

Dude Harley turned toward the crowd that swirled about the faro table, and, through a momentary parting of the crowd, he saw the form of young Alfred Naylor, erect and graceful before the dealer. A red-faced man went by, shining with perspiration, his mouth set in a fixed smile.

"That's the gent that owns the dive," said the miner. "Looks kind of sick, don't he?"

"The kid has nicked him pretty deep," said the Dude. "He's gone to get in some more hard cash, maybe!"

"Most likely," said the miner. "The kid will live high for a coupla days now, maybe."

"Maybe he'll save it," said the Dude.

"Him? Didn't you see him?"

"I seen him. Sure. What about him?"

"He ain't got a savin' look. He's got a lot more of a spendin' look, I'd say. Who is he?"

"I dunno. Some youngster, that's all."

The Dude tasted his beer thoughtfully.

He had not yet been able to make out the character of this boy. For two days he had followed him closely, and all he could say was that the boy was alert, keen on the trail, a good rider and an excellent shot. For the Dude in person, from over the top of a ridge, had witnessed the killing of a rabbit with a snap shot from a revolver. Now young Naylor was busily engaged in the game of faro and having wonderful luck. What would he do with his luck? And in what manner could the strange aversion of Molly Loftus for this good looking boy be explained?

Quickly he turned these thoughts in his mind, and looked up as he heard the miner saying:

"It ain't only money that old Patterson went for!"

The miner was pushing back his chair.

"What's the matter?" asked the Dude.

"Look! There comes the powder!"

"Where?"

"Yonder by the door, sneakin' in."

"I don't see."

"Him with the yaller handkerchief around his neck is one, and there's another, with a ten-gallon hat. And there's the third one. Him with the big shoulders and the head that sticks out forward."

"What about 'em?"

"They're Patterson's man eaters. There's Patterson himself, the damn sneak! I'm gunna get out of this."

"What's up? A fight?"

"Sure. They'll never run the kid out without a lot of trouble. There'll be guns out, most likely."

"Will there?" asked the Dude gently.

And he looked thoughtfully toward the three men.

They had passed into the crowd, but all were drifting gradually toward the faro table. He watched them in their passage-making, and he knew that the miner was right. There would be trouble in that house before long.

Patterson went by again, returning toward the faro game with a buckskin sack in his hand, and a real smile upon his features, now.

"You see?" said the miner.

"Sure I see," said the Dude.

"So long. You better come along out with me!"

"I'll stay along here," said the Dude. "It's a long time since I've seen a free-for-all."

"You call it a free-for-all — three agin one?"

"You and me could make it three a side."

"He ain't my son or my nephew, neither. So long!"

The miner withdrew, and the Dude lolled back in his chair contentedly.

He loved trouble as a mother loves a child, and a battle he could not do without, whether it were with hands or knives or guns.

Now he knew that the battle was about to be joined.

He waited. It was not that he intended to let

the boy go unaided; but only if that boy should in the first place prove his worth. If he had courage and grit, and the fighting heart, the Dude would instantly be with him and redeem his promise to Molly Loftus.

In the meantime, he lolled at ease, his head dropped on the back of the chair, and his cigarette smoke drawn deeply into his lungs.

He saw the upward drifting of a hundred other thin columns of smoke which pooled above the heads of the drinkers and gamblers and tangled among the rafters, and disguised, or concealed them quite. When there was a stir of air, through a violent opening of the big front door, it often looked as though the place were on fire.

There was no sound of footfalls, no matter how many went back and forth, for the floor was no more than hard packed earth, constantly wetted down and rolled; and even through the thickest of the crowd, all night long, went industrious mozos, with fine-toothed rakes and baskets, gathering up cigarette butts. This feel of the ground underfoot was a welcome and a pleasant thing to most of the men within the big enclosure. It made them feel at home. It was like being on hand at a great rodeo.

And what men!

The world was gathered here, in a handful of

representatives, hard, keen, reckless men. The Dude looked them over, as a stallion looks over a wild herd. He was their lord and their master, and all the sweeter was his kingship because it was unrecognized.

And then, through the hum and cheerful stir of voices, he heard an ugly noise, like the barking of a dog. The crowd about the faro table spilled back, and he could see the broad-shouldered man with the forward jutting head standing before young Naylor, shouting!

CHAPTER 16

The Dude, standing, stretched himself without raising his arms, but so that every muscle in his body grew taut in turn, and relaxed; and he told himself that he was fit. For he was one of those gifted people who are strong without the necessity of labor or of training, as a cat is strong, or a caged bear.

Then he stepped lightly forward.

In the meantime, there had come two shifts in the crowd.

The clients of the place had fallen rapidly back, for that angry, yelping voice promised trouble and serious trouble at once – guns, and bullets flying. The other movement was a stirring forward of the waiters, and the other attendants. And the Dude could guess that a signal had been passed around, covertly, to pass this troublesome young winner at faro out of the front door and place him in the street.

He was still at a little distance when he saw

the broad-shouldered man jerk his hand into his clothes. The Dude brought out his own weapon with the speed of light, and with a little, startled oath.

He had not dreamed that they would go as far as murder!

There was no need for him to fire, however. The fist of young Naylor was instantly in the face of the bouncer, and the latter went backwards with long, staggering steps; from his sprawling fingers a gun dropped down to the floor.

It was not the end. As the Dude, hurrying forward, could well have guessed, more trouble was making at the boy from either side, though Alfred Naylor, intent upon his first enemy, gave no heed to it.

But he of the lofty hat and the man of the yellow neck-cloth now drove at Naylor from either side, and he went down in a tangled heap under their rush.

The attendants, by magic, formed a confused cluster around the combatants. When the Dude strove to break through, two ready shoulders thrust him back.

"Is that the game, the good old game?" said the Dude, smiling.

And while he smiled, he smote a bulky half-breed under the ear, watched him fall, stepped upon his inert body, and met another rushing enthusiast with a steam-driven straight left. It landed on the man's mouth with a crunching sound, and the fellow sat down, spitting teeth.

The others held back. They were there, as it were, to throw up a smoke screen; it was not their business to give serious battle, and the very sound of that second blow had been discouraging to all but experts.

The Dude stepped on. He found young Alfred Naylor on his back, his fist in the face of one of the bouncers, but a pair of thumbs thrust deep into his own windpipe. His mouth gaped open; his eyes bulged. And the Dude waited no longer.

The short man, his balance recovered after the first blow, came swarming at this interloper, but the Dude picked him lightly out of mid-rush, and whirled with him. It was an old wrestling trick, and there was none more handy in a free-for-all. He cast Shorty into the heap of three, and the tangle dissolved under that impact.

Out of clinging arms and gripping hands, the Dude drew the boy forth and set him on his feet. He staggered, but he kept there, swaying — swaying towards the bouncers, the Dude noticed with a shrewd relish.

The others came fiercely to their feet; they faced the guns in Harley's nonchalant hands —

and backed up in haste.

"Get out of here," said the Dude, "or the roof'll drop on us in a minute. Watch my back, and I'll watch yours."

The boy stooped and straightened again with a Colt in his hand; and so they went hastily out of the place, back to back, ready to shoot. The big front door slammed behind them, and there they were in the open night with the lights of the houses looking wan and small and distant. For there had been a heavy wind earlier in the day, and the air was still thick with the incredibly small dust of a sandstorm.

The Dude sneezed.

"Come on," he said. "They might sneak out after us."

He took the boy's arm.

"By God, they've cleaned me out!" said Alfred Naylor, reaching into a pocket.

"Well, of course they have."

"Let me go!" said Alfred, struggling.

"Where?"

"Back in there!"

"What'll you do?"

"Get what's mine."

"You'll get a slug through the head. Don't be an ass, old timer. You come along with me."

"They've robbed me," said Alfred. "By God, they've robbed me, and I'm going after them!"

"They'll break you in two," said the Dude.

He locked the arm of the smaller man more firmly within his. There was strength in this youngster, and the vigor and the speed of a wildcat, but all the advantage of weight and seasoned power was with the Dude. Alfred Naylor went with him, perforce.

"I'm going to smash that dive!" said the boy.

The Dude felt the tremor of his body and smiled.

"You better talk soft," said he. "Whatever you want to do, they's no use telling a world full of sheriffs about it."

"Who are you?"

"I'm some luck you run into."

"Who helped you?"

"I helped myself."

"To handle all three of them?"

"You can break a whole bundle, if you tackle it a stick at a time," said the Dude, and chuckled again.

The boy braced his feet and stopped their progress.

"You've saved my life!" said he.

"Don't be a fool," said the Dude. "They wouldn't of choked you to death — unless they had to. All they wanted was to roll you for your wad, and when they done that, they just wanted to gentle you enough to get away."

Alfred Naylor groaned.

"I had almost five thousand! I'd really cleaned up more than that, I guess. I had—"

"Who'll believe you? The police?"

Suddenly the boy straightened and took a great breath.

"You're right," said he. "I'm making a fool of myself. I'm making a big noise, too. Well — I'll quit it."

"That's right. You've got sense, kid."

"I've known you before."

"Maybe you have. I don't recollect."

"Well, I'll be getting on," said the boy.

"Are you trimmed?"

Alfred Naylor laughed.

"I've still got a gun," said he.

"Is that bed and supper for you?"

"The world owes me more than five thousand. This town owes it to me," said Alfred.

"And you'll take it?"

"Why not?"

The Dude raised his head and looked at the dim sky, faintly pricked with stars, here and there. And as he stood there a thought grew slowly up into his brain.

"Well, you come along with me," said he.

"I'll go my own way."

"You'll come with me. We'll eat and have a talk."

"Will we? I'm not a sponger."

"You talk like a fool, and a young fool," said the other. "Lemme tell you something — it's better to go to bed with a full belly than an empty one."

"Not if somebody else has paid for the meal."

"Suppose that somebody else has a way that you can pay him back?"

"You're kidding me."

"I ain't. I'm straight."

"Well—"

"You'd better come."

"You're good to me," murmured the boy. "You're mighty good to me! Well — I'll go along."

He went down the street by the side of the big man with a gait that changed a little, from time to time, now fast and now slow. And the Dude knew that his heart was quickening and slowing with his pace.

He was amused. This boy made him feel ancient, wise, settled in his knowledge of the world. And then again, he felt that he had taken up a handful of fire. Use it right, and something might be done.

In the meantime — he took the boy by the shoulder suddenly, as they rounded a corner, and jerked him into a doorway. He did not whisper an explanation, and none was demanded. Looking down, he saw the youngster

145

half crouched, tensed and ready as a cat to jump. He had understood in a flash!

A shadowy form turned the corner, came gliding past.

"Get him!" said the Dude.

And he stood watching, curious, keenly enjoying what he saw. For Alfred Naylor struck the shadow like a beast of prey. There was not even an outcry, but only a soft gurgling sound as, with an arm hooked around the neck of the stranger, he dragged him back into the doorway. With his other hand, he mastered the victim's gun hand.

"Here he is," panted the boy.

"Give him to me," said the Dude.

And placing his hands upon the other, he paralyzed him with his grip.

"What are you?"

The man groaned.

"You dirty rat!"

Like a rat the Dude shook him.

"Don't! I — I was sent. It ain't my fault."

"Who?"

"Patterson."

"What did he want to know?"

"Where you went."

"My friend here?"

"No, you."

"Me?"

"Yes. For God's sake," whined the coward, "don't do me any hurt—"

The Dude turned him and booted him heavily down the street.

CHAPTER 17

The spy, heavily impelled from the toe of the Dude's boot, struck the wall and landed running; but he hardly had taken a step forward when he whirled and bolted back toward the two. A black dog had risen, as it were, from the breath of the night, and threatened him with silent malice.

"Get down, Moses, you fool!" commanded Alfred Naylor.

The big Dude reached out and gathered the spy in from his flight.

"Lemme go!" said the frightened man. "My God, the dog'll eat me!"

"He ain't gunna eat you," said the Dude. "There ain't gunna be a chance of that. Maybe we'll eat you ourselves!"

A shameful sense of pity came to Alfred.

"Let him go, partner," said he. "What do we want with a poor rat like that?"

"There's many a dog knows his business

better than his master," said the Dude. "*He* wanted this gent. Why shouldn't we want him? Come to think about it, we *do* want him."

"Not me," said Alfred.

"Not you, maybe, because you forget that if you can squeeze blood out of an elephant, so you can out of a sparrow, or an alley cat. Keep back the dog. I'm gunna squeeze this bird!"

The captive slumped against the wall, his head canting back on his shoulders. He was sick with fear. This moment of danger had starved every ounce of strength out of him.

"I don't know what you can do with him," said Alfred Naylor. "It makes me sick to see the poor devil."

"I'm thinkin' him over," said the Dude. "We'll take him along home. You hook onto him, will you? I'll show you the way. But first, get that damn dog out of the way. Might as well wear a label wrote on your back as to have your dog trailin' you!"

"Get out!" said the boy to the dog. "Get out of here, Moses. Go home, you old fool!"

He picked up a rock. Moses scurried to a distance, half dissolving in the night.

"Throw it," said the Dude sharply. "Throw it — and don't miss. That's what he needs — a whack on the nose!"

Alfred threw the stone. It missed. His heart

had not been in that business.

"All right," said the Dude. "He'll foller you again. He'll be like a black hand pointin' down your trail. Come along, will you, and bring the sparrow with you!"

The spy pleaded desperately:

"What good could I be to you gents? I ain't nothin'; I can't do nothin'; I ain't worth nothin'."

"Maybe we want to write a letter in blood," said the Dude. "And yours would do as good as anybody's — unless there's too much yaller in it!"

He laughed at this brutal jest, and then he led on down the street, and across a lane, and twisting back and forth until Alfred had not the slightest idea of where the town lay in relation to their present position. The Dude paused before a narrow-faced two-story house, newly put up.

"Ain't this Marlowe's Boarding House?" he asked of the spy.

"Sure it is," said the other, with humble eagerness to please. "This here is Marlowe's, but he ain't opened it, yet. He ain't got a cook."

"He's got rooms, though," said the Dude.

"They ain't half furnished."

"They'll do for me and my friend, and for our talk with you."

"Look here," proffered the spy. "You come

along with me and I'll show you to a—"

"To a rat-trap, sure you will. But this here will do."

He stepped to the front door and rapped. There was no answer. He rapped again, and Alfred could hear the echo rattle through the flimsy house, sounding hollow in distant chambers. He looked up and down the street, keeping a careless hold upon the arm of his prisoner. They were on the very edge of the town. The flat of the desert stretched away from them, opening out either end of the little street; and on both sides, far off, he could see the mountains cloudlike against the stars.

"There's nobody here," said the Dude, with an oath.

"Marlowe, he'll be off at Patterson's, playing. He likes his turn at faro or poker dice."

"Will he?" answered the Dude. "I'll try again."

He whistled sharply, thinly. And, almost at once, an upper window opened and a rough voice said: "Who the hell's there?"

This voice seemed to have a magic effect upon the captive. With wonderful dexterity he spun about and twisted himself out of his coat. The boy leaped at him; a knife flashed like quicksilver in his eyes, and as the stroke missed, the captive fled.

He ran fast. His lean body seemed to have

151

the speed of a greyhound. But fifty yards made his knees sag. He whirled about again for a last, desperate attack; and the boy's fist beat him to the earth like a club of iron.

The Dude came up, panting, cursing. He threw the limp body over his shoulder and said almost bitterly: "You'd let him go, would you? The poison cur! I'll teach him before I'm through with him!"

He strode on down the street; Marlowe was still leaning from the window.

"I want a room for the night," said the Dude.

"Ain't the whole sky big enough roof for you?" asked Marlowe harshly.

"Pretty nigh," said the Dude, "but that roof leaks. Your house looks good to me."

"Does it?" said Marlowe. "Then you stand there and fill your eye with it, son!"

He started to close the window.

"You're a black cloud," said the Dude without bitterness. "Ain't you got any silver lining?"

The head of Marlowe thrust suddenly out of the window again.

"Whacha say?" he demanded.

"You heard me," said the Dude.

"I'll tell you what," said Marlowe, "I'd be glad to take you in, but the fact is, partner, that I ain't ready to bring in guests. House ain't fixed up, and I'd give myself a bad name if I started in business now!"

"You'll give yourself a bad name with *us*," said the Dude pointedly, "unless you open that front door pretty pronto."

Marlowe hesitated. Then, muttering, he disappeared from the window, and presently the front door yawned before them. Marlowe stood within, holding a lamp.

"Who are you?" he muttered as they came up the stairs.

He was a man of middle age, brutal of face, lowering of brow. He had one of those deformed, bunched ears called a "cauliflower," and his nose had been beaten to a shapeless sponge. Obviously he had served his turn inside the ring.

"We're gents that are tired of standin' in the dark," said the Dude. "Give us a room and a light, will you?"

"What's that?" asked Marlowe.

"That's a sack of chaff," said the Dude.

"I ain't gunna have any dirty work started in my house," said the other grimly.

"Sure you ain't," said the Dude. "We're Sisters of Charity. Look how we bring the helpless in out of the cold night, eh?"

Suddenly Marlowe grinned broadly, wickedly.

"All right," he said. "I guess you know your own business."

"It's the only business that means anything to us," the Dude assured him.

"Then foller on behind me."

He led them up the stairs, which creaked beneath their steps, so new was the wood, so raw the grip of the nails upon the half-wet boards.

"Some place where we ain't gunna be bothered," suggested the Dude.

"From inside or out?" asked Marlowe.

"From either way."

"Here's your best bet."

He went to the end of the upper hall and cast a door open. They passed into a blank chamber with only a pair of cheap wooden chairs, and a kitchen table in it besides a narrow cot of which only the frame was present. There was one window, looking out into the thick darkness of the branches of a big tree. This the Dude regarded with a gloomy attention.

"All right," said he. "I guess that this will do. Fry us a bunch of eggs, will you, and a slab of bacon and stir up some coffee."

"Do I look like a damn Chink cook?" asked Marlowe fiercely.

"You look like a good-natured guy to me," said the Dude in his gentle way. "Run along, brother, and show us that you got a heart."

Marlowe hesitated. His eyes fixed keenly upon

154

the face of Harley, and then he stared as keenly at the limp body of the captive.

"All right," he said at last. "I'll take a chance on you guys, I suppose."

He backed into the doorway, still hesitant, then he turned suddenly and went off down the hallway, and Alfred noticed that the step of the owner of the house made not a sound.

His own experience in the world was not wide, but if yonder were a keeper of the law, then he felt that he had no judgment whatever!

The Dude, in the meantime, stretched the captive upon the floor. The face of the spy was very white; on the corner of his jaw there was a distinctly purple bruise.

"You give him a beaut," said the Dude, with a chuckle. "Where'd you learn to handle yourself, kid?"

"I learned from a hard-boiled blacksmith who used to be in the ring," said the boy.

"He taught you!" agreed the big man, interested. "He taught you how to soak!"

"If I couldn't hit him away from me, he used to get in close and tear me in two. He had a short right rip that used to loosen my ribs for me!"

He laid a hand upon his side, and then nodded.

For the captive, with a gurgle and then with

a gasp, sat bolt upright, tearing at the air before him with both hands.

"Lemme out – oh, Gawd – oh, Gawd!" he choked. "I – I thought I was buried alive!"

"Maybe you are," said the Dude cheerfully. "Sit up and watch out for yourself!"

CHAPTER 18

The good nature with which he said this caused the prisoner to look at the big man with hope; but there was something in the face of Harley that removed his content at once. He staggered to his feet and stood in the corner, bracing himself with one hand against the wall.

"Did you fan that baby?" asked the Dude of Alfred.

"No."

"I'll go through him, then."

"I got nothin' on me!" cringed the spy.

Dexterously, swiftly, the Dude "fanned" the other; and he laid upon the central table a slingshot, and a small keen knife, with a blade no thicker than a sheet of paper.

"This'd cut a throat without no pain at all!" said Dude Harley. "Pretty, ain't he?"

"I'd forgot them," said the spy. "I – whacha want with me, Big Boy?"

"Your kind attention," said Harley. "Sit

157

down and roll yourself a smoke out of this. It ain't poison."

The other hesitated. Then he slunk into a chair; Harley immediately took the other and faced his prisoner. It left young Naylor free to move about the room.

"What's your name?" asked Harley.

The little bright eyes of the spy jerked from one side of the room to the other, as he licked the flap of his cigarette paper.

"Jackson," said he.

"If you lie to me again," said the Dude, dispassionate and grave, "I'll take your scalp off — and I won't use a knife to do it, either."

"My God," said the captive, "I don't mean no harm. How should I guess my name made no difference to you? I'm Morris. I'm Blinky Morris. I—"

He paused, his fingers tangling and untangling, slowly. The Dude had raised his brows.

"You? Morris?"

Blinky fairly jumped in his chair.

"D'you know me? D'you know me?" he gasped.

"No wonder that Patterson gives you the job of running us down," said the Dude slowly. "So you're Blinky, are you? You're the one and only Blinky?"

The spy cowered; and then a grin flashed.

"Nobody else wears that monniker that I know nothin' about," he assured them. "Whacha heard about me?"

Again the Dude overlooked the question. He rested an elbow upon the table and leaned impressively closer.

"I thought you was just a low bum," said he. "But now that I know you're Blinky, I'm changin' my mind about you."

Blinky licked his lips and drew deep on the cigarette. He nodded. In fact, his head was continually in movement, ducking up and down a little, or shaken from side to side. The man was helplessly in the grip of bad nerves.

"Look here," said Harley. "How come that Patterson had a guy like you workin' for him?"

"Me?" said Blinky.

Then his face twisted into a knot.

"He got me when I was down."

"And then how come that he sicked you onto me? It wasn't me that trimmed his faro table and made the dirty dog start the roughhouse."

"You mean – this gent?"

Blinky jerked a thumb contemptuously at Alfred, and his pale face grew rosy with anger.

"I mean him."

"The boss never would bother about him. He rolled the kid for his wad. That was all."

"And then he started you after me?"

"Nothin' much. Only, he *seen* you."

"Oh."

"Pickin' his best men up and heavin' 'em around like footballs. That's what he seen. Y'understand? Patterson was scared. As if you'd swiped the key to his safe."

"That would be worth having," said the Dude.

"Would a hundred thousand in cold cash be worth havin'?"

"Is that all that he carries?"

"Hey! All? Ain't that enough, I'd like to know? A hundred thousand to run a game in a rube town like this here?"

"He gets some heavy plays, though."

"Sure he does. But none that crowd him that bad! Aw, he's made of money, that skunk!"

"And when a kid comes in like my partner, here, he starts in and rolls the kid, if he wins too much?"

"Aw, not always. But tonight it got him kind of nervous to see the way the money was dribblin' away at that table. He didn't know that the kid had a friend like you!"

"Or he would of sent more after him?"

"Sure. A whole flock. He don't take chances. He ain't a gambler; he just sweeps up the coin that other gents drop."

"This here floor-cleaner," said the Dude,

"gets more and more interestin' to me. How about all of us throwin' together and cleanin' up his safe for him?"

Blinky rose from his chair, stiff with terror. The big man pushed him back into his seat.

"You mean it?" gasped Blinky.

"Sure."

"You're crazy, then!"

"Why, maybe I am. But I feel pretty secure, havin' you along with me!"

"Me? I ain't with you. Not in a million years I ain't with you!"

"How come?"

"Patterson? Nobody ever can get that guy. He's too damn mean to be got! His safe? Why, man, they's never a time when it ain't watched."

"Ain't there?"

"No, never."

"But there must be a way up every hill, old timer. You gotta think of that."

"Is there?" sneered Blinky. "You find it, then."

"With you helpin'."

Blinky threw out both his hands.

"You wanta go get yourself bumped off? All right. That ain't my business. But don't ask me in."

"Don't make no mistake," said the Dude. "I ain't *askin'* you."

161

Blinky shrank smaller in his chair.

"Whacha mean?" he demanded.

"I mean, you're in! You're in with me. When you come up here, I was half of a mind to burn you slow and sure over a small fire. I was half of a mind to cook you. Well, I still am. But not if you throw in with me and the kid."

Blinky moistened his white lips.

"That's the how of it, is it?" said he.

"That's the how of it," agreed the big man.

Blinky was silent.

"All right," he said faintly.

He added: "What practice have you had, anyway?"

The hand of Harley rose to his face and lingered there a moment, plucking. It came away with his moustache, and at the same time he rubbed hard with a moistened handkerchief and took out a certain shadow in the hollow of his eyes, certain lines that ran past his mouth.

Then he lowered his hands. He was ten years younger, and he was smiling at them, a handsome and careless youth, indeed.

Blinky gaped, amazed, curious. But young Alfred Naylor burst out: "The Dude!"

"Hello, Alf," said the Dude. "You recognized me, finally, eh?"

Blinky stretched out a shaky arm.

"You're Dude Harley?"

"That's my name."

"By God!"

"Well," said Harley. "Now how do you feel about old man Patterson's safe?"

"You could, if anybody. But nobody could."

"Lemme hear."

"It ain't in a bank. It's in the gambling house."

"That don't make it harder."

"Wait a minute. It does. It's in a little room right behind the big bar. There ain't a time when there ain't three or four gents wandering around in there."

"How about three in the morning?"

"They've got a gang on cleaning up, at that time."

"A cleaning gang don't look at safes. It looks at dust."

"Maybe. But they're always around. And then there's the watchmen, too."

"A hard gang?"

"Harder'n you ever laid eyes on in your life. All picked because they shoot first and think afterwards. They love a fight. That's why they're there."

The Dude leaned back in his chair and half closed his eyes.

"I gotta think," he said. "It ain't the size of the wad, though a hundred thousand ain't to be sneezed at. It ain't that. It's the fact that

Patterson owns it that makes the coin look so sweet to me! A hundred thousand iron boys, all rollin' out of his pockets—"

He shook his head.

"We gotta have it! Kid, what you say?"

The boy had been listening in a species of horror until he heard the total sum. And then he could remember. A certain number of thousands were necessary to his father, to save him, to tide him over certain ruin, to enable him to face the future and prepare to rebuild the dam, if possible.

So a flash of fire burned through him, and he answered:

"I'm with you, Dude. I'm with you to the limit! I'd shake on that—"

The Dude rose softly and suddenly from his chair and held up a hand.

He said in a rapid whisper: "Listen! Something's comin' through that door — whatever happens — keep Blinky here with you!"

He glided to the window, and there, turning, Alfred Naylor saw the eyes of the criminal turned to yellow fire. Then the Dude leaned out the window into the darkness, fell, and there was a swishing of leaves in the wind. He had taken to the tree. At the same moment, the door opened.

CHAPTER 19

It was a little, dusty, withered looking man who stood at the entrance to the room, smiling a faint greeting to those within.

Blinky Morris croaked enthusiastically: "Hey, Sheriff Axon, I'm glad to see you!"

"Are you, Blinky?" said the sheriff.

"Me? With a thug like this one?"

The hand of Blinky Morris flew up and touched his chin. He glowered fiercely, maliciously at young Naylor.

"He's not a thug," asserted the sheriff. "He's not a thug, I suppose. You're Alfred Naylor, ain't you?"

The sheriff looked kindly upon Alfred, and the boy blushed. For the recent hope of robbery which had been in his mind seemed like an act of treachery and a lie in the presence of this mild-eyed little man of the law.

He could not speak, and the sheriff went on: "But I'm glad that you're glad to see me," said the sheriff to Blinky.

"Glad? They'd of taken my heart out of me!"

Blinky trembled with fury.

"Would they?" asked the sheriff in interest. "Is that right, Alfred Naylor?"

Alfred did not have a chance to answer before Blinky Morris went on:

"I'm beaten up! I been knocked down and kidnapped right here in the streets of this town, where the law is supposed to be roamin' up and down and lookin' out, and takin' care of people! That's what happened to me — and since you're the sheriff, maybe you'd like to know a little about it and who done it?"

"Of course I would," said Axon gently. "Did young Naylor have anything to do with it?"

The laughter of Blinky Morris was like a shriek.

"Did he have anything to do with it? My God — look here!"

He showed his swollen jaw.

"Where he smashed me — when I wasn't lookin' — the sneak!" said Blinky.

The sheriff shook his head.

"That's pretty bad," said he.

"He done it! He done it!" yelled Blinky. "Why, damn him, if you wasn't here, I'd clean him up for that!"

"Well, I'm glad I'm here," said the sheriff,

"because I'm a friend of his father's."

"You are, are you?" said Blinky. "Well, he's a crook — this kid. He's a thug. He's no good. I tell you that! Damn him, he'll rot in jail, that's what he'll do."

"I'm mighty sorry to hear that," said the sheriff. "What did he do? Just walk up and hit you?"

"He did — he did — he jumped out at me—"
Blinky shook with rage.

"Is that so?"

The sheriff directed his question to Alfred Naylor.

And the boy answered quietly:

"I was playing faro at Patterson's place."
The sheriff nodded.

"While I was playing, I won a good deal. As a matter of fact, I think I had between five and six thousand dollars rolled up, when three of Patterson's hired thugs jumped me. I would have been murdered, I think."

He fumbled at a crimson place upon his throat.

"They were choking the life out of me. Then a fellow came out of the crowd and scattered them, and got me away. But not before the thugs had taken the money I'd won — and all the rest of the money I'd brought in with me!"

"Ah, well," said the sheriff. "I'm sorry to hear about that!"

"Can't something be done about it?" asked the boy angrily. "Five thousand—"

"Did anyone else know how much you had?"

"No. I suppose not."

"Could you identify any of the money that was paid out to you?"

"No," said the boy sullenly.

"Could you swear which one of the three picked your pocket?"

"No, I didn't know when it happened."

"It might have happened before the fight started, then?"

Naylor was silent.

Fiercely he told himself that the law was a joke, a mere foolish gesture. It wrecked people, it never helped them. But he did not complain aloud. There was a certain professional ease and logic in what the sheriff had had to say.

"You see how it is?" said the sheriff. "It's hard to get anything on these gents that run gambling houses. That's why I don't like 'em. I've played in 'em myself. But I don't like 'em!"

He added: "But what's this about your kidnaping of Blinky Morris?"

"I was going up the street with the man who saved me—"

"Who was that man?" yelled Blinky savagely.

"Who was he?" repeated the boy, uncertain what he should do.

"Dude Harley, I suppose?" said the sheriff. Alfred Naylor flushed.

"Well—"

"It *was* the Dude!" cried Blinky. "It was him — it was the thug himself. It was him that carried me into this crooked dive."

"Was it?" said the sheriff in his usual mild manner.

"They carried me in here. They beat me silly, and they carried me in here! What could I do agin the two of 'em?"

"No, that would be kind of hard," assented the sheriff.

"Sure it would!" said Blinky, trembling with his grievance and his fury.

"Now you?" said the sheriff to Alfred.

"As we were going up the street, this fellow came dodging after us. We caught him. He confessed that Patterson had sent him after us to spy us out. And the Dude thought that we'd better talk to him and find out what Patterson had in his mind."

"I thought it would be something like that," said the sheriff.

"It's a lie," said Blinky wildly. "I was just walkin' along and all at once, before I knew—"

The sheriff raised one finger, and Blinky was silent, gaping upon the next word.

"That's about all from you, Blinky," said the

169

sheriff. "Sometimes when I see you, I wonder how come that you're still alive. It's a pretty good proof that they's a lot of decency in folks, that they don't put their heel down on you! It's a wonder to me that they don't step on you and squash you."

Blinky writhed.

"That's what I get from the law," he said. "Ain't my word as good as this kid's?"

"No," said the sheriff. "It ain't. It never was. It never will be. Your word ain't worth a handful of fire in hell! That's what it ain't worth."

He turned to the boy.

"I thought that I might find my old friend Dude Harley in here."

Naylor was silent, his eyes steadily upon the face of the sheriff.

And the latter went on genially:

"But I see that there window open, and a tree pretty close. Well, I've missed a chance to have a little chat with the old Dude, it looks like."

Still Naylor was silent.

"He heard me comin', did he?" said the sheriff. "And I could of swore that nobody had an ear that could know I was slippin' up the hall!"

He laughed cheerfully.

And again Naylor wondered at him. This little man was as quiet and as gentle as a mouse, but he did not need to be told that the sheriff was filled with strength and with danger. And through his mind there drifted out of the past echoes and rumors of the great deeds of this fighting sheriff — deeds of heroism that were worthy of a poet's recitals!

And this dusty little man was Axon, the great Axon.

"Well," said the sheriff, "if I've missed, I've missed. So long."

"So long," said Naylor.

"When you see your father agin, tell him that I was askin' after him, and that I was right sorry to of heard about the busting of the dam — and if I can get on the trail of the low skunk that done that job, I'll — well, that's a promise!"

"Thanks," said the boy.

"So long, again. But I'd like to say something to you, young man."

Alfred obeyed the beckoning finger and came closer. Upon his shoulder fell the hand of the sheriff, and from under the sun-faded eyebrows, keen, level eyes looked veritably through him.

"Don't do it, son!" said the sheriff.

He turned and started for the door; Blinky Morris crowding at his heels. But the hand of the boy caught Blinky by the shoulder and jerked him backwards, and flung him against the wall.

"Hey!" choked Blinky, wild with fury and with fear. "Whacha mean? Hey, Sheriff Axon – hey, sheriff! Hey, look at! He's got me agin – are you gunna walk off and leave me – hey! Oh, damn you all, I'm gunna let the world know about the way you hold up the law! I'm gunna poison your soup, you swine!"

For the sheriff had walked out through the door and closed it gently behind him, regardless of the appeals of the spy and sneak thief.

Left deserted against the wall, Blinky cowered into a corner, his haunted eyes fixed upon Alfred Naylor, one arm raised before his face to ward off the expected blow.

"I was only jokin', kid. I didn't mean nothin' – *you* know!"

The boy paid no attention to him.

He had a greater concern. For it made his heart ache one moment and the chills fly up his spine the next to recall what the sheriff had said to him in parting.

"Don't do it!"

What did he mean? What did he know?

Suddenly this world appeared to the boy a most mysterious place, where all others had sources of information which were shut off to him. One thing at least was most certain – the sheriff had penetrated the disguise of the Dude, and from that moment onward, the life of the latter would be in a greater danger.

The Dude himself suddenly re-arose at the window and climbed in like the big, smooth-muscled cat that he was. He nodded and smiled at them both.

"Good work, kid," he said to Alfred Naylor. "We got the old grey shark himself after us, though, and from now on we're gunna need all of Blinky's brains to get us out of danger!"

CHAPTER 20

Upon one part of this speech the spy seized.

"You got the old shark after you!" he agreed with a sort of cringing malice. "And he'll have his teeth into you, before long. Oh, God, he's gunna do you both up — quick, I hope!"

The Dude regarded the unhealthy face of Mr. Morris with the mildest of eyes.

"He would have, maybe. But we got you to help us out, Blinky!"

"Me?" said Blinky, his mouth twisting. "I'm apt to, ain't I?"

"You hear Blinky talk," said the big Dude to Alfred, with a soft chuckle, "and you'd think that he didn't give a rap for coin, wouldn't you? You'd think that he tumbled into five or ten thousand every day of his life."

Blinky stiffened and looked almost like a man.

"Five or ten thousand?" said he. "Do you mean that? Five or ten thousand?"

"Sit down, boys," said the Dude. "Sit down and be friends!"

Blinky slipped instantly into his chair. He looked like a child expecting a sweet cake or a fairy story, or both. But Alfred made a gesture of disgust and turned away toward the door.

"He's young and proud," said the Dude, "but you and me, Blinky, we ain't proud when it comes to bringin' a hundred thousand into the hands that could use it the best!"

"Ain't we?" asked Blinky, with a croaking laugh. "I guess we ain't!"

"Even if it has to come out of the safe of your old friend, Patterson?"

Blinky made a sour face.

"I'd rather take it from him than from the devil," he declared passionately. "But the fact is that you'll walk a thousand mile barefoot through cactus thorns before you'll get anything out of him. He wasn't born unlucky!"

"It ain't unlucky to be operated on by us, Blinky," said the Dude. "It's the other way around."

Blinky raised his snaky head, and waited for the answer to the riddle.

"You take him the way that he is," said the Dude, "and he's just an ordinary common or garden, nacheral sneak and crooked gambler. Who knows him outside of this here corner of

175

the state? Why, nobody does. But when we get through with him, he'll be crowdin' his way onto the front pages of some of the biggest and best papers in the country. They'll be talkin' about this Patterson in New York, and they'll have him for table talk in New Orleans, too. That's when the pair of us get through cookin' his stew!"

Blinky gaped and swallowed. Then he laughed with a snarling joy.

"If we could—!" said he, and drew in his breath through his yellow teeth.

Alfred Naylor could look at the man no longer. The fellow reminded him too keenly of a poisonous rat.

Then the Dude went on: "What goes on in that room of the safe that you was telling me all about? I mean, ain't there a regular guard there all the time?"

"Yes. One man," said Blinky.

"Only one?" asked the Dude, hopefully.

"Because Patterson says that when there's two, they both leave it to the other fellow to keep awake, and both of 'em go to sleep."

The Dude nodded, with eyes that twinkled with appreciation.

"This here Patterson interests me," said he.

"He knows how to get interest out of everybody," said the spy, with a sour grin.

"Does he lend money?"

"He does everything that's rotten."

"He's built up a big business," said the Dude.

"Sure. By brain work, as he says. He's a self-made man. First he started workin' on a ranch. Ten years ago."

"And now he's got a lot!"

"He's got more'n half a million — outside of the slug of coin that he keeps in his safe."

"It's a lot!" sighed the Dude. "He has brains, all right. How did he plant a crop of that size?"

"I'll tell you how. He found a fool of an old maid school teacher that had twenty or thirty thousand on her life insurance. He married her, and she died of pneumonia the first winter after. There's some that do a lot of guessing about the way that she developed that pneumonia. Well, I ain't one of those. She died. He got the dough. That was his start. He showed he was a bright boy, right away. He got to sellin' minin' stock back East—"

"Worked all sides of the country, eh?"

"Sure. The further he was away from some of those mines, the more he knew about 'em. He left every town just before the mob got him. He come back West with his twenty or thirty thou' growed into a hundred. He was gettin' fat, y'understand? Then he got a swell system for fixin' jockeys and went to the track at New Orleans to work it. He worked it for a few weeks, and then he dodged a couple of shotguns and boarded the train back West. He had a quarter of a million, all said and done, and then he opened this shop of his here. He ain't the sort that will ever have bad luck, I tell you!"

The Dude rose and hastily paced the floor, up and down.

"It's a facer!" he said, stopping short at last.

"What's a facer?" asked Blinky. "His layout? Sure it's a facer. It ain't the first time that a yegg has tried his hand on that safe, and they've all muffed it bad. There's four men in the penitentiary that are gunna stay there most of their lives, on account of gettin' curious about the inside of Patterson's safe."

"Are there?" murmured the Dude.

"I'll tell you what kind of a bird Patterson is. District attorney wasn't good enough for him. He hired a smart lawyer to work in the background and feed the district attorney's hand. That's how he got such long terms secured for every conviction. That's the kind of a guy that he is — poison!"

"Of course he is," agreed the Dude. "But we'll get to him, Blinky. The more that have tried and failed, the better the chance for me."

"How come?"

"The more that have failed, the more of his good luck has been used up!"

"Well," drawled Blinky, scowling, "that's true, too!"

For this sort of argument appealed to his superstitions.

"But what puts me back on my heels is: Why does the son-of-a-gun keep so much in his safe?"

"What you care?"

"Because it looks pretty mysterious. That kind of a bird would be more likely to keep his coin in a big bank!"

"There ain't a big, safe bank in town," said Blinky. "There ain't a bank that has a safe that he would trust as much as his own. And he's gotta have that lump of money right there under his hand, all of the time."

"What for?"

"Why, because of the quick loans that he makes. Suppose that some gent comes to town and wants quick cash — for anything — for the payin' of a gamblin' debt — to buy a hoss that's caught his eye — or the buyin' of a piece of land, or a mine, or a bunch of cows — or anything that a man might want quick and not have the price with him, why, that's the kind of a business that Patterson does. You gotta take security along, when you talk to a bank. Well, you don't have to have security when you talk to

Patterson. He gambles on you. He sizes you up."

"He must lose a lot."

"He does. He loses a lot, but them that run out on Patterson generally wish that they'd run into hell fire instead. He makes their trail so hot. He spent a whole month runnin' down one poor sucker that only had got to him for a hundred dollars!"

"He deals as small as that, does he?"

"He does," said Blinky. "He deals as small as a squirrel or as big as a grizzly."

"I like this job better and better," smiled the Dude.

"It'll spoil your digestion, and I'm warnin' you," said the spy. "All that'll be exchanged between you will be the skin that you leave on his claws."

"Maybe so. What sort of interest does he charge?"

"That depends. Get a big fellow that means something and that only wants the coin for a few months, and maybe he'll let him go for only twenty or thirty per cent."

"What!"

"The only ones that come to him are the ones that are plumb thirsty for money," said Blinky. "They think that they're dyin'. It is only after he's brought them back to life that they realize he's drinkin' their blood."

"Blinky, you ever have a turn to stand guard in the room where that safe is?"

"I do," said Blinky. "But believe me, son, I ain't gunna start anything."

"He lets you stay on as a guard?"

"Why not? He says that I can yell as loud as any man!"

Harley laughed cheerfully.

He seized Blinky's coat and ripped it almost from his back. He took off his hat and kicked it against the wall.

Then he raised the hat from the floor and presented it to his staggered guest.

"You've just busted away from me," said the Dude. "You managed to get away, and you faded as fast as you could."

Blinky gasped and nodded.

"From here?"

"Hell, no," said the Dude. "From the street, where we took you. We was gunna cut your throat. Anything you please. You managed to twist away."

"From you and the kid?"

"Sure. And you run all the way back to the shop and bust in on Patterson to show him your spoiled face and the bump on your jaw, and your ruined clothes. You oughta get a thousand out of the skunk, for what you've been through."

"If I get a fourth-hand suit of clothes, I'll be lucky, and some good advice for healin' my jaw!" snarled Blinky. "Kid, I'm gunna work with you. But if you catch the bird, what part of the meat comes onto my plate?"

"Some of the white, Blinky. Some of the white," said the Dude. "We'll fix that later, when you show me that you're with me!"

Blinky went slowly toward the door. There he paused, scowling at the floor, jerked the door open and was gone without a word.

"He's going to double cross you," said Alfred.

The Dude shook his head.

"He thought about it, but the thought wasn't no good."

The front door closed softly; quiet steps went along the board walk. Then, from well down the street, a wild scream rang through the air, followed by yell upon yell, fading out toward the center of the town.

"That's Blinky," said the Dude with a grin, "started on his way and trailin' his little cloud of glory!"

CHAPTER 21

No sooner was the sound of Blinky's yelling gone in the distance than the Dude jerked the door open and shouted loudly: "Marlowe! Hey, Marlowe! Hey!"

His voice had turned, from its usual softness, into an iron, ringing quality that roused the deep-throated echoes far off in the flimsy house.

Hasty footfalls thudded up the stairs and down the hall they rattled. Marlowe himself came into the room.

His humor seemed rarely pleasant, but now he was in the temper of a wild bull.

"Who's this yelling? Who's makin' all of this racket?" he demanded. "Are you maybe the sheriff, or are you only God A'mighty?"

The Dude moved without seeming speed, and yet his hand was as inescapable as the striking head of a snake. He took Mr. Marlowe by the breast of his coat and thrust him into a corner. Marlowe reached his right hand into his clothes, but that hand was caught at the wrist by a grip that bruised his flesh against the bones of his arm. His hand turned to a nerveless lump. And instantly he lost all thoughts of resistance. His bright, angry eyes changed, and became mild, doubtful and curious.

Said the Dude in a terrible voice which Alfred hardly could recognize: "Are you the leader of the orchestra in this here town?"

"I dunno what you mean," said the keeper of the house.

"You mangy skunk," said the Dude, "if there was a shade more of hair on you, I'd skin you for your hide and sell it for four bits. What in hell d'you mean by letting Axon in on me?"

"Axon? Axon?" said the other with a convincing astonishment.

Then his jaw fell.

"Hey! You don't mean the sheriff?"

"Don't I?" sneered the Dude.

"My God," said Marlowe, "I'm queered, then, before I'm started! Axon! What's he got on me?" he inquired anxiously.

The Dude loosed his double grip and let the other go, but Marlowe did not take advantage of this opportunity for offensive measures. As one who has felt the paw of the lion, he remained passive and stroked softly the bruised right wrist where the grip of the Dude had rested.

And Alfred Naylor, watching them both, wondered not a little. He had known the Dude from his boyhood, from a time when strange rumors and odd talk circulated about the big, handsome, soft-spoken youth. And no matter what tales reached his ears of the dangers that lurked under the surface of this fellow, he never could believe them. The truth always had seemed to him apparent in the gentle manner of the man.

But Marlowe carried his index number written large upon his face. He was a man of action. In the West of that date, it meant a man of guns. And Marlowe was dangerous. He was no barking dog which does not bite. The man had every indication of a hard and bitter temper. He had a quick eye, and a hand to match the eye.

And yet the lazy, care-free Dude had mastered the man without a serious effort, as it appeared.

And suddenly Alfred Naylor remembered all of the tales which he had heard about the Dude. It was not that he had been sent to the penitentiary. Good men may find their way within stone walls for no very serious fault. It was not that. But suddenly the light had shown through upon the truth about the man, and that truth froze the blood of the boy.

He could have held his breath, like a child

when strange tales are told of heroes. The Dude was a man apart. He was leisurely and careless because to him the perils which daunt common people were as nothing. He was at ease because the world held no dangers which to him were worthy of a second thought.

And as all of this realization flooded suddenly upon the brain of the boy, he was stopped, checked, bewildered. He listened in a haze to the rest of the conversation, which was brief.

"What's he got on me?" their host had asked.

And the big Dude answered calmly: "What he's got on you, I dunno. Plenty, maybe. But as long as you ain't disturbin' the peace, I suppose that he ain't apt to make you any trouble. But you let him in on me, which is what counts."

"I didn't," said Marlowe rather feebly. "I didn't let him in on you. What should I for? What would I want to for? And if I did, why didn't he walk away with you?"

"You didn't let him in?"

"No."

"You'll go to hell, for that kind of a lie!"

"Will I? You're a fool, to think that! I'm tellin' the truth."

So it seemed to Alfred. Never had he felt honesty for that moment, at least, so breathe from a man.

But the Dude seemed unconvinced. His rage

seemed rather to gather to a head.

"It was a chance that after I come here, the sheriff come in after me, eh? He got in without makin' any noise, did he? He got up them damn creakin' stairs and to my room without any noise? Eh?"

The landlord scratched his head, despairing.

"You know Axon," he feebly offered.

"I know Axon, and I'm beginning to know you!" said the Dude fiercely. "You sneakin' devil, you invited him up here. You wanted a part of the blood money on me!"

The face of Marlow flushed. Suddenly he said: "I wanted the blood money? I want it? Why, damn it, you talk like a jackass!"

"Get out of here," said the Dude. "If I didn't have a doubt about you, I'd wring your neck. But I got the doubt. And I tell you this. If anybody else breaks in here, I won't ask no questions. I'll just go and break you in two, you damn yaller coyote, and I'll feed the pieces to the town dogs! That's me!"

He waved his arm.

"Get out of here!"

Said Mr. Marlowe:

"Look here, Dude. I know you, I know myself. What I got to gain by blowing on you? It won't clear my card for me. Everybody knows what I been and done! But the fact is that I didn't know nothin'. I didn't ask the sheriff in. I never took blood money in my life, though there been times when I was near starved and could of got it fat and rich. You're doin' me wrong, old timer."

Alfred looked from man to man, wondering how the affair would come out. Marlowe was still dangerous. The Dude was still enraged.

Suddenly the latter melted.

He said, staring at Marlowe: "I believe in you. You're all right. Marlowe, I believe every word that you said."

Alfred himself was paralyzed with wonder. A moment before, it had seemed that the Dude desired nothing so much as trouble. But the astonishment of Marlowe trebled his own. That gentleman looked at the Dude as if he were a new world.

"The fact is, Marlowe," said the Dude, in his usual voice, which was wonderfully gentle, "I may of taken a wrong steer about you. It sort of riled me when I saw Axon walk into the room."

"But how in the name of God," said the other, "did he come away without you?"

"I faded through the window. I heard a couple of squeaks down the hall," said the Dude.

Marlowe beamed.

"You got the ear," he announced. "I'd give something for that!"

"Maybe you would. Anyway, I'm sorry that I was a grouch. We'll shake on that, if you want to, or else, I'll beat it now."

"You mean away from here?"

"Of course."

"You stay with me," said Marlowe, his jaw setting, "and if anybody else gets in here you or the kid can poison me. That's all that I mean!"

They closed hands, seriously, slowly. And Alfred knew that they were friends indeed.

It was a new world to him. He studied the pair, and could draw no conclusions.

"All right," said the Dude. "But look here, Marlowe. Before you go I want you to understand something. The kid and me are like one."

Marlowe turned and looked deliberately at Alfred. Never before had the boy been under such a surveillance.

"You mean that he's all right?"

"That's what I mean."

"I'll take your word for it," said Marlowe dubiously.

"And what he says goes, the same as me."

"I'll take that, too. But—"

"So long, Marlowe. I ain't even gunna lock the door, while I stay in your place."

Marlowe paused with his hand upon the door-knob.

"You ain't noticed that there ain't no locks," said he.

Then he vanished.

Young Alfred Naylor looked upon his companion with befitting awe.

"All right," said he, "but I don't understand."

"I don't want you to," said the Dude.

"Will he play square?"

"Him? He'd rather lose his own head than mine, just now."

Alfred nodded.

"I think that you're right," said he. "But what about Blinky Morris? He looked like a sneak to me!"

"He is a sneak."

"Are you going to ask him into the game?"

"Blinky," said the other, "is one of them gents that always hates the fellow that he gets his pay check from. That's why we can bank on Blinky."

"He won't crook us?"

"Not a chance, unless he gets something better from the other side. And there ain't much chance of that. Blinky is ours, until this game is through!"

Said Alfred suddenly: "What did you know about him?"

"Nothing," said the other.

"You put everything in his hands," cried Alfred, amazed.

"Sure I did," said the Dude. "That flattered him so much that he's sure to play straight — for a couple of days. And that's all we need."

"Is it?"

"Sure," said the Dude, "because you're well known, now, in this town."

CHAPTER 22

Into Patterson's gambling room, the following night, walked a man of such a presence that the guard at the door bowed a little, and said: "Good evening, Colonel!"

The stranger paused. He said in a singularly pleasant and deep bass voice: "Do you know me, my friend?"

The doorkeeper blushed. It was the first time in years that he had enjoyed that novelty.

"I reckon I do, sir," said he. "Step back, there, Jerry, will you? Give the Colonel room to pass!"

The big man went on, smiling his gratitude to the doorkeeper. He was as handsome a man as one would care to see. He might have been thirty-five years old, but he gave an older effect, due to the size of his thick black beard. His hair was long, flowing richly out from beneath the brim of his wide hat, and gathering into clustering curls. His complexion was swarthy-sallow; he wore a long coat of a rather antique style which did not matter, because the Colonel would be sure to create his own fashions; and if there was one jarring note, it lay in the contrast between the color of his hair and that of his eye. For though the hair was so black, the eye was distinctly a grey-blue! It was such a contrast as would hold an observer for a breathtaking instant, since he seemed to be looking at a new soul in an old skin.

The announcement of the doorkeeper spread. It went like magic through the room, and since the play was at that moment dull, and the crowd small, most heads turned toward the newcomer.

He took his stand toward the center of the room, and there he looked majestically about from side to side, in search of something or of someone.

Presently he saw, in an obscure corner, the little form of Sheriff Axon gathering up the hand which had been given him by the poker dealer. He started, hesitated, and then went on again in haste. Coming up to the table where the sheriff was sitting, he waited until the hand was finished. Then he asked the pardon of the others for interrupting them, and finally he said slowly to the sheriff:

"Are you Sheriff Axon?"

The sheriff was not a very mannerly man; but now he rose from his chair and looked steadily into the face of the stranger.

"My name is Axon," said he.

The other nodded.

"I've heard of you," said he. "I've heard a great deal of you. And I couldn't resist the temptation to come over here and shake hands with you, sir. I couldn't resist the temptation because I come from a part of the world which is not so far west, sir, but which is wild enough! You have wild mountains here, sir, and you have wild horses; but in my state, sir, we have wild men!"

"What state — Mr.?" began the sheriff.

"Ah, sir," said the Colonel, "from the old and beautiful and unfortunate state of Kentucky, sir! And we have a need of such a man as you are, sir! It has been a pleasure to take your hand. I bid you good evening."

He bowed to the sheriff, and he bowed to the others at the table, and then moved easily away, with all eyes trailing after him.

"There," said the poker dealer, "is a first rate gent, if ever I laid eyes on one before. If he ain't a gentleman, I'll eat my hat, and the hats of the crowd. What's the matter, Axon? Did he hypnotize you?"

The sheriff sat with a far-away look in his eyes.

"I was just thinkin'," said he.

"Of what?"

"Oh, nothin'—" said the sheriff. "But he give me a sort of a chill. He seemed to remind me of somebody that I had knowed before!"

Across the floor of moist and well-rolled earth, the Colonel went on his leisurely way until he came to a door which carried beside it a small legend:

OFFICE

Private

And underneath was printed: "Don't open this door!" as a warning for those who could not understand generalities.

As he paused, a boy who had been trailing behind him started up at his side.

"Wanta see Mr. Patterson?"

"Who is Mr. Patterson, my son?" asked the Colonel.

"Him? Why, he runs this here show. All of it!"

"Then he's working on a big scale, isn't he?" said the Colonel with a smile.

"Not so big as you, maybe," said the boy, flushing, "but pretty big for Double Bend. We reckon him the biggest man in our county, Colonel!"

"Of course, he's a big man," said the Colonel.

"And for that matter, I *would* be glad to see him, if it could be arranged. You might tell him now."

His hard knuckles were instantly rapping on the door; a voice growled inside, and the boy dragged the door open. It showed a small room, and on the farther side of the room there was a desk with a roll top, above which Mr. Patterson looked at his guest, being visible only above the bridge of the nose.

"There he is," said the boy. "Mr. Patterson, here's the Colonel come in to see you."

Mr. Patterson rose and came forward with a ready hand. His palm was moist and rather warm; his smile possessed a soothing sweetness; and his eyes almost disappeared in the wrinkles of his pleasure at meeting so distinguished a guest. He sat the Colonel down in the chair beside his desk. His time was at the disposal of the gentleman, absolutely. Perhaps the Colonel wished to make a round of the tables? Or should they sit and chat in the office?

The Colonel preferred to sit and chat; and he had hardly finished expressing this preference, when a hand beat on the door, and a boy looked in, sweating.

"Farnum's roulette wheel has gone bust," he said.

Mr. Patterson rose with a smile which wrinkled

his face and left his eyes sober.

"Another few thousands snatched away," said he. "You see the sort of a life I live, Colonel — walking on the edge of a precipice, sir. Walking on the edge of a precipice!"

He excused himself, and unlocking the back door of his office, he stepped out into a larger room beyond.

It appeared to be a sort of passageway between two parts of the establishment. There was a continual drifting of waiters here and there throughout the day and the night, as they carried drinks from the bar into the game room, and other people continually lingered about. In the center of this room stood an old safe, finished in rustproof nickel, and bright as a new-minted dollar. That was the safe in which the gambler kept his capital for quick investment. He took from his pocket two big keys connected with a light chain, and now the Colonel leaned forward to watch.

He saw the first key pushed into an upper keyhole; that key had an acid stain on the handle, distinguishing it from its fellow. The second key was also introduced into its notch, and turned, after which the thick door of the safe opened with a deep groaning sound. There were revealed a series of little trays, and one of these Mr. Patterson drew out and, without examining the contents, dumped them into a canvas bag which he was carrying. The Colonel could see the fluttering of the edges of greenbacks!

This bag Patterson now gave to the boy — and a single glance he gave the youngster at the same time, which made the hand of the child freeze to iron around the throat of the canvas. He turned and went gingerly away. Mr. Patterson closed and relocked the safe rapidly, and as he turned back toward his office, the interrupted line of waiters again flowed unbrokenly.

The Colonel was sitting back in his chair, shaking his head a little.

"I don't want to intrude rash advice, sir," said he. "I only want to suggest that that's not an up-to-date safe, sir — and in an exposed position, if I may dare to say so."

Mr. Patterson smiled again. The wrath he had felt at the loss on Farnum's table had left his face blotched with white.

"Well, Colonel," said he, "as long as the people keep flowin' around that safe, they won't have time to stop and open it. The danger to that safe is kept juggled, and up in the air, d'you see? There ain't a time of night or day when that room has a chance to be lonely."

"Ah?" said the Colonel.

And his brows raised a trifle.

"And yet one never can be sure!"

Mr. Patterson struck his desk with his fist, and his nostrils flared a little.

"I'll tell you this," said he. "I'm going to make a prophecy. That safe will never be opened by anything but my keys!"

"They might be in the hands of another man," suggested the Colonel.

At this, Patterson shrugged his shoulders.

"Look there!" said he.

He pointed across the room, to a place where an iron disk two feet in diameter hung upon the wall, with a white line painted across its face and up and down it, so that they crossed in the center. The disk appeared much battered, and in the center, the white lines were practically worn out.

"They have their gunmen and their desperadoes," said Mr. Patterson. "A lot of drunken fools and half-wits, really. Well, Colonel, once or twice one or more of those fellows have broken into my office. But I didn't have to call for any help. I spend a solid hour every morning blazing away at that target. It fills the room with smoke. The wind will hardly blow it away, but it keeps my hand in, and there's something to be said in favor of that. The gunmen know it, Colonel. They get themselves brave with red-eye, now and then, but their courage evaporates before they get to the door of my office."

He laughed in an ugly manner, and nodded his head.

"Young Jack Deems fell dead beside the door. That's the nick in the wall that the bullet cut. It went through his throat. Denver Phil Harrison fell over the back of that very chair you're sitting in, squealing like a pig. No, Colonel, I ain't afraid that anybody else will get his hands onto my keys."

And he laughed again, a gloating light in his eyes.

"Well," said the Colonel, "suppose I confess that I've come here on a matter of business?"

"Well?"

Mr. Patterson raised his head with a new glint in his eyes. His visitor took out a twist of chamois leather which he unfolded, and laid upon the desk a big yellow diamond!

CHAPTER 23

Mr. Patterson took up the jewel and examined it with affection. He loved all precious things, and he saw at once that this was neither glass nor paste but, actually, a very fine stone. He weighed it with expert fingertips and appraised it as a three-thousand-dollar stone. He might make a small error in one direction or the other, but he felt that he was not far wrong. If he counted it by the carat, it would be worth this sum. It had no flaw other than a small one at the base. It was well cut, and the color was rich and sparkling.

He looked up from the diamond to the face of his visitor and carefully regarded the eyes of the other.

"Well?" said Patterson sharply.

He could not help that tone of sharpness. He had been pleased to sit and talk with a man who was called by such a title of respect or of real authority as "colonel," but now that business was introduced he altered, as a starved dog alters when it smells raw meat.

"I haven't any money left," said the Colonel with perfect simplicity. "And I must go back to Kentucky at once. I need money to do that. I need, I should say, about five hundred dollars. Very well, I didn't want to trouble you about such a small affair; but there's no pawn shop in Double Bend — and I hear that you occasionally lend money."

He had stated his needs so quietly and so directly, and the sum wanted was so small for such security, that Patterson almost went at once to get the sum.

He remembered in the nick of time that business is business.

He picked up the diamond without saying a word, turned it in his hand, laid it down again.

"I suppose it is worth that much?" said the Colonel.

"Do you?" said Patterson.

He sat back in his chair and shrugged his shoulders.

Then he added: "I don't deal in jewels."

The big Colonel stood up.

"I'm sorry," he said, and picked up the stone.

Patterson bit his lip. Usually, men who wanted money were importunate; this abruptness upset him and all of his methods. He wanted that yellow diamond. He saw himself with the flare of it on his brightest necktie. The picture pleased the gambler.

"But," said Patterson, "I like to make exceptions — I mean, for gentlemen."

"Thank you," said the Colonel, and sat down again, and replaced the yellow diamond upon the edge of the desk. He waited, polite, attentive.

"The other way of it," went on Patterson, "is that I'm short. I'm sorry, but I'm short."

The Colonel said not a word. But his grave eyes dwelt steadily upon the face of the other. As though this merely were thinking aloud, and not bargaining.

"It kind of makes me ashamed," said Patterson. "Fact is, I generally have plenty on hand. But I've had bad luck. They're cleaning me out in this business. I've gotta leave it!"

Still the Colonel said nothing, and Patterson began to perspire a little.

"But I can't let you be stranded," said he. "I might rake up the money — for a month, say?"

The Colonel murmured something in surprise.

"That's not very long," he said aloud.

"In a month, I'll need every penny I can put my hands on," said Patterson, "if I'm not cleaned out in the meantime. Well, I could let you have the five hundred for a month. That'd give you a chance to get back there, and mail me the money."

He had calculated carefully. If this man were able to raise five hundred with ease at home, he would be able to get it, also, by telegraph. No, the man would find it hard to get five hundred.

"Suppose that you sign a note, promise to pay six hundred in a month — I keep the diamond for that time — and mail it back to you when you send me the money."

He was scratching out a note in legal form, in the meantime. He pushed it across the desk as he spoke. He dared not look up. He was asking twenty per cent for a single month!

Then the calm voice of the Colonel sounded and quieted his fear.

"If I found it hard to get the money together —"

"Oh, of course! I could give you extra time. Matter of form —" said the gambler.

Matter of form? There was no mention of extensions of time in that little note to which the visitor was now appending his signature.

Smoothly, gracefully the pen flowed on and the paper was pushed back to Mr. Patterson.

He read:

"Anthony G. St. O. Wilton."

What a signature! It trailed clear across the page. Patterson folded the paper with care and wrapped it around the jewel. That jewel was his. He knew it. Pleasant electric thrills flowed up and down his spine, and prickled on the surface of his skin.

"Well, then—" He rose and turned to the door.

He passed out into the next room, and as he did so a smile flashed in the strange blue eyes of the Colonel, and went out like a snuffed candle.

Again Patterson unlocked the safe; again he drew out a drawer, but this time more covertly, selected from it a small bundle of bills, and then in another place put down the yellow diamond.

He closed and relocked the safe door and then turned to a narrow-shouldered, long-faced man who lingered near.

"How's things, Blinky?"

Blinky scowled and touched his bruised jaw which had swollen greatly.

"Things look all right for you, Mr. Patterson," said he.

Patterson hung in his stride as he turned away.

"I'll tell you something," said he. "If things look good for me, they look good for you and all the rest of the boys, and don't you forget it! I keep you boys in mind, all of you!"

"Yes, sir," said Blinky, and looked down suddenly to the floor, for there was that in his eyes which could not be seen without danger.

Patterson went back into his office with a smile springing to his lips and to his eyes. He had in his heart the sense of virtue which comes to most men after they had done a good deed for the sake of another; but to Patterson that warmth about the heart only occurred when he had filled his own pocket or tripped up an associate. He never looked backward upon his past, but forward, turning corners to shut out disagreeable memories.

Now he gazed benevolently upon the colonel.

"Here you are, Colonel," said he. "Five hundred dollars, you'll find it in good order, I trust."

"Of course," said the colonel. "And now about another thing, Mr. Patterson —"

He was interrupted by a sudden stir of voices; and then silence.

Patterson roused himself and canted his head to one side.

"Somebody's made a big winning — and he's playing again!"

The noises from the game room did not come distinctly through the thick walls of Patterson's office, but they came as the voice of the sea comes inland at a distance, reaching over the tops of the orchards, murmuring in a strange language across the meadows. So that the noise of the gamblers reached into the office of Patterson, usually with a sullen mumbling, but sometimes cutting in thin and sharp when some boy laughed, his pocket filled with gold; or when some man yelled out, mad with bad whiskey.

Those sounds were all familiar to Patterson. They made a pattern of music, as it were, and from it he drew a strange comfort. "Big men are steam rollers," he was apt to say, "and God help the little fellows that get in their way. I'm a big man, I hope. All right, I squeeze out some blood. If I didn't, somebody else would get the suckers. Fools are like ripe apples. They gotta fall. All I do is to give the tree a bit of a shake. People say I'm hard. Well, maybe I am. I don't care. I'm looking to the future. There'll be a time when I've got enough. Take a hell of a lot, but I'll get it. Then what'll I do? I'll found a college, or something like that. I'll found a college. Turn out a thousand boys a year that'll look up to me as if I was God. That's what I'll do. Won't call me a hard man, then. Call me simply a smart man, a big man. That's what I am."

In exactly those words he had expressed himself, on an evening when a few glasses of liquor went to his head. But now and again a touch of drunken exultation flashed across his mind. It did now, and he said, genially: "Somebody's won! That'll make him play bigger still. Probably lose it all. But he's won. He's up. Everybody in the room is up. They wanta pull me down. They want me under their feet. But they ain't going to get me there. I sit back and wait for the fools to dance till they drop. They'll always drop, in the end. They'll always drop, I tell you — and the bigger the winnings, the bigger the crowd that comes in the next day to be picked!"

"Of course," said the colonel amiably, and his strange blue eyes rested with wonderful thought and steadiness upon the gambler.

A hand rattled hastily at the door; there was no pause to wait for an invitation to enter, but that door was jerked open, and on the threshold appeared one of the errand and handy boys of the place, his face flushed, his eyes dancing with joy and with mischief.

"It's him come back!" said he.

"Who, you fool?" asked Patterson.

"Him that made the great fight at the faro table the other night. Him that was mobbed — I mean, that Al Naylor! He's back! He's back agin!"

Patterson lurched forward a long step, as though he would go personally to look into this matter. But he checked himself with his usual prudence.

"He's at the faro table?"

"Yes. He's playing big — he's winning again!"

"The damn young fool!" said Patterson. "Where's Gil Bunch and young Rooney?"

"I dunno."

"Go find them, you jackass. Don't stand there and moon. Go find them and bring them here by the ears. Is that hog, that other fellow — is he in the place?"

"Everybody's looking for him; he ain't been seen."

The boy vanished through the door, which closed with a thud, and the owner of the gaming house stood fixed, listening to the rush of many feet. Everyone in his establishment was drawing out from the offices, from the bar, from the kitchen, from the by-passages, from the private gambling rooms, to see the picture of the dare-devil youth who had come back to tempt his fate.

But something else interested Mr. Patterson. He began to feel that he dared not turn and face the Colonel again. He felt that the Colonel was laughing softly and savagely, in triumph, and Patterson broke into a hot sweat of agony!

CHAPTER 24

It was not that any clear idea of danger had come into the mind of Mr. Patterson, or that he could see any reason or possibility of harm. The time was the broadest daylight. The gambling house was full. His fighting men, his trained helpers and assistants of all kinds, were scattered throughout the crowd. There was surely no possibility of harm of serious proportions.

And yet a sudden flash of danger had leaped red across his brain, and he turned suddenly about, breaking through his chill of apprehension.

Then he saw a long, blue-barreled revolver in the hand of the Colonel, and a smile upon the Colonel's lips, and a bright, gay light in the Colonel's eyes.

Mr. Patterson caught his breath and even thought of snatching at his own gun; but he changed his mind—

"Just in time," said the Colonel, filling in the very thought of Patterson.

He added: "Lie down on the floor and lie there on your face with your hands behind your back."

It was an awkward moment for Patterson. He had his reputation as a rich and successful business man. He had also his reputation as a great man of battle, and the second half of his frame was dearer to him, almost, than the first.

"If you ain't gunna do it," said the Colonel, lapsing suddenly into vernacular, and his very voice changing, "I'll let a streak of light through you from one side to the other. Get down on that floor!"

Patterson got. He remembered that life was sweet and that much of it lay before him, and many a lamb was yet to pass under the fleecing edge of his shears. He lay down, his hands were caught together behind his back and a light pair of iron manacles was snapped together to secure them. Another pair of the shackles bound his ankles, and then with a length of stout twine, the Colonel bound the heels and the hands of his victim together.

Patterson recognized the touch of experience in this work. He could not move, now, but he still could shout. That opportunity, also, was lost to him.

"I oughta break your head open," said the Colonel, "because it'd be quicker. You twenty-per-cent a month hound! You inside the law crook! But I gotta do this, instead!"

And he crowded Patterson's own balled up handkerchief, twisted together with a quantity of twine, into his mouth, distending the jaws until they ached.

Mr. Patterson strove instinctively to speak; he could only gasp. He strove to use his tongue and swallow, but he nearly choked. And he realized that all he could do would be to lie there, careful of nothing except that his breathing was regular and easy until he could be released.

And what would the Colonel do?

The Colonel sat down quietly on the arm of Patterson's own chair, dangling in his fingers the keys of the safe.

The keys of the safe! With the ashes of despair in his soul, Patterson remembered that he had been warned by this very man — this devil of a man! — that exactly this thing might happen, and his keys come into the possession of another. He had derided that possibility at the time, and now it had come about that the fatal beauty of the yellow diamond had made him, deliberately, turn his back upon the danger which had now undone him.

And all had happened so easily – he had not been able to strike a blow or offer a single stroke of resistance! He had enemies. He knew that. And they would make his downfall famous through every far corner of the range. Mr. Patterson could have died of chagrin, if the danger of actually choking to death had not been so near as to keep his mind half occupied by the process of breathing.

Said the Colonel, balanced upon the edge of the chair:

"It ain't always true that you can put a price on time. There was a three-thousand-dollar diamond, that you could of got, you thought, for five hundred. Well, it was worth the loss, d'you see? Because it gave me the time that I wanted. It'll almost leave me kind of sad, Patterson, to take away the diamond along with the rest of the boodle in that safe of yours. I gotta touch of shame in me, old fellow. You might learn, if you'd listen to me. But you ain't that kind. Besides, I'm short, and I need every penny that I got in that safe of yours. Everything that you been keeping care of for me, for so long! I'm grateful for that. I'm a tender-hearted man, Patterson!"

He smiled as he said this, and rolled a cigarette.

"If I wasn't a tender-hearted gent," he went

on, lighting the cigarette, "I'd sure kick your head in with the heel of this gat. That's what God A'mighty must be askin' me to do. But I'll leave you to die in your own poison, you snake! While I sit here and have a little chat with you and wait for the time when your gents outside get their minds all occupied—"

There was a sudden roar of voices outside the office. And then guns barked, sounding strangely far away. A man yelled in agony, another in fear, and the roar of many trampling feet and cursing voices gathered.

That instant the light in the office went out.

The same darkness seemed to have blanketed the people in the game-room as well, for they, in turn, were hushed, and then Babel broke loose in a louder key than before. All was a madness of confusion. And Patterson strained his hands at the shackles which held them, and struggled until the sudden closing of his throat warned him that he would stifle himself with the effort.

Then he was aware that the Colonel was standing over him. The bright flare of a flashlight blinded his staring, bulging eyes, and he heard the stranger say:

"We've got you where we want you, old timer! So long."

A door was torn open, the door to the room

214

in which the safe stood, and an hysterical voice called: "Hey, Big Boy! Where are you? What's keepin' you back, in God's name! I got the room all empty and waitin'!"

It was the voice of Blinky Morris, and at this bit of recognition, Patterson went blind indeed with rage and consuming desire for revenge.

Through his blindness, he was able to see the big form of the Colonel passing through the door into the room where the safe itself was discernible, glimmering faintly in the light of a candle held in the trembling hand of Blinky.

"Bump off that ——" cried Blinky. "Why don't you bump him off? I'll do it myself!"

He lurched through the doorway. The candle he held was the light by which his face was revealed like the face of a devil incarnate, and Patterson knew that he lay on the brink of a horrible death.

Then a big arm barred the way to Blinky and brushed him back.

"None of that, son," said the Colonel. "We wanta do this job quick and clean. And there ain't a thing in the world so apt to make you slip as blood on the floor."

The door to the safe room was therewith closed. Darkness fell upon the gambler. He heard the lock turned with a click of finality. And he was a hopeless prisoner in his own office.

Not necessarily hopeless, however, no matter how black was his present moment. He was alone, to be sure, and he was secured hand and foot. But still, something might be done—

Like a half animate lump of flesh, with his straining knees and elbows he worked his way across the office floor.

Now the swift hands of the Colonel would have turned the second lock, the door of the safe would be opening with a groan upon its rusted hinges, that noise which so often had been music to his very soul—

At the side of his office there was a fireplace, built in of bricks, and now he strained and labored toward it. The effort made him breathe hard and fast, and the speed of his breathing made him well-nigh strangle. But gradually he drew closer to it, and he was able to bring his heels and his hands against it. Across the rough edges of the brick he chafed the twine which bound them back and forth. It parted.

And he was free, then, to roll like a log, swiftly, across the floor to the door which communicated with the game room.

Inside of this place, there was a pandemonium growing louder every moment.

And at that very moment a prolonged knocking came against his door.

Mr. Patterson smote upon the door with both

of his shackled feet, and with such force that he drove out the entire lower panel of the door.

The light of a lantern shone in upon him, and this was reinforced, dimly, but the flickering of many other, more distant lights.

Through the gap in the lower part of the door, young Erskine forced his way, leaned over his employer, and gasped as he recognized him and his condition.

Then he plucked forth the gag.

Mr. Patterson attempted to say: "You jackass, don't waste time here. Get into the safe room! Get into the safe room! They're robbing the safe!"

He cried it out at the top of his lungs, but young Erskine merely backed away, and looked in amazed fear at the head of the house.

He stammered: "What's happened? What's happened to you, Mr. Patterson? That young fellow – that young Naylor. He came back. Shorty and a couple of the boys went for him – with guns – he shot out the lights –"

Suddenly Patterson realized that the first command which he had given had not been properly uttered at all. The words had formed in his brain, but from his paralyzed tongue and throat only a mumbling scream had poured forth.

Now he gripped his aching jaws together.

Then he shouted, making sure of articulation: "Damn you! The safe room! The safe room! They've got the keys! The Colonel! Damn you — quick! Quick!"

Erskine swayed this way and that.

He started for the door of the safe room at last.

"Jackass!" yelled Patterson. "They'll shoot your head off! Go back into the big room and get more help! Get help! Stop them — I'll make you rich — ten thousand — twenty thousand dollars—"

Erskine did not need the urging of any money reward, held before his eyes. He plunged through the broken door like a ferret down a rabbit's hole.

And Patterson heard his voice bellowing in the big room:

"Saunders! King! Jerry! For God's sake! Come here. Hey, Saunders—"

Then Patterson closed his eyes and smiled in an agony of expectancy.

Would they be in time? Would they be in time?

And, if they were, in what fire of oil and damnation could he torment the soul out of the body of the "Colonel" if that gentleman were caught?

CHAPTER 25

It is necessary to go back to young Alfred Naylor, a little earlier in that evening.

He was seen to be wandering down the main street with a gait a trifle uncertain. His hat was at an angle over one ear. His necktie was twisted to the side and the ends of it blew in the hot wind over his shoulder. One button of his coat was fastened — the second button being hitched into the first button hole, with the result that the whole coat was crumpled and bulging at the chest.

In a moment he was noted, regarded, and apparently understood.

The youngsters of the town were the first to spot him. They are the keenest gatherers of news because they have the sharpest eyes and few preconceptions. Most grown people see little more than their own thoughts, but a child goes through the world with the eye of a hunter, and above all he loves to find trouble.

Their eyes were attracted to Alfred Naylor because he had secured in that town, at one stroke, the reputation of a hero.

Mr. Patterson was not popular. Gamblers rarely are, and, above all, those who take no chances in person. His place and the income it brought to the town were too important to be dispensed with; otherwise a committee of irate citizens long ago would have headed the man for the more open spaces. But they knew well enough the methods of Patterson, and there was little doubt in the minds of anyone that young Naylor had been mobbed by the express orders of the owner of the establishment. Nothing was done about it, because nothing could be done. There was no proof that could be held up against Patterson, as Sheriff Axon in person had pointed out to that young man. But the minds of the townsmen were hot. They loved fair play, and they hated its opposite.

All of this was known to the boys in a town where the children ate at the same table with their parents. They knew every phase of the fight in Patterson's place, and they knew that the man, with empty hands, had beaten down one of the hired bullies of the house and had then been swarmed over by a sneaking flank attack.

So when they saw Alfred Naylor on the street

they were drawn to him as iron flies to the magnet. And a moment after they began to swarm at his heels, they were aware that he was apparently in an odd condition. He had the dress, the gait, the manner of a drunkard.

And the boys began to laugh.

Particularly when he leaned against a telephone pole and talked in a rambling fashion to the broad, strong arms above him, that supported the many wires! Grown men saw the little mob and the center of it. They paused in turn. They did not openly join the procession but they drifted before it, behind it, to the flanks.

There was one burning question in every mind. Would this boy, in his present condition, enter Patterson's place? If he did, he would probably be shot down like a dog!

He paused and turned in at Steve Graham's saloon, and there it was noted by the bartender that the face of the young man seemed neither flushed nor pale, nor was his tongue apparently thick. But indubitably he seemed uncertain upon his feet, and his talk was wild, and his manner extremely careless.

"He's about two sheets to the wind," said the bartender. "Something oughta be done about it!"

He found a chance to confer privately at the

end of the bar with Bud Langdale, the cow-puncher. And Bud's advice was given instantly, from the wealth of long experience in similar cases.

"This here kid is a wildcat, with his claws all made of iron," said Bud. "No, the thing to do is to get him plumb poisoned with red-eye. After that, we can handle him pretty easy, without getting chawed up on the way. Don't let him get to Patterson's!"

It was a vain proposal, simply because Alfred Naylor refused more than a single drink, and then wandered out into the sun with the announced determination of seeing how Patterson's looked.

And toward Patterson's he went.

He was on the street corner before it, when Langdale and two other punchers barred his way.

"Old kid," they said to him gently, "you better stay shut of Patterson's. They's trouble for you in there. Stay out here with your friends!"

Naylor propped himself with one hand against the hitching rack.

"I don't know you!" he said. "I ain't got time to know you, because I'm on my way. Back up, old razoos, and lemme through!"

And as he swayed forward, they hesitated, being brave men, and then gave way, being discreet men, also.

He entered Patterson's.

The doorkeeper was a scarred and grizzled warrior, famed for his many battles. The instant he saw the boy, he knew his duty and tried to do it.

"You ain't wanted here," said he. "Get out, Naylor! Clear out! You can't come in!"

There was a silver flash of light; the muzzle of a Colt rested against the stomach of the doorkeeper.

"Say it over again and say it slow," said Alfred. "That sounded like a foreign language to me."

The doorkeeper, his hands above his head, shuddered.

"Go on, then," said he. "Go on in, and God help you, kid!"

The "kid" went on.

Once inside the door, he paused, as though to let his eye grow familiar with the inside of the house. And presently he saw the faro table in the distance, in the corner where the big electric line passed through the wall into a box of switches.

That pause permitted a small crowd to surround him. They were the men who had swarmed behind him on the street, and they now entered Patterson's place as fast as they could file by the doorkeeper. That man was half unnerved; a chill was in his vitals. And instead of trying to keep the crowd back, he merely passed on word to the "Boys" that trouble was coming, and probably coming big.

And that was the signal which flew like magic from one end of Patterson's busy place to another.

And that was the time, as well, when a thick murmur of voices crowded into the big game room, as the "Colonel" and Patterson himself could distinguish in the latter's office.

The other games were suspended, and all eyes were concentrated upon the young man who crossed the earth floor with an uncertain step toward the distant faro table. By the time he had reached it, most of the men of Double Bend were in the gaming house; and every gambler, and every waiter in the place, and the guards, and the idlers, and the dealers, and the cleaning corps, and the errand boys, had flocked in a great, loose circle to see the fun.

Fun or tragedy it was sure to be. Young Naylor, however, was apparently drunk, and the staggering step reassured those who did not want to see him fall.

The guards themselves were puzzled. It was hard to shoot a drunken man; it was hard to manhandle an armed fighter who was still sober enough to shoot. And the experience of the doorkeeper was quoted in muffled voices.

However, the hardier spirits drew closer and closer, elbowing their way through the crowd. Their duty was obvious. This man was not wanted, and they would have to throw him out!

Already the faro dealer had looked up long and steadily into the cheerful eyes of Alfred Naylor.

He saw the bet laid; and automatically he opened his game.

Naylor lost.

Another hundred went the next moment.

And five hundred came in to him on the next play. He was making it come big, as he had in his other experience at this same table. And the crowd, seeing him rake up the pile of chips and immediately place more bets, grew excited for a secondary reason.

It was at this moment that Hendrix, a hired gunman, came straight towards the boy.

Hendrix feared neither God, man, nor devil. No tremor ever had entered his heart, and none ever would. He was a bull of a man who knew nothing but combat, and he called out as he came: "Hey, Naylor! You ain't wanted in here. Understand? You ain't wanted. Get out."

Alfred Naylor turned toward the speaker. He had not moved a hand towards a gun, but the blind beast had taken possession of Hendrix, and he dragged forth his Colt and began shooting.

At the first shot, Naylor plunged head first to the floor, as the crowd scattered back from expected bullets with cries of horror.

That cry was repeated with a louder note of rage and disgust when they saw Hendrix deliberately level his gun again at the fallen figure.

But Hendrix had seen what the others had not, and that was a subtle movement of Naylor's hand as he dropped. Furthermore, he had begun to fall before Hendrix's weapon exploded for the first time; so that the bullet had whizzed over his head. Now he lay on the ground with his own Colt stretched forth before him, resting on the crook of his left arm — a perfect support for steady, accurate shooting. And he answered Hendrix's second shot with a bullet that drilled its way through both of the gunman's thighs.

Hendrix toppled backwards with a shout; and young Naylor turned on one raised elbow in time to face the faro dealer.

That gentleman, willing to try a shot for the sake of the house which gave him both salary and commission, had risen from his chair and was levelling a sawed-off shotgun that surely would have blown Naylor's back in two, when the latter exploded a revolver shot almost in his face. The dealer fell backwards, sprawled over his chair, and rose cursing, half blinded by the smoke.

The next instant, he was in a more real darkness, for Naylor, shooting again, had driven a forty-five calibre bullet into the delicate mechanism of the switch box, and the whole gambling house was lost in a total darkness.

The fusillade of bullets and the outbreak of shouting seemed to drive everyone mad, in the blanket of darkness that followed.

Fear had started, and it raged like wildfire in the total lack of light. Yonder someone was scratching with a match and making a pale glow come up from a lantern. A candle was started in another place like a star in the wide, dark sky. But this illumination was as nothing to the general darkness, or only a production of shadows worse than the utter dark itself.

Alfred Naylor had drawn back under the shelter of the faro table, as he saw the flood of legs and feet come trampling and stamping about him.

Then he got up and drove himself like a football player into the crowd, charging low and hard, and going for a definite goal which he had plotted in his mind long before a shot had been fired.

CHAPTER 26

It seemed an eternity that he was wading through the mass of the crowd; somewhere he heard men shouting: "Clear the way for the sheriff! Get clear for Sheriff Axon!"

The little sheriff was there, then. Yes, he had seen him at a side table, rising, hurrying towards the scene of the shooting just at the end, before the bullet through the box of electric connections had dipped the big room into darkness.

And Axon made a most serious complication. However, it might be that the very size of the jostling crowd would keep him from action.

Finally, the boy reached the side wall, and there he took from the bulging breast of his coat a linen over-all which he slipped into. It had a hood that fitted tightly over the head and left capacious eyeholes through which he could look. Into his hands he brought a pair of guns, and now he stood prepared for the actual role of a robber. Up to that moment, he had been merely the accidental disturbance which allowed the others to do their work. Now he was actually stepping out into the presence of the law.

And yet it meant very little to him.

He felt that it was both the greatest and the happiest moment of his life, and all that he wanted, seriously, was to plunge deeper and deeper, and lose himself in this joy of action.

The over-all was a dark grey, and it made him well nigh invisible among the shadows. Unless he had to spring into action with those guns!

It seemed to him that there had been time, there had been centuries for the Dude and Blinky Morris to accomplish their ends. But still he could not be sure.

They had only one man and two rooms to secure — two rooms from which he had stripped the defenders. Big Patterson was the main difficulty, and yet the boy was reasonably sure that the Dude would be able to handle that problem.

He *must* handle it!

In the meantime, there was nothing more that he could do in the big room. He must get out into the street.

But how could that be managed, when the doorway was thronged with a jumbled mass of men, fighting, cursing?

They seemed to be held back as if a terrific

blast of wind were pouring into their faces. Sometimes they actually receded! But it was only the effect of their own blind struggling to get out. They were not men. They were sheep in a panic.

He looked at them with an odd abstraction, an odd amusement. Then he turned to the window beside him.

It was barred across by irons, and the ends of those irons were sunk in concrete. He sent a bullet through one of these settings, and kicked the bar out that end. In an instant it was detached from the other, and with this as a lever, he wrenched at the next and the next, until a gap had been formed.

And so wild was the excitement in the hall that no one appeared to notice him.

In another instant he was in the street.

It was filled with a swirl of excited people. Some were pouring out of the madhouse of the gaming room; others were the townsfolk, who were flocking to the scene of the disturbance. And every man had his voice raised to offer suggestions as to how this affair should be managed, or as to how it might be done, and there were questions asked and answered, and hallooings to friends, and the forming of defensive groups, as if a general battle were under way.

Someone yelled "Fire!"

That threw the crowd into a greater consternation than ever. The boy thought that he never had seen such wild faces, as they pressed away from the wall of the suspected building.

However, there was no fire!

But yonder to the side there was happening a thing which had great importance to young Alfred Naylor. Through the jam, a man actually had succeeded in bringing three horses to a hitching post, and there he tethered them.

Naylor saw, and took careful note that these were no ordinary mustangs, but long-legged, long-necked animals. Once give them headway across the open country, and old Sheriff Axon could use his brains as best he might! He would not get far here!

One thing remained for the boy to do. He had done his share in the game room; he had extricated himself from the place; now he was slinking down the wall, hardly guessed at by the others, on account of that enveloping mantle of mist.

But he reached another barred window with a door beside it, and pressing his face against the bars he called out softly.

He heard the jangling of the lock.

"Kid!"

"Yes?"

"The damned door can't be opened. It's barred

and locked on your side — and it's iron!"

"Oh, my God," yammered Blinky Morris, almost in hysterics, "we'll never get out — and they're bustin' in the other door — they're bustin' in the other door!"

The battering at that door at the moment drowned the sound of Blinky's voice, until the latter shrieked out a few words which Alfred Naylor could not understand; but he recognized the fear in them, and the sweat stood on his forehead.

Then a canvas bag was suddenly crushed through, between the bars of the window, and fell at his feet, and he heard the deep voice of the Dude, saying: "There's the loot. Cut and run with it, kid; and let us go!"

"No! No!" screamed Blinky.

But at that moment, the actions of the boy were a sufficient answer, for he took the heavy iron bar which had been his own means of release from the gaming room, and fixing it under an end of the central upright bar of the window, he tugged with all his might.

But unfortunately, the concrete in which these bars were sunk was of tougher stuff than that which had been used on the window of the game room. The bar gave only a little, and then the lever which the boy was using sagged in his hands!

It had yielded more than a little. He felt that a second effort would perhaps break or bend it hopelessly. And, desperate, he chipped at the stubborn concrete with an end of the bar. It was clumsy, awkward work, and the concrete held like granite. He cursed the honest labor which had mixed its due portion of cement in that compound.

With his half bent bar, he tried again. There was a shriek of iron sliding through yielding concrete, and the bar came away at the lower end with a jerk. He worked it back and forth, and presently its own leverage made it give way.

There were two bars, now. One of them he passed inwards to the mighty hands of the Dude. With the other, he worked from the outside, and uniting their efforts at one point, they quickly ripped away the bars until there was a sufficient gap.

What happened in the crowd, at this time?

There were more than seven score men and children, jamming the street upon either side, and there were a hundred weapons which, if they had been drawn, would have blasted away the life of young Alfred Naylor as a chip is floated off upon a torrent of water. The small of his back tingled and twitched with his consciousness of the danger behind him, beside him. He could hear the murmurs, the shouts. Those behind were pushing to get forward, and half of those in front were saying:

"Hey, Joe, pull your gun and go after 'em. We'll be behind you! Look what they're doin'! They're robbin' the place! Hey, Jimmy! Bring your shotgun over here. Let's rush 'em! You start, Big Boy! We'll be with you! Start something, somebody!"

But no one started.

The unhurried, business-like methods of the man outside the bars, the labor of those within, combined to make the spectators feel a plan in this affair. They could not be sure. Others might be waiting nearby. The first attack upon the marauders would have resulted in a fusillade. And if that happened, in the densely packed mob, every bullet would go home.

Besides, it was Patterson's house. That was the key to the situation. Who cared?

So those in front pushed back, and those to the rear urged forward, but nothing happened, until the door between the game room and the chamber in which the safe stood went down with an audible roar — audible even in the noisy street.

Then guns sparkled inside the dark window. Someone shrieked with pain. At the door, not daring to rush in, Patterson's men were firing in, at random. There was another loud yell. Then, through the gap in the bars, the big Dude passed the limp body of Blinky Morris.

Alfred Naylor received him and tried to stand him up. It was like trying to stand up a dummy loosely stuffed with sand. There was no starch in Blinky. There was no timber in him. He did not cry out, but his eyes had doubled their size, and his face was luminous with pallor.

"One of 'em's gone. Close in!" cried someone in the crowd.

And then, far in the distance, a bellow like that of a wounded animal:

"Lemme through! Lemme through! You damn cowards! Oh, damn you! Lemme through! I'll pay fifty thousand dollars! I'll pay fifty thousand, I swear to God! Fifty thousand for 'em alive or dead. Alive or dead! Hey, help! Lemme through! Oh, God! You rotten yellow quitters—"

That was Patterson screaming and raving.

But fifty thousand dollars?

The calm voice of the Dude said beside Alfred Naylor: "It looks like we've got something worth having, from the way that old Patterson is belly-aching!"

CHAPTER 27

It was a different crowd, now.

A sluggish horse may win the race, if the spur is driven deep enough, provided that he has a touch of bone and quality. And there was plenty of courage in that assembly. It was only that they were indifferent to the outrage upon the gambler.

Now, they had felt the spur.

Fifty thousand dollars! It was enough to reward fifty men, richly. And suddenly, they wanted to be in at the death!

In the meantime, big Harley knew well enough the change that had taken place. He was holding up Blinky Morris on one side, and young Naylor was holding him up on the other. Like three ghosts they went, clothed in grey to their heels. But the Dude had insisted upon that. He could tell stories of men who had had their heads thoroughly masked and had been recognized by the design of a patch upon their overalls. In certain details, the Dude was a stickler in his craft, and worked according to a meticulously close pattern. He had insisted upon those coverings, partly, as he said, because it made other people half feel that ghosts were walking.

But one of these three ghosts was no longer an erect and gliding spirit. He staggered and wabbled too humanly, even if one could not see the red patch which grew upon his side.

They reached the horses; they heaved Blinky up in the saddle, and as he wavered there, Alfred flashed onto the back of the black mare and supported the wounded man by passing an arm under his shoulders. With his free hand he held a six-shooter. He could thank his God, then, that he had so thoroughly mastered the mare that he could guide her merely by the sway of his body, the pressure of his knees. She worked for him like an obedient spirit. She was a part and portion of his thoughts!

At that very moment, the crowd broke towards them. And surely they would have been overwhelmed in that first rush.

The Dude bellowed, close to Alfred's ear: "Shoot — but for God's sake shoot over their heads!"

Long afterward, Alfred was to remember that. It came even in that moment of excitement as a strange pacification to him, a criticism of his spirit from a loftier soul, as it were!

And then he turned the heads of the horses down the street and began to fire rapidly, just over the heads of the crowd, as the big man had told him to do.

Blinky began to laugh hideously. He, too, took out a revolver, and, holding it in both hands, he fired blindly, reeling in the saddle as he pulled the trigger.

His shots, too, were high.

But the Dude was like a madman.

He swerved his horse straight back at the thickest mass of the crowd, and with a dreadful yell that would have done credit to a Blackfoot in mid-battle, he rushed into them. He had a gun in either hand. His bullets seemed driven into the very faces of the mob. The boy, looking back, actually saw a man struck, and trampled down by the horse — heard his scream—

Then the crowd broke and surged wildly back. Hats, hands, staggered against the light further down the street.

So it went with the Dude in his charge to the rear. But in front of Alfred Naylor, his shots and those of Blinky Morris seemed to have little effect indeed. Some cowards bolted. Others, brave men, dropped on their knees, guns in hand.

The finger of death reached for Alfred, but merely flicked the top of his mask, ripping it open at the crown. And again, it brushed his side.

Once more, and this time it struck, with a solid impact which the boy could hear, the body of Blinky Morris.

The sneak-thief doubled limply back over the strong arm of Alfred, and he heard a yell of gratification from the men before him.

Then, sweeping from the rear, the Dude struck that mass, and he split them apart as the lightning splits apart the mists of the clouds. Blinky and the boy were small forces. But there was no doubting of the reality of the Dude. The very trampling of his big horse meant something. And to either side these hunters for the fifty thousand dollar reward gave back suddenly.

The Dude did not keep straight down the street. He swerved to the right; the crowd thinned upon that side, and suddenly Alfred Naylor saw before him a narrow-throated alley, dark, close, leading to he know not what.

But the Dude was leading in that direction, and he blindly followed, pushing his horse forward, trying to support the wounded man and control Blinky's horse with one hand. It was a task that defied every resource in his

powerful young body. His back seemed breaking in two with the sidewise wrench, but he
would not give up.

It was partly that he was naturally loyal. It
was partly because he knew that the Dude
would not have approved if he gave way to the
labor.

For the figure of the Dude was becoming
more and more important, taking on a sort of
legendary significance. He could not be called
in any fair sense a good man, because of course
he was a professional yegg. And yet the very
swing of his shoulders and the holding of his
head told the boy that this was the man to be
trusted in a crisis.

Those shoulders turned. Having broken the
way in front, big Harley came thundering
back, with foam dripping from the mouth of
his horse, and flung himself in the face of the
pursuit.

"You're crazy – they'll shoot you to bits!"
screamed Alfred Naylor.

He rolled his head and his eyes frantically
back, and he saw the Dude coming again.
Guns were crashing, guns were roaring down
the alley, but they were drawing away. They
turned a corner, and suddenly the sound was
dimmed.

There still was danger. But the hoof beats,

the shouts, the barking of the roused dogs of the town, all clamored in the rear.

And now the whole adventure seemed unreal to the boy. It was as though he had passed through a pasteboard show. Otherwise they would have torn him to bits, that crowd of savage men. But they had stood like lifeless silhouettes, and seen him do as he would.

It had been odd that only now had the barking of the dogs begun — those dogs of a Western town, ready to prick their ears at the first strange sound, ready to howl at the next.

But then it occurred to him that the real explanation was that all of this had not taken much time.

To the lightning processes of his feverish brain it had seemed like minutes and minutes. It had only been seconds from the time he had fallen as the first bullet was fired, through his own shot that crashed out the lights, his frantic plunge through the crowd, and then that terrible time when he was clawing at the bars which kept him from the Dude and Blinky.

Even that time was not long, as he could see, now.

And he could understand the crowd. They had seen a man issue suddenly. They had seen the tearing at the bars of the safe-room window, and they had hardly realized what was happening, until the three men were in retreat, and the screeching, frantic voice of Patterson was yammering over their heads, promising fortunes for the arrest of the fugitives.

But here they were!

The burden of Blinky's body was taken from him. The Dude was on the far side of him, and the Dude's mighty arm was beneath the shoulders of the wounded man.

"Dude—" gasped Blinky Morris.

"We're gunna turn in and rest here," said the Dude briskly.

And deliberately he turned his horse and Blinky's into a grove of pines that filled a big vacant lot.

At the same time he called quickly to the boy: "Here, Alf! You take this saddle-bag of mine. Ride like hell. Make for Tangle Butte. I'll stay here a minute and fix up Blinky so's he can get along — then I'll follow you and meet you at the Tangle—"

He threw the saddle bag at Alfred, and the boy caught it, and hooped the loop over the pommel of his saddle.

He reined in his horse, bewildered. And then he saw the body of Blinky sag suddenly toward the Dude.

It was not in the expectation that he would soon be following that the Dude had given him the loot. It was simply that he would not abandon a comrade — even a rat of a man like Blinky — that made the Dude order the boy away. He, the Dude, would stay there and comfort the hurt man, though all the while he knew that danger was closing in around him.

And the heart of the boy expanded, and a dimness passed across his eyes. He could remember the times when he had looked upon the Dude as a worthless criminal, a mere idler, a lazy, useless fellow. He could remember how he had laid down the vices of the Dude to bad blood, to mental weakness—

But now he passed into a great self-shadowing valley of humiliation and with a mild heart he rode in after the Dude, into the thickness of the little wood.

"You damn young fool!" he heard the half-stifled voice of the Dude, before him.

But he knew that he was right. He knew that if the Dude had been in his place, he would never have deserted in that hour of danger.

In the heart of the wood, where the trees stood back from a little open circle, they dismounted. He took the weight of Blinky in his arms, and the wounded man opened his eyes and cursed him in a whining voice.

"You damn young botcher, you, you clumsy jackass!" said Blinky to him. "I hated your liver, from the first time that I laid eyes on you!"

The boy did not answer. With the ready help of the Dude, he laid the body as softly as possible upon the ground, and all that Alfred felt, instead of anger or shame, from this reproach, was a sense of chilly awe.

For he knew that Blinky would not ordinarily have used such language. He would not have dared to. And it was the coming of something new to Blinky that gave him the courage to abuse a stronger man than himself.

Alfred could guess what the new thing was.

But just then a rush of mounted men went down the street, came closer and closer, made the ground shake with the pounding of the hoofs of their horses, and began to pour past.

His tightened nerves relaxed a little. They were driving past. And here they were, the three of them, with the money safe — and the deed done.

Then he heard a voice cry:

"Here's these here trees. Why not give 'em a look?"

CHAPTER 28

Blinky Morris had heard the same voice and he reached out for the Dude.

"Don't let 'em get to us, Dude!" he breathed.

"Steady, old timer. They'll miss us," said the Dude.

And his voice was as calm and as sure as that of a father calming a nervous child afraid of the dark.

This was not mere darkness.

Black as was the space inside of the trees, searchers were coming through. The twigs snapped under their feet. Their voices boomed closer and closer, and the boy knew, by a sure instinct, that if they were found these searchers would no longer prove the cardboard figures which they had seemed in the street in Double Bend, not a minute before.

There is a virtue in aggression that stiffens the nerves and fortifies the mind. That virtue was now on the side of the hunters and all against the fugitives.

He drew both revolvers, and quietly reloaded them, and he was busy at this when the big hand of the Dude reached out and took him by the shoulder.

"No shooting, now," said he. "No more shooting, kid!"

He could not answer. And he could not resist.

For he was controlled, not by the superior wisdom or the superior strength of his companion, but by the greater moral force of the yegg. And suddenly he knew the difference between robbery and murder. Once the law hanged thieves; but the law never had a right to hang such a man as Harley. He was no killer. There was more law in his little finger than in the whole soul of many a man who never had transgressed enough to stand in the danger of the law. He, Alfred Naylor, would have shot and shot to kill, without a thought of doing otherwise, rather than meekly surrender — because, forsooth, they were nailed down in one place by the helplessness of a comrade.

The steps came closer. The voices were like a snarling thunder.

"It's dark as the devil — mind where you're stepping, will you?"

"This way!"

"Never can find anything in this damned wood."

"They ain't here. Never would stay this close in."

"You can't tell. Foxes that think out a thing like they done — they're able to be up to anything, I tell you."

"Tell it to the sheriff. I don't believe you."

"Where's the sheriff?"

"Never where he's wanted!"

"Come on, boys, hunt the wood clean!"

The speaker emerged suddenly from the trees into the little circle. Plainly he could be seen, a shadow disengaging himself from the shadows, and as suddenly lost to view again.

Had he jumped back behind a tree? Would he open fire? Or merely summon them to surrender?

And then his voice was heard again, calling his comrades further on. The whole search poured away.

And as it poured off, Blinky stammered:

"Are they gone?"

"Ay. Gone away, Blinky!"

"They're gone! They're gone! Then why don't we start on, Dude? I feel a lot better — I—"

"Because I want to have a look and tie up that hurt place—"

"Hurry up, then. Don't be so slow. Hurry up a little, will you, Dude?"

The Dude lighted a match, and by that light Alfred saw that the whole side of Blinky's drapery was covered with blood.

The cloth was drawn up, the coat parted, the skirt drawn away by the Dude's dexterous hands.

Then, with a knife, he slit off long strips of the grey veil and with it he made a pad and pressed this over the side of the hurt man. But the boy saw this dimly. He was holding the matches, now, screening the light with his hands as well as he could, and making only a thin ray pour onto the hurt. But he had seen the welling of blood, like water forced up from a spring, and the sight sickened him, and made his eyes dim.

"Go on and make the bandage," said Blinky in a fierce whisper.

"Sure. Wait a minute, though. Wait till the bleeding is stopped for a minute, Blinky. That's the best way."

"The bleeding! My God, am I still bleeding?" gasped Blinky.

"Aw, just a trickle," said the Dude.

"It — it ain't anything?" asked Blinky's trembling voice.

"This here? Why, it ain't any more'n a

scratch," said the Dude.

"I kind of thought for a second — hell, what funny thoughts come into a gent's head. Let's get a hurry on, Dude."

"What's all the hurry?" said the Dude, in seeming impatience. "You lie still, will you? It's the best way. How many wounds have you taken care of, you damn welcher?"

The familiar abuse made Blinky snarl, but he did not protest again.

"Besides," went on the Dude, "it's kind of slick, us stretched out here, takin' it easy, while they hunt up and down for us and ride their hosses ragged. Afterwards, I'll tell you what, we'll ride through 'em like nothing at all!"

"Sure, sure," assented Blinky grudgingly. "Maybe they's an idea in that. You got a head, Dude, damn your old heart!"

"Then shut up and do what I say."

"I'm doing it, ain't I? Quit your hollerin', will you?" said Blinky.

And again the boy was amazed by the unusual boldness of the sneak-thief.

"You, kid," directed the big Dude, "you get over there and stand at the heads of the hosses. Pull their heads all right in to them. Hold 'em by the bits, so the bits won't rattle, and keep workin' those bits a little. Understand? If a bridle was to shake and a bit rattle, or one of those hosses to stamp, we might be snapped. Keep drawin' their heads in and out. That'll keep 'em occupied!"

Alfred went without a word to execute this order. He was wonderfully glad, for some reason, to be away from Blinky. An unaccountable horror lay upon his spirit, and the smell of the acrid sweat of the horses and the faint glimmering of their eyes in the forest shadow eased him. He was surprised to find that his hands shook, and that it was so much easier to breathe, now that he was standing up!

He heard Blinky say, quietly, with a sneering chuckle: "Kind of a weight, ain't he, the kid?"

"He's young," said the Dude.

And the boy flushed. But he felt no resentment. There would be a need of greater insult than this before he would feel resentment toward the Dude.

"While we're lyin' here, takin' it easy," said the Dude, "I can't help thinkin' what this is gunna mean to your folks, Blinky."

"My folks? What folks you mean?"

"Why, your wife, and—"

"Wife? Me? Say, what d'ya think I am?" demanded Blinky. "I been a fool a lot of times, but I never been a *damn* fool!"

"You never married?"

"Sure I never did. Did you?"

"None of 'em ever would take me," said the Dude.

"Plenty would of taken me — any time that I was flush," said the sneak-thief. "But I know 'em. They couldn't pull the wool over my eyes, the damn, dirty—"

"Well, you got other folks," said the Dude.

"Say, what you drivin' at?"

"I was just thinking that you're gunna have more money out of this than you ever could spend all on yourself, Blinky!"

"Was that your idea? Well, I ain't."

"No folks at all?" said the Dude, carelessly.

But the boy, in a sudden, dreadful flash of understanding, knew what the big man meant. Of all of that money of Blinky's, he would never spend a penny, to be sure. He lay there dying, unaware of the nearness of his death, and the Dude, with a woman's tact, was trying to draw from him the name of an heir.

Alfred, very sick, clung to the mane of the black mare, and felt his brain spin.

"No folks at all," repeated Blinky.

"Aw, you got a mother and a father, or a brother, maybe!"

"The old man and woman are dead. Never had no brothers but one that got himself bumped off in the Klondike. That's all. Never

251

bothered each other. We lived too far apart."

"No brother, no sister, no nephew or niece, even?"

"Say, what are you gettin' at?"

"I was wonderin' if you was like me — no relations at all, in the world!"

"Me? Exactly like that. And glad of it! What you want? For me to split up what I've made tonight? Not me! It stays put with me. Who else took the danger for me, and the risks, and done the planning? Nobody but me, and nobody but me is gunna have the spendin' of the coin!"

"Aw, go on," said the Dude. "I'll tell you what. I've heard guys like you talk hard, before this, but you always come through in the end like a fairy story, and spend your coin puttin' up a church, or some such foolishness, or establishin' of some beds in a hospital!"

"Me? I'd see churches in hell before I'd ever build one. What did churches do for me, or hospitals, except to charge me ten prices, damn 'em! I'd — hey, I — I—"

His voice trailed away.

Was he dead?

"That was funny," said the voice of Blinky, mumbling. "I sort of — sort of dropped away — to sleep, sort of — I — whatcha think of that, Dude?"

He spoke like a child to its father.

"Aw, you're all right," said the Dude. "You're tired. So'm I. I can hardly keep my eyes open, I tell you."

"Are you that tired, Dude?"

"Sure I am."

"Kind of funny, though. I thought — that I was faintin', Dude."

"That's a joke. You faint like a fool because you got a scratch along the ribs?"

"I gotta move, though," said the sneak-thief. "I'm sort of chilly inside. I'd like a slug of whiskey. About four fingers would be all right with me, along about now!"

"We'll have plenty of whiskey, when we get shut of this racket," said the Dude. "I know the first bar we'll hit in the mountains. A good snug place where the prices are right, and so's the liquor."

"I'll lay aboard about a gallon, when we get there," said the thief. "What made you so tired, though? I thought you never got tired, big boy?"

"It was rememberin' the way they taught me how to talk in school that tired me out," said the Dude. "Wore me clean down, tryin' to talk like the Colonel. They called me the Colonel, Blinky."

"Sure they did. Didn't I hear 'em? A sap come

runnin' in to me and says: 'You oughta go there and see the bird that just blew in. Kentucky Colonel!'

"I went to the door and what do I see? You in your new front. I had to laugh. 'He looks like a swell guy,' says I.

" 'Sure he is,' says this sap to me. 'You can always tell the real article from the made up moonshine. That's Kentucky, son. I come from there, myself!'

"It's a funny thing, what a lot of saps there are in the world, Dude."

"It sure is," said the Dude.

"I'd like to know," went on the sneak-thief, "what kind of a—"

His voice stopped short.

"Dude!"

"Ay, Blinky."

"My God — there's something stirrin' in me — ice cold — oh, God!"

"Aw, you got a bit of a chill, Blinky."

"I — can't — hardly breathe — none at all!"

"Sure. That's from bein' nervous. Always hits a gent like that—"

"I can't see none, Dude—"

"It's the night, you poor fool—"

"Dude — hold onto my hand a bit, will you?"

"Ay, Blinky. There you are."

"I don't hardly feel you. I'm like a shadow

under a windy tree, sort of all adrift — I — I — ah-h-h!"

And the silence continued through two dreadful heartbeats. Then the boy heard a faint scuffing on the grass, a gasp. And silence again.

His knees sagged beneath him. He knew that Blinky was dead.

CHAPTER 29

The voice of the Dude sounded at his ears —
deep, hollow, distant, like the roaring of a sea
in a cave.

"Hello, kid," said the Dude. "We'd better get
ready to blow."

"All right," said the boy.

But his voice was only a whisper.

The Dude gripped his arm and shook it,
roughly; Alfred wakened under the stinging
fingertips.

"What in hell is broke loose with you? You
answer up like a girl," said the Dude. "Are you
scared?"

"I felt a little sick, was all," said the boy.

"You felt a little sick, did you?" said the
Dude. "Well, you're gunna feel a damn sight
sicker, if you don't wake up and look sharp
around you. I ain't your nurse. You gotta look
after yourself, now!"

There was an unnecessary cut to these words,

the boy felt. He was quite willing to admit that Harley had been the brains of the enterprise, the guiding spirit. But he felt that he had fairly well accomplished the share that had been put before him. And, to an extent, it was the most perilous part of all — to enter that game room, where hired guns were fairly sure to be ready for him, to focus all attention upon his sole self, to shoot out the lights — to do all of these things single-handed had seemed Herculean before the effort was made, and enough to take his breath away even after the job had been accomplished.

Therefore the speech of the Dude cut him to the quick and turned him hot with a sudden anger. But he said nothing. He was too filled with respect for other things this man had done and said that evening.

"All right," he murmured.

"Jump, then, kid! Get onto your hoss. What you waitin' for?"

"Blinky—"

"You'll have to wait for him to come back from hell, where he's gone to," said the Dude.

Was this the womanish tenderness which had chased the thought of death, the dread of the end from the mind of the cowardly sneak-thief until death itself had throttled the man?

"Are you — are we going to just leave him there?"

"We just are. Wanta dig his grave with your hands, then? Don't you be such a fool. Let's get out of here. We're gunna have our hands full, at that!"

"I'll do what you say," said Alfred.

"You're talking sense. Now, mind you, no matter what happens, shoot at their feet, shoot at their hats, but never shoot to kill."

"Maybe we can slip out."

"Without being seen? Maybe. I don't pin no hopes on that. Old Axon was in this here town this evening, boy, and maybe he's here still."

"He seems sort of sleepy and dull," said the boy.

"Him? Well — you're young, that's all."

With this contemptuous murmur, the Dude pushed his horse ahead, taking the one that Blinky had been riding in tow. He pushed straight across the little wood, and halted when the blink of lights came glimmering between the trunks.

Alfred checked the black mare beside him.

"Gimme the stuff," commanded the Dude.

Deeply hurt, more deeply filled with wonder, the boy handed over the stuffed saddle-bag. It was light, and yet he had every reason to feel that it contained a fortune.

"If you'd done what I told you," said the Dude, "I wouldn't have you and the money on my hands, now! I'd only have myself to think for!"

"Go on, then," said the boy. "I won't hang on your hands. You go this way, and I'll cut back through the other street—"

"And get yourself cut up, eh? And be a damn fool hero, and pull all the attention on yourself, eh? You talk like an ass! Shut up. I gotta think."

The boy was silent. But every muscle in his body was leaping and hardening with rage. There would be an accounting, afterward, for this manner of talk!

He promised himself that, bitterly.

He heard the Dude murmuring:

"There oughta be a narrow street. An alley half a block down. Tin Can Alley, but we could get through it. Then a low fence. Might be that we could jump it. Then a strip of woods. Then the creek. That damn creek. Could we manage it?"

Wonder made the boy speak.

"How do you know all of this? Ever live here, Dude?"

"I been mappin' the town in my head for months," said the Dude. "You think I walked in here like a mouse into a trap? Come on!"

"Hadn't we better take off this stuff?"

"And get yourself seen?" demanded the other. "No, you do what I tell you to do from this on. Understand?"

With that brisk command, the Dude forced his horse forward, the lead pulled back, then went ahead with a stretched out neck.

And as they issued from the dark of the big pines, Alfred saw a narrow street before him, winding, as though the houses had followed the line originally laid down by some idly wandering train of cows. The houses themselves, built along this road, seemed to face each other awkwardly, all a little out of angle, and their fences and their yards were out of line, one with the other.

They were little homely places, each with a careful garden in front, many of them with lawns, and upon those lawns, Alfred saw the uppermost sprays of water tossed by sprinklers, appearing as mists of silver that continually pulsed upward and died again into shadows.

But that was not all that held his attention.

In front of each house the family was out, not to take the air of the evening, but in serious groups, the women and the children in the background, sitting close together under the light of the porch lamps or the electric lights, but the men to the front, each householder leaning with his neighbors, discussing something of the gravest importance, and Alfred could guess what was on their minds.

Conversation alone he could very well have endured, but there was something more serious to note, and that was that beside each man appeared a twinkling line of light, almost undistinguishable, but vastly significant, for he knew that each one of these glimmering lines represented a rifle, probably of the Winchester make, which throws fifteen balls, and the last with as much accuracy as the first.

The Dude, to his amazement, showed no haste. Neither did he cling to the line of the shadows, but he trotted his horse briskly out into the middle of the street, where the bars of lamplight from the open windows and the doors of the houses frequently crossed, and every bar of light was like an arm thrown out before them, barring the way.

Onto the road the Dude, therefore, pushed his horse, and the thin, light dust rose upward from under the impact of its hoofs and of the led horse behind him, and the smell of it was acrid with alkali as it floated in the breeze. The boy began to sneeze. He would almost rather have choked than to have made any undue noise, at this time, to alarm those waiting rifles, but he could not help but sneeze, and sneeze again.

And still the convulsion continued.

Suppose that they were attacked then, it was no need for the Dude to caution him against shooting to kill, for in his shaking hands, no gun could have been held true.

But they passed a house, they passed another, and another, and still nothing happened, and he could hear the deep murmuring of his voices of the men, and he could even hear the whispering of the water sprays as they fell down upon the grass, and the light, quick laughter of the children. It reminded him, oddly enough, of the unreasonable sound of rain showers upon the roof, when one is first in bed, chilly from the touch of the sheets, and waiting for sleep.

Then someone shouted from the right hand side of the street:

"Who's that? By God, it couldn't be—"

Then another voice: "Hey, hold on there! You two, hold up and let's have a look at you!"

The Dude barked back over his shoulder: "Ride like hell!"

And spurred his horse forward.

So sudden was his start, that even through his hand whipped the reins of the led horse. And the boy, pitching sidewise in his saddle as a bullet kissed the air beside his cheek, caught at the flying reins, got them in a firm grip — and was almost pulled backward to the street as the led horse gathered way, and then gal-loped freely beside him.

He heard other bullets whine high above him. He saw the dust knocked upward into little puffs from the ground, where the light from the windows streamed across the way, and he thought, instinctively, two things — that he was mad to have risked his life for the sake of capturing a led horse, and secondly, that those who shot at them must be mad, also, or they would not have fired so low.

Then he saw the Dude dart to the left from the street, into the darkness, and he followed as hard as he could ride.

CHAPTER 30

Very well and truly the Dude had mapped the town in his mind. Here was the dark alley to the left that gave them refuge from the bullets for a moment.

Before them, a fence rose; and big Harley put his horse at it. They seemed flying clear of it when the horse dipped, like a bird dipping on the wing, and the next instant the boy saw the flourish of the tail and heels of the animal in the air.

He heard a deep groan, whether from the horse or the man, he could not tell.

He was straight behind them, coming at such a pace that he could not pull up, but he swung a little to the side and jerked at the head of the led horse. It was a strong, willing roan, and it actually pricked its ears at the fence, and ran lightly forward to meet the jump with the reins hanging loose. The black mare was a different matter. He had put her over many a jump before, but in the dark, the fence seemed to loom large to her, and she flattened her ears and shortened her stride.

He leaned to her, shouted, caught her with the sway of his body and a whip stroke at exactly the right instant. So she rose, cleared the fence, and dropped down short, while the good roan sailed on like a bird and again almost yanked the boy from the saddle by the freedom of his jumping.

But he was looking down, with a sense of disaster, at the sight of the Dude's horse lying in a twisted heap, plainly with a broken neck, and the Dude himself, flat upon his back.

He could snatch up the money and go on. There lay the saddle-bag, flung toward him as though in a gesture of offering. But he did not think of it. Without the Dude, he felt like a child exposed naked to the rigors of the world; and then a rage rushed up from his heart at those who were hunting them, at those who had pressed the Dude, perhaps to his death.

He turned and saw shouting men bursting toward them across the face of the alley, running hard, swinging their guns.

They shouted. No doubt someone had seen that fall!

And then, forgetful of everything that he had been told by the Dude, the boy whipped out his two guns and opened fire, not to warn off the men of the law, but to kill them; for they were not as men to him, but rather as spectres and ghosts and demons whose black shadows raced forward, leaping, bounding, seeming to dance in a hideous glee because a gallant horse had died, and a brave man might be dead, also.

From either hand, the guns of the boy barked rapidly. He sent a sweeping shower of lead across the lane, and he heard a wild yelling of pain and of fear in answer to him.

They were tumbling back, almost without firing a shot, as though it were a machine-gun which had opened upon them in this unexpected manner.

Scorn and rage mingled in the heart of the boy. For such men as these had driven the big Dude to his death, perhaps.

He turned. The big man lay as motionless as ever, and when the boy dismounted and sprang to his side, there was no stir of response to his voice and his hand.

Furious with despair, he tugged at the total weight of the man, lifted his head and shoulders, and then heard with joy a deep, groaning sound. The Dude, fumbling, his weight like that of loose sacks of lead to the boy, came to his feet and stood swaying. His arms hung from his shoulders as though attached there by wires, and his head dropped forward and swayed from side to side in a manner horrible to behold.

It was too dark to see how badly the big man was hurt. He might have broken ribs, or a broken head. It might merely be a knockout.

"Dude! Dude!" cried the boy. "Will you wake up? Will you try to help yourself a little? Dude!"

And then he paused, breathing hard, feeling like prayer, if God were watching over thieves as well as honest men, upon this night. And as he stood there in the dark of the yard, he could hear the man-hunters swarming down on either side, working along the fenced paths close beside the houses, and calling to one another, and assuring each other that the criminals were indeed still there.

As surely as a trap ever was closed, so this one was being closed around him, and still the Dude swayed back and forth from heel to toe, like a scarecrow rocking in the wind!

Alfred cried out to him again, bitterly, and the Dude mumbled something that had no meaning.

It was in the hope to stir the giant — partly it was in sheery womanish vexation for which he hated himself, but Alfred, with the flat of his hand, struck the big man across the face as hard as he could.

The sting seemed to bring some strength of pride back to the half senseless man. He raised his head with a jerk, muttered something, and behold, climbed back into the saddle upon the roan gelding which had jumped so well.

The boy scooped up the fallen saddle-bag and hooked it over the pommel of the roan's saddle, for he had a perverse determination that he would not prosper by this lawless labor unless the big man prospered also.

But they were both far from prosperity at this moment. For as they mounted and pushed on, they heard voices shouting from either side, and even one yelling before them.

He looked through the darkness toward the Dude and saw that the monster was rolling in his saddle like a child that could not reach stirrups and did not understand how to hold on by a knee-grip. And then he knew that he would have to try to handle the Dude as the Dude and he, earlier, had handled Blinky Morris.

He rode close beside him, his hand on the shoulder of the Dude, steadying him. There was another fence just before them, but by grace they found the gate and the latch pushed down with a screech of rusted iron. Then they were through and in the woods.

And not a shot had been fired! By a miracle

they had come safely through, thus far, but perhaps it was no miracle, after all, but rather the effect of the thick dark.

They worked through the woods then, and still it seemed that the Dude never would come to himself, for he swayed in a sickly fashion in the saddle, and a stumble of the roan almost threw him head foremost to the ground.

He could not talk, either, and in response to the occasional questions of the boy, he returned mere mumblings.

Abruptly, they found themselves on the steep verge of a bank, and at the base of the bank there was the rushing of water. But the dark was so complete that Alfred could not make out the depth of the descent, the actual angle of the slope, or the width of the water, except that he knew the Dude had seemed in doubt about that creek.

Beyond that stream there was a promise of freedom from immediate pursuit, if only they could get safely across.

A little time would give him a chance to explore. He threw the reins of the black mare and sprang down, then paused an instant to listen, and heard distinctly behind him the trampling and the voices of men coming through the wood.

Hastily he started down the bank, but hardly

had made a step when the ground loosened beneath him, and he came down with a crash into icy water.

He staggered, half choked, back to the bank, but had to wade up many yards before he found a place where the surface sloped sufficiently to let him up.

If he could climb up there, the horses could slide down.

He went back to the place where he had left the Dude and saw his dim silhouette as he bent forward in his saddle, his two hands gravely clasping the pommel.

"Dude!" he called. "Here goes our last chance, our big chance! Can you help yourself?"

The Dude said not a word!

And, in the meantime, the sound of voices through the wood was like the crashing of guns behind them. Once those voices had the range — it would go hard with them both!

He found the place by which he had ascended. The pitch of the bank looked dreadfully steep, staring down it, and the ground which had supported his weight, might easily yield under the tonnage of two big horses! That would mean a fall in the creek, broken bones, death by drowning for the Dude, of course!

They started down, he with a feverish hold upon the arm of the Dude, and hardly had they started when the treacherous earth quaked beneath them. They shot forward and the cold water dashed above their heads.

The black mare stumbled, fell — water closed over the boy, but before he could extricate himself from the stirrups, the good mare was on her feet again, pushing forward, climbing.

He reined her in.

Where was the Dude?

Alfred was blind, muddy water was in his eyes and he could see nothing, and he ventured to cry out above the roaring of the water: "Dude! Oh, Dude!"

But he felt it was a folly. The Dude was gone, carried off through the rush of the stream which even now was staggering the good mare.

But then a voice boomed close behind him.

"Good idea, that ducking. It cleared my head up, kid. What the hell are you ridin' straight upstream for? Come along!"

The boy did not answer. But his sight cleared at that moment, and he could see the stream, the far bank, and the mighty form of Harley riding beside him, with a dim curling line of foam along the side of the roan where the force of the current struck them.

They went forward, and suddenly the mare was lifting out of the strong hands of the creek, and clambering into shoal water, slipping over the broadfaced stones.

She tried the bank. It yielded before her. She side-stepped, testing the bank with a tentative forefoot — and there went the Dude, heaving upward, while big stones rattled back behind him. The next instant the mare had found a proper place, also, and she was up the bank.

They were in an open grove, big, round-headed trees scattered everywhere about them, and good, level going for the horses, while behind them the voices of the hunters were shut away in a thick veil.

There was no whisper from the town. Beyond the trees, the hills rolled wonderfully black, toward the east, and now a pale glow was pushing up behind a hill.

"Dude, you're not hurt badly?"

"Me? Wait till my head stops ringing. Just now I think I'm a church bell, but I don't think that the old bell is cracked!"

CHAPTER 31

They lay on a softly grassed bank with the long, thin arms of a willow tree swaying above them, softening the sun with the tenderest of shadows. A shack lay below them, and behind the shack, a boy was leading the roan and the black mare up and down.

"That'll take the stiffness out of 'em," said the Dude. "Nothin' like walkin' to put a hoss back in shape. They trotted us a long ways, last night!"

It shocked the boy to hear the very words — *last night*. Last year, last life, last eternity! There was no fence of time between him and Double Bend, but a whole new nature had grown up in him.

He sat up, laughing softly.

There, where the little stream rounded a bend, was a bearded man with a fishing line — fishing to catch enough for himself, his son, and above all for his two notable guests. Behind

273

that black beard reigned silence.

"You can trust that black-haired devil," the Dude had said quietly, when they first came to the house.

"Look here," said the boy, "how's your head, Dude?"

"Sore, kid. Sore, but all in one piece."

"Well, that's good."

He reached out a hand to touch his companion, and then checked the impulse.

"Poor Blinky!" said he.

The Dude rolled flat on his back and shrugged his great shoulders.

"Roll me a cigarette, kid, will you? I'm lazy."

The boy rolled the cigarette, passed it to his friend, held the lighted match. And he looked fondly down into the handsome face of the Dude, the careless, lazy, half-sleepy face of the Dude.

He knew what was behind that seeming casualness of the man. He could value the coin not by its imprint, but by its weight and the purity of the gold. This was fine as fine could be, and he had seen the metal tested.

He had been tested, himself. He had been tested in the company of this man, and each knew the other. Each knew that the other was brave, true, loyal to death, large-hearted. Compared with this, what was his knowledge of other men? Of his mother, his father, his sister? No, he knew none of them. They were strangers to him, compared with the nearness he felt with this slangy safe-breaker. In one night of grim adventure they had been welded together closer than heat and hammer blows can weld iron. They were of one piece.

So he smiled down at the Dude and a warmth of tenderness, and affection, and pride in himself for having such a friend, came up out of the heart of the boy, as water comes up from an eternal spring.

He knew that he was enriched, and not with money alone but with something of an infinite value. Something had been added to him that was more vital than bone of his bone and flesh of his flesh; for this day he was a new man, a new heart, a new spirit.

These great thoughts, these great, vague emotions, surging through him in immense waves, made a moisture spring into his eyes, and he looked down the stream to where the bearded man was fishing. He was wet to the knees, and the sun flashed on the wet overalls as from burnished metal.

"I hope he catches twenty," said the boy. "I could eat ten."

"He'll keep on fishin' and never get tired, till you're filled up. And his wife'll keep on fryin' till you're filled up. And the boy'll keep on passin' you chuck and coffee till you're filled up, and not one of the three of 'em will ever stop smilin' and askin' you to go right on."

"By jiminy," said the boy.

He paused, and his breast heaved.

"That's the sort of people to have around!" said he. "Friendly people, Dude. They're worth all of your high-priced hotels, your slick waiters, with their made-up smiles and their fishhook fingers. You take in a big city, you can just feel the money flowing out of you, without pain, the way this water goes sloping down that creek bed. And what do you have afterward? Well, a stomachache because you've eaten what you shouldn't, and too much of it. Or a headache, because you've drunk what you shouldn't, and too much of it! But this is different. These people are your friends! I'd like to have friends like that. I don't suppose they ask much, either!"

"Money, you mean?"

"Yes, of course."

"You try to pay them! You'd never try again! They'd turn you out of the house!"

"Would they, Dude?"

"Of course they would. That's a man, and his wife is a woman, and don't you forget it!"

"I didn't mean to speak lightly of them. Only — they're poor, you see. We're taking a good deal from them!"

"You can always find a way. The kid admired your layout of guns. Well, you've got three, counting the one in your saddle holster. Slip one to him as you're going away."

"I'd like to do that."

"Well, that's the way to work it."

"You've never given 'em money?"

"Never a penny."

"That's great, Dude. They have hearts."

"Well, they break pretty even on me. You can't go on always taking from people and still keep them as friends — unless you've seen them go through the fire."

The boy looked away, and flushed with purest pleasure. He knew what it meant; he knew it was meant for him. *He* had been put through the fire, and therefore all the rest of his life he could take from the Dude, and never a word would be said; or the Dude could take from him. He would like that! He would like to have this friendship which he felt tested by all that could test it!

"But how do they break even, Dude?"

"Well, take the first time I met them. I was loping across these hills bound south. There were about twenty men behind me, and they all happened to be riding the way that I was going. They were dead set on going the way that I went. They would have done anything to get up with me, in fact. Well, I had a thousand-dollar pure bred gelding between my legs. I pulled up at this house and saw a mean-looking mustang in the corral.

"I said: 'I'll trade you.'

"He looked behind me at the hills. And he grinned.

" 'This is a thousand- and that's a hundred-dollar hoss,' I told him. 'You could take a chance of hidin' this one of mine away in the hills.'

"Well, he took the chance, and I got away clean on that tough devil of a mustang, and he saved the high-priced hoss. I come around here six months later. I still happened to have that same mustang, because it was a tough devil, for sure. He says to his kid the next morning: 'Go saddle the gentleman's hoss!'

"When I walked out, my saddle was on the thousand-dollar beauty. I said: 'A trade is a trade, old timer. You can't give me charity, as well as my hide, which your mustang saved.'

"After that we were friends. I've never given them a penny. Once, when they were down and out, I sent over a whole load of chuck to get them through the winter. You gotta do things for your friends, you know."

"Good old Dude," said the boy, affectionately.

"Kid," said the big man, "the whole range

I've got spotted with the same kind of friends. Glad to see me come, hate to see me go. That's why I'm still navigatin' these here waters when a whole lot of other craft have sunk on the reefs."

"You've got a way about you, Dude. You know how to do things."

The Dude shrugged his shoulders.

"You ain't asked about the insides of the bag," said he.

"No. I didn't know you'd be ready to talk about it today."

The Dude dumped the contents on the grass.

Little brown semi-envelopes contained packets of bills, closely wadded together, the ends a little rumpled by the rough usage they had had in the bag. The boy gasped.

"There's a terrible lot there!" said he.

"Only a hundred and twenty-eight thousand," said the Dude.

Alfred took a great breath.

"Is that all?" said he, and then he laughed.

"Poor Blinky," he repeated.

"Leave Blinky out," said the other. "He was the worst rat that I ever run into. Leave him out. But all of this money ain't ours."

"Who else? Blinky didn't have any relatives."

"Marlowe."

"That's right."

"We'll give him the spare eight."

"Eight thousand dollars? Whew!"

"When you make big, you pay big, in this game. You take the eight thousand into town."

"I?"

The boy sat up, startled.

"Yep. You."

Alfred swallowed hard. He felt a protest rising, hot in his throat, and yet he felt that he could not argue against the justice of the Dude.

"Well, I'll take the chance," said he. "But couldn't we send in word to Marlowe to come out here and take the coin?"

"Of course we could, but that ain't the point."

"What is the point, Dude?"

"You've gotta show yourself back in that town, before you're missed very bad."

"I do?"

"Yes, you do."

"I suppose they'll jail me?"

"Maybe, but they won't hold you. By my way of thinkin', they won't have anything on you. And they'll have to take you in. They may suspect a whole lot, but they ain't going to snag you any too hard. You see what you got up — your reputation as an honest man!"

"An honest man!" said the boy, bitterly. "No, I never can pretend to be that!"

"Because you took something from Patterson?"

"Well, I broke his safe — and the law!"

"He soaked you, didn't he?"

"Because he broke the law, that doesn't let me out," said the boy earnestly.

"Well, you can argue it that way. But the thing for you to do is to hop back onto the right side of the fence."

"Jail or no jail?"

"If you're jailed, there's more than a hundred thousand to get lawyers to pay your way out. You go back to Double Bend. Don't argue with me none! That's what you got to do!"

And Alfred submitted, with a rebellious heart.

CHAPTER 32

The house of the Naylors was not brightly lighted, but because of its position, the lamps from its kitchen and dining room threw a wide light over the desolation of the valley. It was to the dining room that Hugh Loftus was admitted. There sat his daughter and the three Naylors who remained at the house.

Loftus was a tall, grim-faced frontiersman; to a stranger he was the most silent of the taciturn; to an old friend he was as mellow as good French wine.

Now he entered the room with a smile and a nod for everyone. Mrs. Naylor looked at his rough boots and his dusty jeans with a wrinkling of her nose. But her airs had gone from her under the impact of the misfortune which had fallen upon them; as for Rosamund, she was as though all her life had been limited to this little valley alone. So Loftus quickly was made at home.

He was seated at the table. He was offered food, but he refused.

"Got to hankerin' after some roast meat this afternoon," said he, "and shot one of them pigs that's been runnin' wild these last couple of years up at the side of the valley, through the oak woods. Doggone me if I didn't have the best mess of roast hog-flesh that you ever put a tooth into, Joe!"

"I wish I'd been there," said Joseph Naylor, with interest.

Molly Loftus flushed a little at the somewhat gross language of her father, but she was too proud to disown her own flesh and blood and she looked steadily into the face of her father until she could smile freely at him again.

He could not eat anything, but he would gladly have some coffee. She served him with her own hands and remained for a moment behind him, her hand resting upon his broad, lean shoulder. He looked up at her with something of a scowl.

"Doggone me, Joe," said the woodsman, "but ain't my Molly growed up into a corker?"

"She's a regular girl and a half!" said Joe Naylor seriously. "We wouldn't of got along without her anyways at all, lately."

"And you needing her so bad at home!" said Mrs. Naylor with an apologetic gesture.

The two girls looked at one another and smiled at this interchange of foolish courtesies.

Said hardy Hugh Loftus:

"I'll tell you the way that it is. I rustled and found and fed for myself, in the old days, when you could shoot a buffalo for the sake of one meal — I mean, when you was marching hard. I found for myself in them days, and I never cottoned to the idea of havin' too many women around me. Neither Molly's ma nor Molly was very much of a comfort to me for housework, savin' maybe after dinner, when I gotta admit that the ache in a man's legs makes it kind of hard for him to up and swash into the dishes."

The women looked at one another and nodded slightly.

They were amused now, and when they were alone, they would laugh over this.

Joe Naylor said: "I'll tell you what, Hugh. When a gent is takin' care of himself, there ain't so many dishes, neither."

"There ain't, at that."

"You get a good deep tin plate, and it'll do for soup and meat and everything else."

"You men, you men!" said Mrs. Naylor. "You'd eat ice cream out of a beefsteak plate, I do believe!"

"And why not?" said her husband. "Take a chunk of bread and give the plate a couple of good swipes, and it's as clean as soap and water would ever make it!"

"Dad," said Molly Loftus, breaking in, "you've got something on your mind. What brought you over here tonight?"

Her father looked sternly at her.

"I'll tell you how it is," said he to his host. "I'll tell you what its comin' to, Joe. A man ain't got any mind of his own, any more, but his women folks has gotta read it out like it was a newspaper. Speakin' of that, I suppose that you *do* know the news. No, you don't, or I'd of heard talk of it before, when I come into the house."

They looked earnestly at their guest, waiting.

And Joseph Naylor said: "No. We got no news since the flood!"

He grinned a little at his jest.

Said Loftus: "There might be nothin' in it. That feller, Slim Harry Mackay brought it over to me, and I never put no trust in him."

"Slim Harry is a rat," said Joe Naylor with conviction.

"What Slim Harry told me, there might be nothin' in," said Loftus, "but I reckon that you and me had better go and talk it over alone, Joe."

Mrs. Naylor jumped in her chair.

"It's Alfred!" she said, "It's something about Alfred."

"Catch hold of yourself, ma," said her husband, who was very pale in spite of his gruffness.

"Alfred – he's hurt – he's dead!" cried Mrs. Naylor, beginning to tremble violently.

"Hey!" said Loftus, "he ain't nothing of the kind, by the last reports!"

"By the last reports? Is Alfred in danger, then?" said Rosamund.

Molly Loftus said not a word. But she found a chair against the wall and slipped heavily into it. There she sat with a hanging head, and a chalky face.

"Look here," said Joe Naylor. "You got the women all buzzling like hornets, and you'd better talk right out. If you tell it private to me, ma will blast it out of me afterward. I know the kind of steel that I'm made of, and I ain't sound proof, Hugh! There's Molly, too, lookin' kind of as though she needed something to pick her up."

The father turned in his chair and regarded his daughter with a stern glance. In vain Molly straightened herself in the chair and smiled. The whiteness of her face and her hollow, haunted eyes were a sufficient betrayal.

"Well," said her father, "the kid is all right. He's well."

There was a universal sigh of relief.

"Only," said Loftus, "accordin' to Slim Harry, that boy has got a good deal of his dad in him, of the old days when Joe Naylor was called up in Montana by the name of—"

"You could leave that out, and no feelin's hurt," said Joe Naylor sharply.

His friend grinned broadly.

"I mean," said he, "that what Slim Harry says is that over in Double Bend, where Patterson has the big gamin' house—"

"I know that Patterson," said Joe Naylor. "I recollect a time when I was out with—"

"Joseph!" snapped his wife. "Are you going to interrupt?"

He subsided into silence.

"Well," said Hugh Loftus, "it appears like your boy walked into that place the other night and started to play faro and made a big killing. So big that that skunk of a Patterson decided that he wouldn't let him get away with his honest winnings, and so he sent some gents to mob him. The boy laid out the first one — his bare fist agin a gun—"

"Ah!" said Joe Naylor, with an infinite satisfaction in his voice.

"But a couple of more of 'em sashayed in and laid him out, pretty near, when along comes — who do you think? Why, he was fixed up so slick that nobody knew him, but they say it was Dude Harley—"

"Oh!" said Molly, in a stifled voice.

"And he yanked one of 'em one way, and one of 'em another, and got your boy safe away, without so much as a scratch on him, but leavin' of his money behind him. The thugs had picked his pockets when they rolled him!"

"Damn their hides!" said Joe Naylor. "And damn their hind sights!"

"Would a real man put up with that? No. And the boy seems pretty real, no matter how old the pattern that you lay him agin! Back he comes last night and sashays right into the same place where he'd pretty near found poison the night before. And he goes right up to the same table. Well, everybody in the place was drawed in to watch the play, guessing that Colts would be aces in that game, and while they was watching, one of Patterson's gunmen drawed on the boy. Got in the first shot, the kid dropped—"

Molly Loftus screamed, a strangled sound.

They looked at her in silence, as though it were a dreadful sound heard in a dream.

"Not hurt," said her father. "Dropped like a young fox, and shot from the ground, and downed his man, and then turned and shot out the electric lights in one smash! And that way, he got clean off. But now here's the point.

While he was gettin' away, and while all the attention was drawed to him, a tall gent that was called a Colonel, had gone in before and had got Patterson into talk in Patterson's own office. And while he was there, when the fun began around Alf, he stuck up Patterson, tied him, and took his keys; opened the safe in the next room and cleaned it out, and Patterson says that a hundred and thirty thousand dollars was taken off!"

"A hundred and thirty thousand?" said Joe Naylor.

"That's right. And then there was the whole town crashing and dashing around, and through them went three men in hoods, like three doggone ghosts. There was a good deal of gunplay, and this mornin' Blinky Morris, a low-down sneak-thief that was guardin' the safe that night, was found lyin' in a hood and dead in a pine grove in the town. That was one of the three. The Colonel was that same slick gent, big Dude Harley. But who was the third gent — him that got away with Harley? Was it the kid? Was it Alf? They looked for him this mornin' around the town, but they didn't spot him there. If it wasn't him, where did he go to?"

Silence lay heavy on the room.

"I told you that I had ought to of told you

this all alone," said Loftus reproachfully to his host.

"It's in the air," said Naylor. "If you hadn't talked, somebody else would of."

Still the silence held. Mrs. Naylor was looking before her with wide eyes, as though she saw a gibbet in her dreams.

Her husband finally rose.

"I'll go out and take a turn in the open," he muttered. "It's kind of stuffy in here."

Loftus, sweating with anxiety and sympathy, rose in turn, but his daughter held him back.

"Leave him alone," said she. "He needs to be alone, for a spell, I guess."

So the father of the family went out alone into the night, and paced slowly up and down before his house. And then he was suddenly aware of a shadow standing behind him. He turned sharply around.

"It's only me, father," said the voice of his son.

CHAPTER 33

Joe Naylor went hastily to the boy.

"Why, son," said he, "doggone me if you didn't give me a fright! Come on in! Where did you come from? Well, I see the mare, yonder! Where you been, anyway?"

"Why – hunting," said the boy. "Hunting for luck, dad."

"Well, come along in and tell us all about it –"

"I want to see you. I don't want to see the rest of them," said Alfred.

"Well, now," protested his father mildly. "And what you got on your mind, Alf?"

"A lot of money, and a little trouble," said the boy.

"Money?"

"You said that you needed fifty thousand to put you in the clear?"

"Why, that's right, too."

"Well, here you are. You'll be back on your

feet and able to make a new start on the dam. Is that right?"

"Fifty thousand? Here in this wallet?"

"Fifty thousand to a penny, and in that wallet."

"Why, Alf, are you turnin' over all of that to me? To keep for you, you mean!"

"No. For you, dad."

"Hold on. How could I be taking a fifty-thousand-dollar gift? You mean that you want a share in the valley, lad?"

"A share in the valley? No, no!" cried Alfred with genuine emotion. "I don't want any share. It's yours. I don't want a penny of that money, but I want you to take it; I want you to use it as you see fit. It − it would be poison to me − that money − I mean, if I were to use it for myself! But it's yours!"

"Alf," said the father gently, "that would be sort of beggarly for me to do a thing like that!"

"What was it," said the boy, "when I spent your money like water when I was in the East?"

"It's a father's duty, when you come to think of it, to provide for his children," said Joe Naylor, "but it ain't a boy's duty to fork up coin for his father, until the old man can't swing a pick or a rope. And I ain't that old and lame, just yet, Alf."

"I spent your money like a fool!" said the

boy, bitterly. "I spent it like a jackass. By God, when I think of what the people were that I wanted to know back there — I wouldn't trade them all for your little finger, dad. You and—"

"And who, son?"

"Why, other men around here — real men — I never knew men before! I never dreamed that there were such men! But I want you to take this money. It's free for you. It's partly to make up for the way that mother and Rosamund and I washed piles of your good cash away in the East."

"Ah," said the father, "a boy has gotta have his fun!"

"Let him have it on the back of a horse, instead of on Broadway, then," said Alfred Naylor.

His father hesitated.

"Well, then, you're dead bent on this?"

"Never so set on anything in my life."

"It goes, then. I take this here as a free gift from you, Alf. It sets me back on my feet. It starts me in, again. And there you are! I put it here in my pocket. But I put in more than that. I put a fine lot of pride in you, at the same time! I gotta tell you how I admire you, Alf! To think that you could step right out in the world, like this, and bring back the bacon — why, this is the work of a big man! How'd you manage it, son?"

"I? I managed it — by luck, as you might say — by taking chances."

"Gambling, I reckon you mean?"

"Yes, it started in with gambling. It was gambling, in a sense, all of the way through, when you come down to that!"

"What stakes were you shootin' for, son!"

"They seem high, just now."

"But you mean that you ain't comin' in?"

"I can't. I don't want anyone to know that I've been here, you see."

"No?"

"Nobody must know."

"Alf, this here all sounds kind of strange to me!"

"Does it? I can't help that. I'm sorry, but I can't help it. I — I'm going back to Double Bend—"

"Double Bend?"

"Yes. Have you heard anything about what's happened there?"

"No, not a word."

"That's strange. I should have thought that the news would come here by this time!"

"What happened?"

"Patterson's place was robbed," said the boy slowly. "Three men robbed it. One of them was killed, getting away. The other two — they got away, and they're still being chased."

"Ah, Alf. I know what you mean. You're one of them that was doing the chasing?"

"I? – Yes, that's it. I've been out trying to get on their heels. Patterson – he's offered a fifty-thousand-dollar reward."

"Look here! Alf, you don't mean that you've run them down already and that you've collected the reward – that this is the money in the wallet?"

Alfred paused. Then he answered in a choked voice: "I can't say that. I'll explain about where I got the money, later on. What I want you to do now is to have it, to use it – you understand?"

"Yes. I understand. Alf, I ain't the man to ask fool questions. Only – you said a minute ago that there was a touch of trouble somewheres that made you want to get back to some place. What sort of trouble, Alf? Man, woman, or – the law?"

He made the slightest of pauses before the last word, but the boy did not notice.

"I want to get back to Double Bend," was all he could say, "and I don't want anybody to know that I've been here. You can make that right, father?"

"Why, sure," said Joe Naylor. "Anything that you want me to say is said. Is that all, Alf?"

"That's all, I think. Only—"

"Well?"

"How are things getting on, then?"

"Why, fair. We're gettin' on fair. Ma is kinda upset, but she's takin' hold, pretty well. You wouldn't think that she'd been one of the fashionable ones in the East, with her son engaged to a fine lady, and her girl to a lord! You fairly wouldn't think it, Alf, to see the way that she lays into the cookin' and the dishwashin'! Rosie, too. She ain't a whiner. And that Molly Loftus, she's a girl that's after my own heart. It's a damn shame that she ain't a man, Alf! It sure is!"

"A man? Molly a man?" said the boy. "Why, that's a strange idea! Why would you spoil such a woman as that by making a man out of her? She's — rather different, I'd say."

"Oh, she's a good girl, right enough."

"When I think of her," said Alfred, half dreaming, "I think of somebody — why, above men, father. Different."

"There ain't any airs about her," said the father. "She ain't a stylish girl, at all."

"She had something about her that sticks in the mind," said Alfred. "Like a burr. Well, goodnight."

"So long, Alf. I'd better be getting in. Goodnight, son. And take care of yourself!"

The older man went into the house, and Alfred Naylor remained at the head of the mare, stroking her muzzle, and vaguely longing toward the lights of the house. All who were in the reach of those lights within seemed to him infinitely desirable. He longed for his mother as he had not longed for her since he was a small boy, and very sick. He was a little sick now, to tell the truth, with the fear of the great world into which he had suddenly been thrust. And he wondered, if news of his downfall ever were known, how they would take it in the family — his mother he could not doubt, his father he would not doubt. But Rosamund? And Molly Loftus? What would they think?

Something stirred beneath the only pine tree remaining near the face of the house. He turned in a flash, gun in hand.

"You sneaking rat," said Alfred. "Get out from that tree, or I'll let a streak of light through you."

Then his blood turned cold as a frightened girl's voice said: "Don't!"

And she came out to him, holding up her hands.

"Molly Loftus!"

He went to her and towered above her in his anger.

"You've eavesdropped, Molly!" said he.

"I've listened," she admitted, and hurried on: "Oh, Alfred, go get the money back from your father and take it to Patterson, and give it back to him, and make yourself straight with the world again. What good would ever come of such a thing?"

"You've heard, have you? You've heard what?" he demanded.

"I know what you've done. You and Dude Harley. That sneak! That fellow who calls himself a man! I wouldn't put such a man in a dog kennel. It's too good for him!"

She was savage with her anger.

"Who! Harley? You think he led me on!"

"I know he did!"

"He didn't. I led him. I mean, he did it to save me from trying it all by myself. Dude — why, the Dude's the finest man in the world!"

"I'd wish for half a minute face to face with him to tell him what I thought of him," said she.

And then she began to cry, choking back the sobs, her hands clenched with the effort, and her head thrown a little back.

The dim light from the lamp in the dining room fell upon her at this moment, and it seemed to the boy that he saw her for the first time, as though a shutter had been jerked open before his eyes and let in the unbarred day.

"Molly!" said he. "Great God — Molly!"

She did not seem to hear. He checked himself, and added, duty bound: "Harley is the finest man in the world. You mark that! The finest man there is! I'd — I'd die for him!"

"You'll have a chance quick, most likely," said the girl. "But I wish — I wish that you'd promise me one thing!"

"I'd promise you pretty near anything," said he.

"Promise me that you'll give him a message, word for word!"

"Well, of course I'll promise."

"Then, you tell him that I hate him — hate him! Because he's a liar. Tell him that I said so!"

CHAPTER 34

All night the black mare ran true and straight across the levels, and toiled up slopes, and jogged softly down the steeps, until the thin lights of Double Bend lay in the hollow before Alfred Naylor like the trembling stars of heaven. To the left were the piled rocks of the mountain side — to the right, a tall grove of trees extended across its shoulder; and riding a little toward the trees, he whistled a high, thin note, twice repeated. It was answered at once, and a big shadow came stalking out from beneath the pines.

"Hello, Alf," said the voice of the Dude.

"I'm back on time, I think?" said the boy.

"Sure you are. The mare is a corker. And how was everything at home, son?"

"Why, well enough. I saw my father. He won't let on that I was there."

"That's right. Didn't see anybody else?"

"Only Molly. She slipped up on us while we

300

were talking. She's a regular Indian!"

"She is," said the Dude with pride. "I taught her how to stalk! She could walk up on a wild antelope in a desert as flat as your palm and tickle his ears before he knew she was inside the same sky line with him. That's how smart she is, kid!"

"Why's she so down on you, then?"

"Is she? That's a way she's got, Alf. A girl like her has always got to step on a man's face to show she ain't under his thumb."

"I never thought she was like that," said the boy, laughing a little. "She was wild, for some reason or other. For one thing, she knows or guesses what we've done in Double Bend."

"Does she?" said the outlaw slowly. "How does she guess that?"

"Perhaps other people are guessing it, too. At any rate, she gave me a message for you."

"She did?"

"Look here, Dude. Do you think anything of this girl?"

"Me? I ain't got time to think of girls, kid."

He told the lie easily, and added: "What's up?"

"She wanted me to tell you that she knew what we'd done in Double Bend, and that she hated you, and that the reason was because you're a liar!"

He finished this report with a chuckle, and

then paused, surprised that the Dude did not laugh also.

"Because I'm a liar?" echoed the big man, thoughtfully. "Well — perhaps!"

"Look here, Dude," said the boy, "this doesn't mean anything to you, does it?"

"Not a thing," lied the Dude. "You breeze on in to Marlowe's place, will you? Hand over the coin to him, and go to bed. Get up and show yourself around the town before the middle of the morning. If anybody jumps you — the sheriff, or some of Patterson's hired men, I mean, stick tight and holler for help. That'll prove that you're innocent of taking a hand in the robbery of the safe. Understand?"

"I'm under orders," said the boy. "Otherwise, I wouldn't go in. I don't like the idea."

While he spoke, he looked earnestly at the other. Then he rode closer, and dropped his hand on the Dude's shoulder.

"Look here, Dude," said he. "The fact is, that this girl means something to you. Is that right?"

"Your head is shaking, kid," said the big man. "She don't mean that much to me. Now, get out of here and go down to Double Bend. Mind you, I'll be drifting around in the background, but I can't show my face. Go on, son. Look everybody in the eye and use that right hook on those that sass you."

He waved his hand, and Alfred Naylor rode slowly on.

He was in great doubt. There had been little in the words, but much in the voice of the Dude to make him feel that the man was greatly hurt by that message from the girl, and he groaned to think that he had repeated such words to a man who cared.

And he looked back to Molly Loftus, herself, and felt a sudden tightening of the heart. What was she to the Dude, and the Dude to her? What was she to Alfred Naylor, too, and he to her?

He could answer one of those questions with an increasing trouble of mind. He knew now what she meant to him, and the knowledge rested heavily upon his mind.

But if the Dude felt for her the same interest, what was to be done?

Something more than concern for his own safety in Double Bend creased the brow of the boy as he rode down the long slope, and he began to feel the pressure of a situation which appeared insoluble to him. One resolution he made, grimly: true to the Dude he would unquestionably be. And while his heart ached, he told himself that there are many women in the world, but only one friend!

The sudden barking of a dog at the heels of

the mare aroused him to the fact that he was on the edge of Double Bend. He forgot the Dude, the girl, and all things except the problem before him, which was to get safely to Marlowe's house.

He made a detour, then to the side of Double Bend, and came carefully up to the place. It was totally black. He could guess the time to be not more than a half hour before the daylight should begin to turn the East grey, and, therefore, there was reason that the place should be dark, but its blackness seemed a foreboding of evil to the boy.

He went first to the little stable behind the house. When he opened the door, the low whinny of a horse inside greeted him, and the warm sweetness of the hay in the mow. But still it seemed to him that there might be more than horses and hay in the barn. And he waited, breathlessly, listening, staring in the dark.

At last, shrugging his shoulders, and berating himself for his nervousness, he fumbled along the wall until he found a lantern, lighted it, and by that light scanned the stalls. He saw the glistening eyes of three horses, heads raised to watch him; the wagging flame in the lantern's throat made the shadows tremble into life; but there was no sign of the danger which he half expected to find here.

He tied the mare into the largest stall he could find, unsaddled her, rubbed her down with wisps of hay, and gave her a feed of crushed barley and of hay.

Then he put out the lantern, and left the stable.

The house seemed less formidable, since he had used the hospitality of the barn, and therefore he went on more cheerfully to the front door. From the porch he looked up and down the street. A brisk wind had risen, and the saplings were jerking their heads to it, and the bushes stirring, but there was no sign of human life.

So he knocked, and listened to the hollow reverberation through the house. He knocked again, and finally, listening, he heard something like a whisper come down the hallway. It paused before the door and the rough voice of Marlowe demanded: "Who's there?"

"Friend," said the boy. "Is that Marlowe?"

"It is."

"This is Naylor."

The door was instantly drawn open.

"Naylor? Hello, kid," said the householder. "Come in, will you? Where'e the Dude?"

"He's not with me."

"No." There was, if not surprise, at least a good deal of regret in the voice of Marlowe.

He stepped back, and as the boy entered,

closed and locked the door behind him.

"Come on in here," said he, "and let's hear how things went with you. Blinky got his, eh?"

He went ahead, led the boy into a small waiting room, and there lighted a lamp.

"Hold on!" said the boy. "What's the idea of this? Somebody may see that light!"

Marlowe turned toward him with an ugly expression.

"What if they do?" he asked.

"Why, damn it, man, we don't want to attract attention, I suppose?"

Marlowe shrugged his shoulders.

"I'll draw the curtains, then," said he.

He went to the window, raised the lamp above his head as though to examine the shade, then lowered it, swung it to the side, and turning, replaced it on the table.

He drew down the shade and faced his guest.

"If anybody in the town was looking this way, that light was seen," said Alfred Naylor, half suspicious.

"Don't worry, kid," said Marlowe. "I'm an old stager. I don't make any breaks. Sit down and tell me all about it. Blinky croaked, eh?"

The boy nodded.

"I want to turn in and get some rest," said he. "That's the first job for me. I'll talk to you, afterwards."

"You will? Well—"

Marlowe hesitated.

"What's wrong?" asked Alfred.

"Wrong? Not a thing, not a thing. What could be wrong?"

"A good many things. But you look nervous."

"I ain't been sittin' on a bed of roses all evening, you might say," answered Marlowe. "Fact is, I been wondering when they'd tie me up to this here job."

"Have you? How can they tie you up to it?"

"There was people that seen me taking the three hosses to the place and tyin' them there. They seen that. They could make up their minds, maybe!"

"Of course they could. But it was dark."

"There's gents around here that can see any hoss in the dark! And them three was worth lookin' at. Did Blinky die hard?"

"The Dude got him hypnotized," said the boy, remembering. "The good old Dude!"

"Why ain't he with you?" snapped Marlowe.

"Why? Because there's no use in his coming in, is there?"

"No? Don't I get a split on this job? Or was he just talkin' through his hat?"

"Here," said the boy, drawing the wallet from his pocket. "There's eight thousand in this."

"Eight thousand!" breathed Marlowe.

His eyes opened wide, but strangely enough, they looked away from Alfred toward the door.

"Is that high enough?" asked Alfred.

Marlowe suddenly loosened his collar.

"High. It's enough!" said he. "If I'd known—"

"What?"

"Nothing. Lemme see!"

And opening the wallet, he began to count the money with fingers which stumbled with greed.

CHAPTER 35

There was such a change in the manner of this man from what it had been when he last saw him that he appeared to the boy almost as a different human being. But he attributed the difference to the effect which the big Dude had had upon Marlowe. In the meantime, he remained quietly watching until the counting of the money was ended. Then Marlowe looked up to him with a grin.

"Eighty-one hundred, I make it," said he, "but we ain't gunna argue and kick about that. Here's the eight thou'. But, look here, kid; didn't the Dude made it an even ten thousand? He ain't the kind to welch like that, when he's so close to a round number!"

The boy said nothing. But he looked so steadily in the face of Marlowe that the latter flushed and suddenly glanced aside.

"All right," said Marlowe. "If that's all I get—"

He made a gesture of surrender.

"It's not enough?" asked the boy, dryly.

"Look what I done!" said Marlowe in argument. "I like to know where the three of you would of been without the hosses, and yet all that I get is the fag end of the loot, when you couldn't of got away in a million years without—"

"We could have paid any stable boy to bring the horses there and tie them up, and you know it," said Alfred Naylor. "We could have paid him a quarter, and he'd have been glad to have it. You get eight thousand dollars and whine!"

"Whine? I dunno that I like your lingo, kid," said Marlowe.

An ugly flash crossed the eyes of Alfred. He could not recognize himself in the rage that shook him.

"My name is Naylor," he said.

Marlowe glared; then he suddenly relaxed in his chair with a feeble laugh.

"All right," said he, "if you wanta get dignified — all right. I don't mind—"

Alfred held up a finger.

"I heard something!" he exclaimed.

"Heard what?"

Marlowe scowled with interest and suspicion, looking again toward the door.

"I heard gravel crunch under somebody's

310

foot outside this window!"

"Come on! How could that be? There ain't a soul up in the town at this time of night. You got brains enough to know that!"

Alfred, standing now by his chair, stared keenly at the older man, and then stepped close to the window. He could have sworn that he had heard a light, stealthy footfall there.

"I don't know," he said thoughtfully. "I thought I heard — I could be reasonably sure that I'd heard someone stepping on the path under this window!"

"You're young," said the other, "and you're about two-thirds fool, at that!"

The boy spun about, and he saw Marlowe sitting behind the table with a gun resting on the edge of it.

He could not believe what he beheld.

"It's not possible," he said slowly.

"Ain't it?" gloated the other. "Get up your hands, son, or right pronto you're gunna get something that'll make you a lot sicker than you look now. Stick up your hands, before I soak a slug into you! By God, it'd be a pleasure to me to spread you out! They got the same price on you, standin' or lyin' flat!"

Sudden thoughts, desperate resolutions, flashed through the mind of Alfred Naylor. But he saw that he was helpless, for the moment. He saw that, furthermore, not many more moments would elapse before he whose foot had sounded outside the window would be in the room. And that would be the end for him. As for Marlowe, it had been a sellout and a trap from the first. He could understand clearly, now, the strange movements of the lamp at the window; that had been a signal agreed on before, and read in the distance.

Still, he might have a little time at his disposal. Those who approached to seal the trap doubtless could not expect to find that the prisoner already had been made a captive, and they would go quietly, softly, on their way into the house. All of this required much patience and many minutes. And before they came, perhaps something would come into his mind.

This he thought out, while he gradually raised his hands.

At the level of his hips they paused. It was his last chance for a gun; he burned with eagerness to take it, but caution prevailed, and he raised his hands still further. They were shoulder high, at the last.

"That's right," said Marlowe. "You just keep 'em there. I ain't one of them that like to see a man's hands clean strained over his head and out of the picture; I like to have 'em low down, so's I can watch what he's thinkin' about. Some folks like to watch the eyes of a bloke. I'd rather watch his hands. Fingers is more important to me than brains!"

He laughed as he announced his doctrine, and the boy smiled a little, grimly, thinking how neatly those fingers of his would fit into the throat of the ruffian.

Marlowe, having the upper hand, grew confidential.

"You thought that eight thousand was a big enough wad to choke me, eh?" said he. "Wrong, kid, wrong as hell. You don't mind me calling you a kid, do you?"

The boy was still silent, thoughtful, and always watching that malevolent face with a careful interest.

"He says he don't mind," leered Marlowe. "I was sayin' that you thought that eight thousand would pretty near kill me of indigestion. I'll tell you that I've lifted bigger wads than that, when I was workin' at my own game. I've lifted a pile bigger wads. In my day! Looks like my day has come back to me, eh?"

He laughed, and nodded his head, but the laughter was controlled so that his hand was not disturbed, and his eyes were always brightly upon the boy.

"You get something from Patterson, I suppose," said Alfred.

"I get something from him? Only ten thousand. That's all!"

He laughed again, through his teeth.

"Ten and eight make eighteen!"

"It makes more," said Alfred.

"More? What kind of fancy arithmetic have you got in your head, kid?"

"Ten and eight make a dead man out of you!"

The eyes of the other flashed from side to side, as though he yearned suddenly to look behind him.

For a fraction of an instant, Alfred was on the verge of leaping at him, but Marlowe recovered almost instantly, though his face had turned pale.

"One of your goddam bluffs, eh?" said he. "Well, let it go at that! I'll tell you what! You got your nerve with you, kid. I could wish it wasn't you that's standing there. I don't mind a nervy kid. But you got a fat head. You gotta get rid of that. The pen is where they'll kick it out of you!"

His upper lip lifted and his teeth flashed.

"I wasn't bluffing," said Alfred calmly.

"No?"

Marlowe raised his dark brows.

"I wasn't bluffing. The Dude will kill you, for this. That's what the eighteen thousand will cost you!"

Marlowe slowly drew in his breath, and expelled it again in a hiss.

"I wish that he'd come in here with you tonight!"

"You clumsy fool," said Alfred. "If he'd come, he would have spotted your clumsy tricks long ago. I almost did. If I'd acted on the touch of the idea, I would have cracked your treacherous head for you, and left!"

Marlowe grinned, but the smile was the merest flash.

Then he said: "I'll tell you what, young feller, you got your nerve. You talk big. But it don't bother me. The Dude will be put away!"

"Some day, perhaps. But not before he gets to you!"

"You lie," said Marlowe. "He'll never get to me!"

"Who but the Dude ever got to Patterson's safe? He managed it. He'll manage you, too, because he never wanted money as badly as he'll want your scalp, Marlowe!"

"Shut yer face!" growled Marlowe. "I got half a mind to flatten you now and step on her face, you pup. Stick your hands up higher. I'm going to have another flash at you. There may be some more money on you, if the Dude was fool enough to pay you off before he sent you in, you poor sucker!"

He came closer, then paused, but something creaked, very faintly, in the hallway.

Then he came on more quickly, and put his Colt's muzzle against Alfred's stomach.

"Let's get through with this quick," said he.

Plainly, he wanted to pick the bones of this victim before Patterson or the law got its hands upon him.

He dipped into the coat pockets of the boy, jerked out a small wad of bills which he found there —

"Look here," said Alfred. "Split the thing with me. You'll never find it, but go halves with me, and I'll tell you where it is. You'd never find it, but they'd be sure to when they search me before they jail me!"

"All right," said the criminal, looking keenly up at his victim. "That's a fair shot. Where's the stuff? I'll go you halves!"

Even as he said it, treachery and greed brightened his pig-eyes.

"Down in my boot."

"Which one?"

"Left boot. Outside of the calf. Reach in —"

"There ain't a thing," said the other, leaning gingerly, his eyes desperately turned up at the boy.

"There is! There is!" said Alfred impatiently. "Dig your fingers in deeper. Hurry up, you fool, before they're in here, and you lose your cut on fifty thousand—"

"My God! Fifty thousand!" said Marlowe.

Deeply he reached after the money. He cursed as his finger tips touched a fold of cloth. Then, for half a second, he turned his eyes down from the face of the boy.

It was time and to spare for Alfred.

With his left hand he caught at the barrel of the Colt, and the shot which it belched split the ceiling above his head. His right hand dropped hammer-like behind the ear of the other, and Marlowe dropped without a sound to the floor.

There was no time to attend to him more thoroughly, for at that moment the door of the room jerked open.

CHAPTER 36

He could not see clearly into the dark of the hallway, but he could make out the tall form and the face of Patterson, now turned as savage as a beast. There were others behind him, and on each side. A finger of red pointed at him, the explosion of a gun boomed through the room; then a chair hurtled from his hand straight through the doorway and he heard Patterson roar with pain.

The next instant he had slammed and locked the door in their faces!

It gave him a few seconds, perhaps. The door instantly shivered and groaned under a heavy blow. They would have it burst in two in no time, he understood well; but in the meantime, a few swift seconds might get him away.

He gave one glance at Marlowe. He was beginning to writhe on the floor, like someone who had been trampled under foot, and a fierce heat of savagery made him want to send a bullet through that blindly struggling body. He shook that temptation out of his mind, blew out the light, and jerked up the window shade.

He leaned out. There was nothing to be seen except the slender heads of the poplar saplings bending in the wind, and the long, faint grey of the dawn beginning to circle the hills.

He whipped through the window and hung by his hands at the same moment that the door went in with a crash. And as he hung there, a gun flashed almost in his eyes and a red-hot pain shot through his body. He could not tell where the bullet had struck him, but all at once he was nerveless, powerless, and his hands relaxed their grip.

He fell in a heap, and saw a long-legged shadow running toward him, with the dull glimmer of a poised gun.

"I've got him," yelled a voice. "I've got him cold!"

His mind was perfectly clear. He could think out the thing exactly, see everything, know everything, and wonder that one little slug of lead could paralyze him in this manner, as the sting of a wasp paralyzes a caterpillar.

"Keep him, Bill!" roared Patterson, from inside the room.

Then another gun sounded from the brush, and the man called Bill went down with a yell of pain and surprise.

A voice shouted from the window above him; but again, swiftly, the gun from the brush spoke thrice, and he heard the bullets crashing into the woodwork about the window.

It must be the Dude. It could be no one else.

If only he could get to that hero!

The numbness left him a little. He found that he could crawl and slowly he dragged his way along the side of the house.

All the time he was thinking busily. This was the other side of the picture of freedom and gaiety which had seemed so fascinating to him. There was the life in the open, the wild rides, the keen adventures, the easy money for spending, the true friends — and there were bullets, also, and either real death, or living death behind prison bars.

Then he cursed his weakness, and this self-contempt suddenly made him capable of rising and walking. He staggered toward the brush.

Behind him, he heard the rapid crashing of footfalls, as men raced through Marlowe's house. Marlowe would be one of them, of course, Marlowe raging for blood, by this time. Slowly as his body could move, his mind worked with that much greater rapidity, and it seemed to him that he was sitting in a courtroom, and looking at the stern face of the judge, and seeing the twelve men of the jury, and hearing the snarling voice of Marlowe — State's Evidence Marlowe! That was what would put him behind the bars. They gave long terms for this sort of thing. Thirty-five years, sometimes, he thought he remembered. Thirty-five and twenty-two made fifty-seven. Fifty-seven and a jail bird. Disgrace. His mother and father would be dead, by that time.

But perhaps the dam would have been rebuilt, and the money he contributed would be the foundation of it!

He hoped that the valley would be richer than ever. His father, the happiest of men, only pitied because his son had gone wrong! Molly Loftus, too, was gone, snatched away from him. The smile faded from her image in his mind, and left her a staring picture. She was gone. Another man would marry her. Some poor, half-starved, half-brutal cowpuncher — well, he would see to it that his father gave that man a start in life!

His father, at least, would have a warm spot in his heart for him. His father, and the Dude. The world suddenly shrank to those two faces, for the boy.

And all of this while he made half a dozen staggering steps toward the brush.

Then a giant leaped out to him, and the

voice of the Dude was in his ear. The trees, the face of the Dude, swam before him, and he began to relax.

The flat of the Dude's hand struck him a stinging blow across his face.

"Wake up, you damn yaller-livered quitter!" said the Dude. "Are you gunna lie down an' die like a dog on me?"

"Damn you!" he said, his mind cleared and nerved with fury. "I'll carve your heart out for this — I'll shoot your head off."

The Dude took him beneath each arm pit and walked beside him.

"Save your yapping, will you? I'll give you your chance, when the time comes," said the Dude. "Now, hold your head up. You think you're hurt. You ain't, though. There's nothin' wrong with you, you poor half-wit. You're just showin' yaller. You disgust me. You plumb disgust me!"

Alfred laughed, thin and small.

"Do I disgust you? I'll remember that, too! We'll have this out. By God, I'll fight you now."

"See if you can get into that saddle, will you?" said the Dude. "If you can't do that, you ain't worthy of getting a fair whack at me!"

He saw a horse before him.

"The mare!" said he. "Dude, I can't leave her behind!"

"You stuck her in the stable, like a fool! I never heard of such a fool! But I took her out. I've got her tied to my own nag, over yonder. Only, she's tired. She can't carry you where you'll be going tonight!"

He got his foot into the stirrup, but his leg had no power. At the knee, it seemed to be a void, without muscle, without nerves.

Then the power of the Dude picked him up, and floated him into the saddle.

Afterwards, a little blank intervening, he was aware that the Dude was riding beside him, and that they were going through a wood. Voices hallooed behind them, around them.

He was like one waking in the middle of a dream.

"Why, Dude," said he, "there's somebody out hunting."

"They're running wolves," said the Dude. "Lemme have a look at you!"

The forest around them was not really illuminated by this early light of the morning. But the trees appeared huge and black, and the sky was an infinitely deep bowl of mist above them. Yet, taking advantage of this light, the Dude reined his horse close and looked at the head of the boy. He touched the head, and a pang shot through Alfred's brain. For the first time he realized that he had been hurt in the head as well as the body.

Recollection flooded over him, and he knew what had happened.

"They tagged me a couple of times, it looks like," said he.

"It looks like," said the Dude.

He did not let Alfred dismount, but he began to work like lightning, pulling open the mouth of a saddle bag, and from it producing the articles that he needed. Alfred opened his coat and pulled up his wet, soaking shirt. Then, to the wounds, the Dude applied what felt like liquid fire. Afterwards, he wadded lint and bandage over the hurts, and pulled the pads tight with wide bands of adhesive tape. He did the same to the two holes in the side of the boy, and to the gash along his head.

It was an agony to endure this. Alfred had to grip the pommel of his saddle hard, to keep from falling in a faint. At the end, the Dude gave him a flask, and he drank whiskey from it, like water.

The stimulant cleared his brain. He looked about him, and saw the daylight far enough advanced to show the green of the trees, and now he could hear the hunt working for them back and forth through the wilderness.

He looked back to the big man. Suddenly his face tingled, where the hand of the Dude had slapped him. And then he flushed, hotly. He could understand. Any insult had been used to keep him on his feet until the Dude could see enough to work on him.

He said: "Damn you, Dude, you've chucked yourself away. You've let 'em close a trap over you, while you worked on me!"

"Oh, shut up," said the Dude. "I never knew anybody that made me half as tired as you make me."

He reined in at that moment and cursed softly. The boy listened, also, and behind them he heard the wavering cry of dogs. He could understand that sound. They had put on the trail intelligences which worked with a keener sense than that of sight!

"It looks like a long trail," said the boy, and he stared blankly at his companion.

The fire in his wounds had cleared his brain. It had nerved his body, too.

"Can you gallop?" asked the Dude abruptly.

"Yes."

"Hard?"

"I can keep up, I think."

"You'll have to. Follow me!"

He turned suddenly at right angles to their former course and began to ride hard. The black mare pulled back on her lead rope, and then swung into her long, raking stride that kept her easily up with the Dude.

The boy, watching that stride, wished with all his might that he were on her back. Instead, he had a horse with a pounding, back-breaking gait. But he had no chance to think of this, for the branches of the trees seemed reaching at his head, and now a bough slashed at his wounded side, and he almost fainted at that stroke of agony.

The big trees shot behind them.

"Who's there?" shouted a voice through a screen of trees.

"Duffy!" yelled the Dude in answer. "They've gone this way, I think!"

"You fool! They've gone straight ahead! Swing to the left — swing to the left!" called the speaker.

"All right!" shouted the Dude.

But he kept straight on.

A moment later, looking back down a long alley, Alfred saw a pair of riders come out from the woods, halt, and look after them.

A wild hunting cry instantly went up from their lips, and they pulled their horses about to take up the trail. He knew that the grimmest part of that ride was just beginning, for the hunters were in sight of their quarry!

He called to the Dude, giving his information; and the big man nodded.

Then he reached down and loosened his rifle in its holsters and looked back in turn.

Never had the boy seen a face so altered.

The usual good nature had disappeared. The brows of the Dude were gathered black; his lips were stiffened. No matter what his instructions had been to Alfred at other times, on this day the boy suddenly understood that his companion was going to shoot to kill!

CHAPTER 37

He who flees is not running away from a specific danger – not even from death. As for prison, loss of all the opportunities of life, these fears could not have wrung from the boy the efforts which he was making now. He was fleeing because he was pursued, and the vast horror which was in him was that which is in the hunted beast.

He had courage enough and strength enough, but if it had not been for the overmastering strength of that horror, he could not have endured for a moment the ghastly pain in his side which doubled him over and twisted him about. And besides, there was the agony of the wound in his head, where the pulse pounded like a hammer.

Sometimes his breath was gone, and he knew that he would die if he took another; and yet that breath was taken, and in spite of the sweat of agony, he lived.

This was the happy life of careless freedom towards which he had yearned! This was that half wild and half knightly existence which he had envied in the Dude!

It seemed to the boy, now, that he always had lived the life of one in heaven. He would have mortgaged all his hopes of the real heaven to be peacefully back in his father's house. And suppose that he had offered to him a long and humdrum existence as a cowpuncher of the range, what would cause him to refuse it, in exchange for his misery?

Still the Dude led on at a terrific pace, remorselessly, never looking over his shoulder, never calling a word of comfort, never asking after his companion's well being.

Several times the boy spurred furiously, to get up beside Harley and remonstrate, but he never could make his horse gain. They were running all out!

Sometimes they seemed to be on hobby horses, rocking to and fro with a dreadful motion, while the hills rolled toward them and sloped away toward the rear. Through a gap in the hills, he saw well to the side of the group of four or five horsemen riding furiously, bent well over, jockeying their mounts as though they were racing for a prize.

And it was a prize, and worthy of the efforts

of the finest thoroughbreds, that money which Patterson had hung on the heads of the fugitives.

And still the Dude rushed his horse on, and the black mare galloped freely at his side. She, at least, had a thought for the man in the rear, twisting her beautiful head to look back at him. And once she whinnied to him, loud and shrill, like the note of a horn.

The day grew bright with a dreadful speed. It seemed to the boy they were rushing into a region of flames, and then the flames died, and all was white light, blown in their faces by the wind of their gallop, as the bellows blows the flame of the forge.

There, again, was a fate which he would have accepted gladly – to labor all of every day at the forge, in the heat, the dirt, the spurting of red sparks of iron, and all for the sake of three common meals a day, and a hut to live in – he would have taken that as the sweetest of existences, to be freed from this agony!

The sun flared in his face. They were riding due east. And it seemed to him that he never had appreciated rightly the coming of night. If that had been a westering sun, he could have endured, he told himself. He could have held on, waiting until the sky turned red, and then darkened, and into the darkness they two could have dissolved and the pursuit would have melted away behind them.

As it was, he could not stay on the horse. As it spurned the ground, he lurched from side to side. His breath continually left him, and to draw it again was to breathe of fire that scorched his vitals. He told himself that he would ride as far as the next hill, where a grove of poplars stood on the windless slope; there he would fall to the ground, pitching headlong, regardless of how he reached the turf. For he felt that the grass would receive him as softly as water.

Then the poplars were behind him, and another hill was before. He rode no longer with hope, but simply from point to point, always telling himself that he must fall soon, and always holding on, by a miracle. He took the reins in his teeth. He clutched the pommel with both hands, and every stride of the horse was a wrenching at his side, until he told himself that he could feel no more pain. Nerves, after all, are mortal things, and after a time they must be worn away, they must become numb and end their work. But these nerves of his refused to stop. They were an electric network, focused in his side and in his brain, and each effort of the horse shot blinding sparks of pain through him, through his body, through his soul.

Suddenly he saw that the Dude was reining in.

Was even the Dude surrendering?

The big man drew back at his side.

"Go on, Dude!" something in his gasped. "Go on. You can't do me any good, now. Let 'em take me. You go on and save yourself!"

The horses trotted through a dreadful moment. Then they stopped. He saw the face of the Dude grow ugly with a sneer.

"Quitting like a baby — like a baby girl!" sneered the Dude. "Bah!"

The Dude stood on the ground beside him.

"Get down!" he commanded.

"Go on, Dude. They'll get you. Why should they get you, too?"

"You fool! They're out of sight. We've lost them!"

Then: "Get down, will you?"

He tried to lift his right foot from its stirrup, but his leg was all lead, and no muscle in it. Only at the third effort he succeeded, and the struggle left him shuddering. He pulled his heel over the hips of the horse and slipped down the side of the animal. His right foot refused to leave its stirrup, but shook there like a leaf.

The Dude knocked it loose. The Dude took him beneath the armpits and lowered him to the earth. At once the sunlight shook and quivered in the sky, and the earth trembled beneath him. Or was it the frantic hammering of his heart?

But suddenly he could breathe. He could rest. The pain which possessed his entire body began to flow out of it, strangely, and comfort began to pour up out of the moist earth, comfort and soothing slumber, if only the Dude would let him alone.

But the Dude would not.

He laid bare the wound in the side and with fingers of fire he began to tear at it, like a wolf tearing at a living victim.

"Almighty – God!" said Alfred Naylor.

Then he shut his teeth hard to keep back the cry of agony, lest the Dude should still further despise him, if that were possible! But the man in him seemed to have disappeared and he was all woman, and weak as water. He knew that if he did not keep a stern hand upon himself, he could cry like a child, weakly, endlessly. Babbling complaints rose to his lips, but the lips were locked like iron and refused to let the words come through.

So the Dude still worked on him.

He talked as he worked.

"A scratch like this!" said he. "And you ready to quit! Ain't there any real stuff in you? Ain't there any man in you?"

He wanted to protest that there really *was* some manhood in him, but he could not venture to let his lips part, for fear that a shriek would come forth, like the raising of a white flag, like an infinite surrender of all his pride!

"This ain't nothing," said the Dude fiercely. "This ain't more than a scratch. I remember up on the reservation, there was a Blackfoot came into camp one day with nearly all of his ribs broke, his head fractured, and all the flesh raked off of one arm, from the shoulder down. he got down off of his hoss and pulled a blanket around himself. 'Gimme a pipe,' said he.

"That was all that he said. No howling, no yelling, no talking about giving in. He'd been out bear hunting, and his gun had missed fire, and the grizzly had closed on him and hugged him a couple of times, and give him a swipe with its paw. He didn't howl. He killed that bear with his hunting knife, and then he got onto his hoss and rode in. Some of the boys followed his back trail and found that bear. It was eleven miles away. That's the stuff that he was made of! You take a fellow like you, you'd lie right down and die the first time that the bear stood up and looked you in the eye. You ain't got any backbone!

"Then I remember a ranger that a lot of yeggs laid for. He got two of 'em, and he got away.

He carried five bullets inside of him, and he rode thirty-odd miles back to his camp. He didn't die, neither. There wasn't a cupful of blood inside of him, when he arrived. But what the hell does a man need with blood, or bones? All that he needs is guts. You hear me talk? All that a man needs is guts! If he's got nerve, it's patch him up, solder busted bones together, join up cut flesh, and make him better than ever. But you gotta have nerve, and you ain't got any. You lie down here and give up, like a sick pup three days old, instead of like a man, like I took you to be! Aw, it's easy enough to flash a gun and make a show. But since you've got yours, any kid will be able to stand up to you and make you take water. That's what I mean to say. There ain't anything in you. You're hollow, like an egg ten years old. There ain't anything but dust inside of you. You ain't worth saving from the pen!"

CHAPTER 38

This speech had been delivered with a perfect calm, the disgust which gave it birth being apparently too deep to allow loud utterance. Coldly, dispassionately, out of a bottomless disgust the Dude issued his judgment, and the boy listened, and forgot his pain as he listened.

He accepted the first part of what was said. He accepted it out of the deeps of his weakness, but as the quiet, scornful speech went on, anger began to gather in the soul of the boy. He forgot his pain, and he forgot his awe in the presence of the Dude. Finally he burst out: "You've said enough! I don't mind criticism. But you've handed me too much of it. Now be still, will you?"

The Dude looked critically down at him. Then he nodded.

"That's improved your color a good deal, kid," said he. "I didn't want to give you another shot of whiskey, this early in the day. Now hold yourself together. I'm going to put on fresh straps."

And, pulling so hard that the boy thought his ribs would crack under the strain, the Dude applied new, long strips of adhesive plaster, to hold the wad of lint in place.

"Now, you lie back and rest," said the Dude, "and don't have anything on your mind. We've dodged these hard riding gents. We've made a set of fools of them and their dogs. Lie back and take it easy. Anything you want?"

"A smoke, Dude."

The cigarette was rolled.

And as he drew the smoke deeply into his lungs, he breathed out: "I was a fool, Dude. I should have known − from hearing you talk to Blinky."

"A slap in the face," said the Dude, "is a dog-gone lot better than a patting of the head. I'll tell you what. They's a lot of men that have been soothed away to death. But damn few that have been done in by roughness. It gets a gent's mind off of his troubles, and as long as the brain is alive, the body'll do pretty well."

The boy agreed, with a silent nod, and then he closed his eyes and let the cigarette go out. In a moment, he was sound asleep, and dreamed that he was riding a cyclone of crimson fire, while a demon rushed beside him and thrust a spear of flame again and again into his side, and another devil slashed at his head with a sword of flame.

He wakened, and found the Dude quietly beside him, smoking a pipe, his hands locked in front of his knees.

"How did you manage it, Dude?" he asked. "How were you able to dodge them?"

"Aw, shut up," said the Dude. "Save your breath, and go to sleep again."

He smiled a little at the bruskness of this order, and obediently closed his eyes, murmuring: "Good old Dude —"

Sleep gathered in new waves above him; a strange heat was generated in his body. He could listen to the beating of his heart, which was thumping hard.

"Good old heart," he said to himself. "Working all the time —"

And then he passed into semi-oblivion, or was it really a dream, in which he heard a wind arise, and hollow voices flying down it.

"Kid!" said the voice of the Dude. "Hey, Alf. Wake up!"

He opened his eyes drowsily.

"Got a funny story, Dude?"

He grunted out the words, as a twinge of pain pulled at his side, smothered in part by the hard pull of the strips of plaster.

"Not so funny, either. Listen!"

He listened, and far off down the wind he heard those dreamlike sounds which had mingled with his drowsiness.

Suddenly he recognized the baying of dogs, the sound blown up on the wind, and dying again.

He sat up, thrusting himself erect with his arms.

"They're after us!"

"They're not going to have us, though!"

The Dude took him beneath the armpits and lifted him gently to his feet.

"How's your head?" he barked.

"Good enough."

"Dizzy?"

"No, not very."

"Why, hell," said the Dude, "you could ride a thousand miles. You ain't badly off, at all!"

And then he pointed to the black mare, which now wore a saddle.

"You'll have her under you, now. That'll make a difference. She's got her second wind — she's all iron, that devil!"

The boy shook his head.

"You outweigh me a ton," said he. "You take her."

"She'd spend her time pitching me on my head," said the Dude. "Thanks very much. I don't like her style! You'll have to ride her, Runt, or else she'll go to waste. Besides, my hoss has plenty of running left in his stomach!"

The boy looked at the gelding. Its coat was staring, and he took that as a bad sign.

"He doesn't look too fresh," he argued.

"Sit down, kid, and we'll talk it out," said the Dude ironically. "We've got plenty of time, I suppose. Those dogs are hunting a rabbit, most likely!"

At that, the boy was silent, and allowed the Dude to help him into the saddle. Even so, there was a necessary effort on his side, and the work of lifting his leg over the cantle of the saddle ripped him in two with a thrust of pain.

He settled into the stirrups, breathing hard; his upper lip was beaded with sweat, and his mouth pursed out. However, he was better now than at the beginning of the ride. The shock of the injury had left him. His brain was clear, and his brain, according to the Dude, could control his body. At least, he would most desperately try to make it.

The Dude had mounted, but he seemed in no haste to start.

He looked around him to every side, then grunted, and sent the horses south between a pair of hills. They went on at a dogtrot.

"Dogs don't run so very fast," said the Dude in explanation.

The hills grew larger, more ragged, and the boy got on very well. Compared with the pounding of his last mount, the gait of the mare was like a caress. Neither did she pull on the reins, but went on softly, her head a little turned, as though she understood that her rider had little strength to spare, and she wished to read his mind to learn the directions.

They came into country of a different sort. The sun was straight above their heads, and it flared and flashed from the ground beneath them and the walls on either side, for they had ridden into a ravine where there was hardly a scrap of vegetation. All that sprouted here were naked boulders, shattered by the fall from the rock walls above them. And those walls reared themselves an ungainly height. The boy looked at their impassible faces with concern.

"We're not riding into a trap, Dude?"

The Dude smiled at him.

"We are, son," said he. "But it's a trap where I hope that we can catch the other suckers, not where we'll be snagged. Keep your head up. There's still some music to be played and a little dancing to do, but I hope that we ain't going to be on the stage!"

He led down the valley until, behind them,

the noise of the dogs suddenly crowded upon their very heels, and the boy jerked his head about to stare back. Even the Dude reached for his rifle, with an ugly frown. But he shook his head, afterwards.

"It's the echoes," said he. "Don't worry none about that. But here's the place, and here's the time!"

They had come to a flat stretch of surface, where the rocks were almost as smooth and as polished as glass, the glare of the sun reflecting blindingly from the stone.

Then the Dude dismounted, and taking a small bottle from his pocket, from it he anointed the hoofs of the three horses, one by one. A pungent odor rose to the nostrils of the boy.

"If they come on fast enough," said the Dude, "they'll get a snootful of this stuff, and it'll throw 'em off of the scent. I dunno. I've seen it work before!"

Then he led the way off the rocks to the side of the ravine, where he entered what looked, at the distance, like the narrowest accidental crevice. It proved to be a cleft wide enough for a horseman to ride through, and inside was a glade upward toward the top of the cliff.

Along this they clambered to the flat of a projecting shoulder.

By this time, the ravine was filled with the

music of the dogs, and the Dude dismounted.

"We'll take a peek at the show," said he. "I've got an extra pair of glasses. Take these and use 'em."

He helped the boy from the saddle. Then they approached the side wall of the rocks gingerly, and looked over.

On the floor of the ravine, far below them, the boy saw a scattering of a dozen hounds, running astray, here and there, each seeming to strike off a new line for himself.

"They don't like the heat of the stones," explained the Dude, "with the scent dying on 'em. They gotta nearly burn their noses, damn 'em, to get any smell out of our trail, at all. They got enough boys to herd those dogs along, ain't they?"

Three men came cantering before the others, holding their horses at a steady lope behind the dogs, and after these came other sections of the hunt, three and four together, all strung out as men were sure to be in the course of a long ride such as this, which proved both horses and riders to the uttermost.

"There's Patterson, the fat pig," said the Dude, pointing to a man well up. "There's Patterson, may he rot! And there's old O'Reilly. Doggone me if it ain't a surprise to see old Reilly out on the trail again. He's got a head on his shoulders, the old man has, but he'll be mighty tired before he ever comes up with us. There's Steve Donelly. Steve is a fighting man, too. I never thought that Steve would ride on my trail, though. But you can't tell. When you pour enough money onto a man, it is pretty apt to wash the white from his skin. There's Bud Malone. I always liked Bud pretty well, but he's married. You never can tell what a man'll turn out like, after he's married!"

He shook his head.

"And there's old Sheriff Axon. Damn him! I'd rather have ten times all of the rest behind me than that old fox! Hey, kid. Look!"

The dogs had struck the flat, polished surface of the rocks. And, instantly, their heads went up, and a new note came into their baying, a sharp, bewildered note of pain.

CHAPTER 39

The boy watched with a hungry interest, and he saw hound after hound jerk its head into the air and then yip with pain. Some of them shook their heads and sneezed to get the fumes out, and some of them ran in widening circles to get the scent which they had lost. Only the oldest hound of the lot failed to get to the place. It wasn't its own fault that it missed the spot. It was the oldest and the feeblest of the pack, and its legs were straining and trembling under the labor which it was calling upon them to perform, but now, as it came laboring toward the rest of the leaders, old Sheriff Axon dropped the noose of a rope over its neck, and the next instant, he had the dog safely across the pommel of his saddle.

The Dude broke into a violent cursing. Never had the boy seen him in such a humor!

"The old four-ply skunk!" said the Dude. "He's doubling on me. He's working out my little puzzle for them. If I could get rid of him, I tell you, the rest of it would be pretty easy sailing. And why not? He can't always go on pulling in the chips. Sometime he's gotta pay for 'em!"

And he dragged his rifle forward as he spoke, and settled the butt into the hollow of his shoulder.

The boy looked about him dreamily. Beyond the ravine, the badlands to the north slashed and streaked the surface of the earth with a coat of many colors, and farthest north of all, the big blue mountains rolled up like smoke into the blue of the sky. It was a peaceful time, and a gentle place, if one looked beyond the ravine, except for half a dozen high spots which were circling in the sky above them.

Those were buzzards, and they had gathered here with their peculiar spirit of prophecy, no doubt. Would they swing lower, when the sheriff fell dead?

He looked down into the valley. The sheriff had not moved. He sat still in his saddle, and he was stroking the old dog, until it raised its nose to his face.

The boy turned to the Dude and saw the muzzle of the rifle wavering less and less, coming to the tenseness of a dead bead. At the base of the Dude's jaw a triangle of muscle heaped itself up until it made a point of white on the skin.

And at that critical moment, the boy touched the big man's arm. Harley turned on him an ugly face, with twitching lips and uncertain eyes.

"What in hell you want?" he asked brutally.

"Don't do it," said Alfred.

"Mind what you say!" said the Dude. "It ain't for my sake. It's for yours. He'll run you down as sure as that sun is shinin', and he'll run you down before that sun goes down. You know what I mean?"

The boy hesitated.

If those riders had actually been in motion upon his trail, no doubt he could not have resisted his fear, but he saw them stationary, or milling helplessly under the sun haze in the ravine; and it happened that the face of Sheriff Axon arose before his mind's eye with a wonderful clearness − the dust face, the uncertain, dusty eyes, the soft voice, unused to speech, and fumbling often for the simplest words. Often he was a man whom a child in the first grade could have pitied, and yet he was called a hero, the last of an old order, a man without fear. He, at that moment, seemed to see the sheriff in his father's old house, the shack − sitting with knees crossed, his eyes struggling with some simple problem of thought.

"I understand," said Alfred. "Don't shoot him, Dude, for God's sake."

"Then let's get out of this," said the Dude, "because he'll have that damn dog on our trail before twenty minutes are up. What makes you so soft on him? Did he give you a stick of candy once when you were a kid? That wouldn't be so long ago, at that!"

This came in a half contemptuous and half drawling tone, but the boy was accustomed, by this time, to his companion's sudden touches of brutality and callous scorn. Yet, when he glanced at the Dude, he saw in the eyes of the latter a curious expression of admiration.

He gave this little thought, for he was occupied by the problem of getting to his knees and crawling back through the rocks. When he was near the mare, he began to get up, but his knees developed odd tremblings and shakings, and he would hardly have succeeded, if it had not been that the Dude suddenly helped him with his mighty hands.

He was swung up until he could swing his leg easily over the saddle, and he settled into it with the slightest of shocks; yet that shock pushed exploring fingers of pain through his whole being.

Blinded and weak, he waited until the Dude

gave the word, and they rode on.

It was difficult country, this of the higher level. It was broken in all directions by the little dry gorges in which water ran only after the heaviest rain, and it required great skill to pick out a course along the water divides without dipping into one of the ruinous tangles of defiles where man and horse might labor half a day to get a mile in any direction. However, the Dude seemed able to pick out a course by instinct, and he went on without the slightest hesitation, keeping his horse at a gentle rack.

The black mare followed, but gentle as was her gait and sure as was her footing, she could not help but stumble once or twice among the loose rocks, and each of those stumbles threw great waves of darkness over the brain of the boy.

They were pushing on at this unhurrying pace, when, over the ridges behind them, they heard the mellow cry of the pack. The Dude looked bitterly at his companion and reined in his horse.

"We've gotta ride, now," said he. "Can you manage it?"

"I'll manage it," said the boy.

"What?"

Then Alfred realized that the words had made no sound. He had to force himself, and his voice was harsh to his own ear.

"I'll manage it," said he.

The Dude said no more, but turned his horse straight down a narrow draw, and he went with his mount slipping and sliding over the stone rubble to the bottom of the ravine.

The black mare followed. She, also, had to slip and slide as the first horse had done, and every time the shock threw the boy forward against the pommel, heavily. He had lost all grip in his legs; he was a loose sack, being jounced forward and back, and his vitals were crushed and broken in the process.

The ravine widened and the footing grew better, and at the same time the heavy cry of the pack entered at the upper end.

Dimness covered the eyes of the boy. Through that dimness the voice of the Dude broke in.

"Look here, kid. D'you see that stretch of trees?"

Obediently he rubbed his eyes, and by degrees he could see something more than his own agony — he could see the tender stretch of green, where trees grew, far before him.

"If we can make to that, I'll beat them yet," said the Dude fiercely. "Now, you keep your head up and follow me, will you?"

"Yes," said the boy, "I'll try."

Suddenly the black mare was galloping. Alfred's sight turned dark. She was carrying him into a region of pitchy blackness, in which he lurched up and down according as the ground rose or fell beneath her.

Then he felt himself toppling to the side. He righted himself with a mighty effort, only to spill towards the other side of the saddle.

After that, he knew that the mare was standing, and out of the darkness he heard the voice of the Dude, saying: "Alf! Damn you, sit up and ride, will you? Are you gunna quit on my hands, when I've got you this far?"

"I don't seem to have much left in me," said Alfred. "If you could tie me into the saddle, maybe –"

His voice trailed, and his thoughts left him and flew far off to where the yelling of the dogs hung in a weird music upon the air. Then he heard the Dude murmur: "My God, my God, he's gone. Hey! Alf!"

"Here, Dude," he said dreamily.

"Look at me, not at the damn sky, will you?"

"I don't seem able to find you, quite," said Alfred.

"Alf, here's the mouth of a canyon. Hold tight. Let the mare carry you in. Then slide off. You hear? Slide off in the shade! I swear to God, I'll come back for you, if only I can lead them away down the ravine after me. Alf – it's been a hard run. We gotta split here. You've done all that any man could of done. I never seen a braver or a straighter partner. But we gotta say goodbye now, I reckon! Alf, so long."

"Give me your hand, Dude," said the boy. "God bless you! You've stuck by me till I'm no good. So long. Ride like the devil and beat them off. Wait a minute. Here's the bit of money that's left to me. You take it. It'll not do me much good—"

His eyes cleared enough for him to see the face of the Dude and it was twisted and white with a pain greater than that of wounds.

"We still got a minute," said the Dude. "I don't want to ride on until they're close on my heels. Alf — suppose — I mean to say, suppose that you was to ride on such a trail — I mean that you was not to come to the end of a—"

"If I die?" said the boy. "Well, I'll die, Dude."

"You ain't going to die, but suppose that — well, if the worst come, and somebody said: 'What did the kid have to say?'—"

"Yes. I don't need to send messages to mother and father, and Rosamund. They know that I cared a good deal about them, I think. Except dad, perhaps. You might tell him that whatever I did, I did knowing it wasn't enough. He'll understand that! Tell him I know that I was a fool. But there's one other. You know Molly Loftus, Dude?"

"Molly Loftus?" said the Dude, in a changed voice.

"Ay, Molly. You know her — if you can manage to see her — tell her what I never did — that I loved her."

"You?" said the Dude in that new and terrible voice again. "You never told her?"

"Once I kissed her — that was all," said the boy. "But now I want her to know that I loved her. I guess that's about all. So long, Dude!"

There was no answer, but the hoofs of a horse rushed down the ravine floor, and the boy knew that he was alone.

He could see the opening of the mouth of the box canyon, and toward it he pointed the head of the black mare. The music of the pack was thundering and booming cheerfully down the bigger ravine.

The mare stopped. He put out his hand and found a rough wall of rock. Propping himself against this, he tried to climb down, but all strength now melted from him, and he pitched sideways to the ground.

CHAPTER 40

On a rocky point which jutted over the ravine, there was a little shack, or rather, the remnant of a shack, leaning back against the face of the rocky wall. In this shack, Sheriff Axon took shelter, because the night was filled with windy gusts of rain which rattled like stones against the thin, sun-warped boards; and when the rain was not beating around him, the wind could be heard howling between the jaws of the ravine.

Inside his shelter, the sheriff, like an old campaigner, made himself comfortable as well as he could. In those cramped quarters he had donned his slicker to keep off the rain that sluiced through the cracks in the roof, now and again, and he gave his serious attention to the little fire which burned, filled the place with smoke, giving off little heat, but enough to bring the coffee pot towards a simmer.

He hummed as he tended this fire, and cherished it with twigs. And now and again he held out a piece of stale bread and his horse, blinking from the smoke, accepted the bread with a scornful toss of its head. It was an old and ratty mustang; but the sheriff tended to it as though he were an Arab chief, and this the swiftest of his mares.

"Hey, Axon," said a voice at the entrance to his shack.

"Hello," said the sheriff.

"Here's somebody come to see you."

"Bring 'em in."

The other stepped a little closer.

"It's old man Naylor," he gasped, "and they's a girl with him, too!"

The sheriff turned his head.

"Girl?" said he. "Naylor?"

He looked away at the fire.

"Damn!" said the sheriff through his teeth. Then he added: "All right. Bring 'em in."

He was squatting on his heels, and he rose to his feet as Naylor came in; behind Naylor, he made out a strained face and bright eyes, like the eyes of an animal, seen in the dark.

"Hello, Naylor," said the sheriff. "Hello, Molly. Doggone me if you ain't picked out a funny kind of a night for this here ride across the hills. Kind of a wet night, I'd say. Set down, will you? There's a stone for you, Naylor. Here's a board you can set on, Molly.

How's your pa? I ain't seen him for months. I hear that you're sure enough gunna start in building the dam again! I hear that you've even let out the contract?"

"Yes," said Naylor.

He looked around him cheerfully.

"You're fixed pretty comfortable here," said he.

"Why, I ain't so bad," said the sheriff.

But he glanced nervously around over either shoulder, almost as though he expected that enemies might be behind him, or at least as though he wanted desperately to get away.

"I reckon that down there in the ravine things wouldn't be so comfortable for a gent lying out without no protection. And my boy's down there – wounded, they tell me?"

The sheriff grew pale and his face twisted.

"This here is a sad thing to have to talk about, Naylor," said he in protest.

Naylor held up his hand.

"I ain't here to beg," said he. "I'm here as a law abidin' citizen that's come to talk over a matter of law with his sheriff. I guess that's sound and right?"

"You got a right to talk to me," said the sheriff hoarsely.

He looked desperately at Naylor.

"But what good'll come of it, I dunno. And

then, here's Molly. What brung you, Molly? What brung you?"

Said Naylor hastily: "I couldn't keep her back at home. She was sort of afraid, I reckon, that I'd be lonely, ridin' out here all alone. So Molly, she come along. She's a great comfort, is Molly!"

The sheriff disregarded this explanation, and he said again to the girl, fiercely: "What brung you here, I'd like to know?"

To this, Molly attempted to return a reply, but when she would have spoken, her lips trembled, and all at once tears were running down her face. She let the tears fall, and looked through them with a misty-bright sorrow at the sheriff.

Sheriff Axon gave his fire a poke that almost put it out.

"Damn!" said he again, and as if in explanation, he added: "Rain drippin' on the fire — can't get that damn coffee to boilin'. Excuse me, Molly, the way that I cuss. Seems like I've lost most of my nacheral decent words, from livin' so long with that ornery mustang, yonder!"

The mustang flattened its ears in pretended hate, and the sheriff shook his fist at it in pretended fury.

"It ain't no Sunday-school influence, that mustang ain't," said the sheriff. "Well, Naylor,

I hope that you'll get on with the dam pretty good. I'd like to lay my hand on him that blowed the dam in the first place, and I got an idea that I'm gunna bring somebody to time for it, one of these days."

"You mean Montana Charlie?" asked Naylor.

The girl started. But the sheriff was fairly agape.

"Him? What made you think that I was after him?"

"You are, ain't you?"

"The treacherous sneakin' hound! What could of made him want to do it?" asked the sheriff. "Him your friend! Boilin' oil would be too dog-gone easy a death for a skunk like him!"

"You want to know what made him do it?" asked Naylor.

"Ay, I'd like to know. Downright meanness, I'd say."

"I told him to," said Naylor.

"You – told – him to?"

The sheriff sat back on his heels. Then hurriedly he made a cigarette.

"Go right on," said he.

"Sounds queer to you, don't it?" said Naylor. "Well, I'll tell you what. When I seen my wife and girl and boy come back from the East, and when I seen how they was spendin' money, and what the spendin' of money was doin' to them, it fair sickened me, sheriff. They wasn't my kind of folks, any more. They was all set on bein' fashionable. And I says to myself that the trouble was caused by the dam, that had made me rich. And so I thought that I'd undo what I'd done. And I did. I sent Montana Charlie up to blow the dam. First he telephoned a warning down the valley to the town. That's how you traced him, I reckon?"

"It is," said the sheriff, bursting with interest.

"And then he touched off the powder. I'd showed him the keystones to blow, and he done it, and there you are."

"You wiped the valley out!" said the sheriff, passing his hand across his forehead.

"I wiped it out," said the other. "What was it to me, compared with the family? Nothin', sheriff, nothin'."

"Ay," muttered the sheriff, "family is a thing that I don't know."

"Mind you," said Naylor, "I wasn't bad busted. I had made a lot from the valley, and from selling out land in the town. I had made a lot and I hadn't kept all of my eggs in one basket. And when the dam busted, I could start right in to build it again."

"Which you've done," said the sheriff.

"But only after I let the family think that I

359

was busted flat. Ma has been workin' in the kitchen again. Rosie has pitched in fine. And this here Alf, of mine. Well—"

He paused. The sheriff frowned at the fire.

"I'll tell you about Alf," said the father. "I told him that I had to have fifty thousand dollars. He swore that he'd go and get it. He did!"

He took a brown paper packet from his pocket and laid it on the sheriff's knee.

"This here is stolen money," said Naylor.

The sweat rolled down on the forehead of the sheriff.

"I knew where he'd got it," said the father. "Though I didn't let on. I didn't know that he was that kind of a hoss, Axon. One that would jump the moon, if you put him at it! But he turned out all made of fire. I struck the match into a light. And he started a fire. Maybe you sort of understand?"

The sheriff continued to look straight down at the fire.

At this, the girl started up suddenly, but Naylor pushed her back and kept her silent with a gesture.

"I understand," said Naylor gently, "that you're pretty upset because the Dude got away!"

"The low sneak," said the sheriff fiercely, taking out his emotion upon an oblique topic, "the low sneak, he went off and saved his hide, and he let his partner lie and rot behind him — oh, damn such a man, I say!"

"Well," said Naylor, "you'll have Alf. That'll be something, eh? I would only ask that maybe Patterson would be glad not to prosecute if he got back his money. I'll pay it all back. This is part. I'll pay him back all of the rest. Cash down. And a bonus, if he wants it — for his loss of time, and his hurt feelin's — I take it that nobody's got nothin' agin Alf except Patterson?"

The sheriff drew in his breath.

"Naylor," he said, "there ain't no malice in me. But law is law, God help my soul! I've swore an oath which I never have broke it. I've held to the law till the coat rotted on my back in the rain, and burned on my back in the sun. I've rode the high trails and the low. Cold wind and hot wind, they never have turned me back. I'm gettin' old. My joints creak. But I won't be turned, and I won't be bribed, not by money, nor by the love of a woman, nor by a father's love! Them things that I see, I tell you plain about them. All the light that I've got is used on this job. Naylor, that's all I can say."

Said Naylor: "I reckon it is, sheriff."

There was a wild cry from Molly Loftus, but Naylor suppressed it my main force, laying his hand over her mouth. She began to weep, stifling the sobs as she heard Naylor ask again:

"He's wounded, sheriff?"

"He is," said the sheriff, his white face toward the fire.

"Might I ask, is he hurt bad?"

"He is," said the sheriff. "He is hurt right bad."

"Well," said Naylor. "I'll be getting along. Appears like clearing, over to the north. So long, Axon."

"So long," said the sheriff.

The two stepped from the shack, and instantly the roar of the rain cut away the sound of the girl's weeping, though the sheriff remained staring with haunted eyes, like one who still listened.

CHAPTER 41

The sheriff stepped to the door of the shack and, pushing it open, he looked out on the night. Lightning, at that moment, sprang across the sky out of the deep billows of the chaos of the clouds; even the dark maw of the ravine was partly lighted by this flash, and he saw the dripping jaws of the cliffs. It was very cold. The rain stung his face, even the backs of his hands, and the wind went by with a howl.

He wanted to turn his back upon this, but being a brave man with a conscience, he made himself remain there in the doorway while his thoughts went down to the bottom of the ravine. Somewhere in that canyon, in one of the boxes on either side of it, was young Alfred Naylor; and his own tried men rode up and down, keeping watch and ward. They kept the ravine corked, as it were. In the morning, he would go down and open the bottle!

And as the rain cut at his face, he thought

of how it must cut at the wound of the boy, and his heart shrank with pain. But the law was a dreadful machine, of which he was the hand of iron, and he would go on with his duty.

He turned back into the shack.

It seemed to him at first merely an upward leaping of the shadow cast by his mustang. Then he made out the tall form of a man, gun in hand.

"Why, hullo, Dude," said the sheriff.

"Hullo," said the Dude.

He lived up to his nickname even at this moment. His throat was wrapped in glimmering blue silk, with a diamond pin thrust into it, holding it in place. His boots were neat. The spoon-handle curve of his long spurs was a glint of gold, and the silver conchos glittered down his trouser seams.

His shoulders were black with rain.

"Kind of a wet night," said the sheriff.

"Never seen it blow up much harder, around these parts," said the Dude, with equal calm.

"There's the coffee, boilin' at last," said the sheriff.

He rescued the pot from the fire.

"Have a cup?" he asked.

The Dude paused a half instant.

"I suppose I might as well put this up?" said he.

The sheriff looked at the gun and, slowly, up to the handsome face of the outlaw.

"I suppose that you might as well," said he.

Straightway the gun disappeared into the clothes of Dude Harley.

"I'd sure appreciate a drink of coffee," said he.

The sheriff went to the door and thrust the rusty bolt home, securely locking it.

Then he poured out two tin cups full of coffee and they sat down to it.

"You done some good ridin' today," he said by way of compliment.

"Thanks," said the Dude. "So did you!"

They smiled faintly at each other, these old enemies.

"By way of that," said the sheriff, "when you was lyin' up there in the rocks, wasn't you tempted to take a crack at me, Dude? I mean, you must of been lyin' there, when the dogs was runnin' wild on that stuff you left behind?"

The Dude sipped his coffee and blinked at the heat that scalded his throat.

"We was up there, all right. The kid wouldn't let me shoot," he added.

"Damn!" grunted the sheriff. "Hot, this coffee," he explained.

But the Dude knew that the explanation was only a ruse.

"Where was the kid nicked?" said the sheriff.

"Him?" said the Dude absently. "Oh, he was cracked along the head, and shot through the body."

The sheriff raised his head, stiffly.

"When did he get it through the body?" he snapped.

"Right in the beginning. When he left Marlowe's house."

The sheriff hastily drank more coffee.

"And then — he kept on riding?"

"He kept on riding," said the Dude.

They became silent, watching the flicker of the fire, which the sheriff began to feed, breaking twigs very small, and cursing the smoke which the wet fuel sent up into his eyes.

"Well?" said the sheriff.

"I was thinkin' things over," said the Dude. "I dunno what there is against the kid, except what Patterson would charge him with. Those he plugged in Patterson's place, well, they needed the plugging. They started to mob him, eh?"

The sheriff canted his head to one side and frowned.

"When you come to think about it, that's right," said he. "The sneakin' rats!" he went on. "I almost wish that he'd burned the place down on 'em!"

"Speakin' of Patterson," said the Dude, "I've

got some of his money here. It's fifty-eight thousand dollars shy. But here's the rest."

He handed a wallet to the sheriff. And the latter laid it on top of the package of brown paper.

"I've got friends, and I can raise extra money," said the Dude, "and give me a little time, and I'll get the whole fifty thousand to Patterson. Fifty-eight thousand, I mean."

"It's all here," said the sheriff. "Marlowe had eight thousand on him that he didn't seem to know how to explain!"

He grinned, with fierceness in that smile. "Another fine kind of a man, that Marlowe."

He spat at the fire, and scowled.

"Well," said the Dude, "what about it?"

"You mean what about turning the kid loose, because all of the money is back? That would buy off Patterson, but it won't buy off the law," said the sheriff.

"You're the law," suggested the Dude, softly.

"I suppose that I am, partly."

"You couldn't see it my way, sheriff?"

"I couldn't see it your way! Have some more coffee?"

"Thanks."

The cups were refilled.

"The kid rode all that way, plugged through the side!" said Axon, dreamily.

"He done that."

"He's game," said the sheriff.

"I never seen none gamer," said the Dude.

Suddenly Axon broke in: "You used to be sweet on a girl by name of Molly Loftus."

"I was," said the Dude.

He made a cigarette and began to smoke; but though the sheriff did not look up, he knew that the face of the Dude had become pale.

"Well," said the sheriff, "I suppose you know—"

"She likes the kid better than she does me. That's not his fault," said the Dude.

"No, it ain't. Well, Dude, I can't take that money, if you want to pay it for him."

"It ain't enough?"

"Money never would bribe me," said the sheriff.

"I've got a higher price to offer you," said the Dude.

"You have?"

"I have."

"Go on, then. I'm sort of interested."

"What did you want the most in that chase? The kid, or me?"

The sheriff smiled.

"You could guess the answer to that," said he.

"I could guess it," agreed the Dude. "Now, I'll tell you what. You've got a pair of handcuffs there in your pocket, I guess?"

"I have."

The Dude held out his big wrists, close together.

And, in silence, the sheriff stared at him, and the Dude looked grimly down at his hands.

"You'd never get loose, this time, Dude."

"I know it," said the Dude.

"They'd put ten men to watching of you."

"I know it," said the Dude.

"It'd be life for you, all right."

"I know it," said the Dude.

"Maybe hanging?"

"Maybe hanging."

"What in hell do you owe the kid?" asked the sheriff, in a passion.

The Dude raised his head, dropping his hands upon his knees, still with them close together, as though they already were manacled.

"I've rode my share of the range," said he.

"Sure you have," said the sheriff.

"And seen my share of gents, black, yaller and white."

"I suppose that you have," said the sheriff.

"You see the real color of the skin, when you live my life," went on the Dude.

"I suppose," admitted Axon, "that your kind of life washes a gent's skin pretty hard. It'd bring out a yaller streak, for instance."

"It sure would."

He paused, considering.

"The kid is white," said the Dude at last.

"There's lots of other white men," argued the sheriff.

"He's young. But he never made no breaks," explained the Dude. "He was game all the way through, I mean to say. And straight."

"The world's full of pretty straight men," said the sheriff.

The Dude shook his head.

"He's my partner, Axon," he said.

To this, Axon made no reply, but rose suddenly and walked back and forth through the little shack a time or two.

Then he said abruptly: "Well, get the hell out of this."

The Dude stood up in turn. At the door he paused.

"Do I leave the money?" he asked.

"I s'pose that you do!" snapped Axon. "So long."

"So long, Axon."

Suddenly they faced each other, and their hands gripped hard, and an electric, burning current of understanding leaped from man to man; and if there had been at that moment some divine judgment on the two, it would have been hard to say whether the magnificent Dude or the little, withered, mouse-eaten sheriff were the greater of the pair.

The next moment the door opened; a burst of wind and rain flung into the face of the sheriff. The fire went out under the impact of the torrent of wet and air; and the sheriff was left alone in the dark.

CHAPTER 42

The explanation seemed perfectly simple to everyone.

In the first pale light of the dawn, while the wind still blew the rain in shrieking gusts across the heavens, there was an alarm at the mouth of the valley. Sheriff Axon, himself on duty there, sent word flying back that the Dude himself had been detected, attempting to sneak into the ravine to the help of his companion, and all men were called away in the pursuit.

They came, obediently. After all, there was no great interest in pursuing and taking Alfred Naylor. It was the famous Dude Harley they wanted, and they rode like mad for three historic days, changing horses repeatedly, but harvesting nothing but the wind, in their efforts, at last.

In the meantime, a small party had slipped into the valley and found young Alfred Naylor, senseless, drenched with rain, the black mare standing over him as though she were trying to shield him from the falling of the rain.

Joe Naylor and old Loftus and Montana Charlie carried him off on a stretcher they had brought for him, and in the Loftus house they concealed him, where Molly Loftus and Rosamund Naylor nursed him through the grim days that followed.

The whisper escaped and ran about the countryside.

But who would interfere?

Patterson no longer offered any rewards. He even let it be known that he did not consider that young Alfred Naylor could have had a hand in the robbery. Marlowe himself had left the country, fleeing far and fast, as though he expected that ghosts might ride the wind behind him. And as for the flight of the boy in company of the Dude — well, that was another matter that did not concern Patterson.

He had his money back!

The sheriff won a good deal of reputation, also. For it was felt that having pressed the criminals so hard that he had recovered the huge spoils, he deserved immense credit.

The winter came. Snow piled on the branches of the trees, and Alfred Naylor, looking out and up through the small window of his room, could see the alternate layers of white and dark. As he grew stronger, his nerves steadied, his brain cleared.

At last came a day when he could go freely to his home. All charges against him had dropped. The sheriff in person had let it be known that he was not interested, any longer, in the case of Alfred Naylor. And the boy went out, leaning on the arm of his father and supported on the other side by Montana Charlie.

They helped him onto the back of the black mare, and she whinnied and danced a little to show her delight, and then the procession started up through the trees, and crossed the hills, and came suddenly into the sunshine and warmth of the valley.

He looked down the valley, and there he saw an intricate tracery of newly made irrigation ditches and checks for flooding the land. He looked up the valley, and there he saw the gigantic face of the dam, which rose higher than ever before, and shining, with the light of the sun full upon it.

"You've done it all again, dad!" he cried, delighted.

"Well," said his father, "real estate is boomin' in town, again. So they say!"

He added: "But it ain't all my doings, old son! There's others that of helped — ma and

Rosie, pitchin' in and workin' in the house — and—"

He looked with meaning at his son, and Alfred crimsoned to the very eyes with joy and with pride.

He could not know the truth. No syllable ever had reached his ears of the return of all of the money to Patterson. And as he looked toward the dam and understood what it meant, humility greater than pride took hold on him. Instinctively he touched the healing wound in his side.

"It's worth everything," said he, "to work together."

"Ay, to be partners," said his father.

Then, as the boy did not immediately answer, he went on: "Or does only Dude Harley rate that high with you, Alf?"

"The good old Dude!" said the boy softly. "He's never come back!"

EPILOGUE

But the Dude did come back.

It was on the evening of that day when Alfred Naylor married Molly Loftus.

The great white house on the hill opened its arms. It did not receive a fashionable throng, but merchants and farmers from the town came out, and hunters and trappers from the woods and the mountains, and spurs jingled, and loud, hearty voices boomed through the halls of the house, and Mrs. Naylor moved through the throng with a blissful face.

Her husband found a moment to say to her:

"It ain't like your New York receptions, ma, I'm afraid."

She answered, unconscious of the thrust: "They're my people, Joe, God bless them; but it took pain and sorrow to show me the truth!"

In the midst of all this rejoicing, a whisper and then a murmur ran through the house.

Sheriff Axon suddenly remembered that he had business in town, and barely waited to wish the newly married couple good luck. The deputy sheriff remembered a similar errand. And the marshal in equal haste saddled and rode furiously away.

When they were gone to the last man, the front door opened, and the hushed crowd saw a tall, handsome fellow dressed like a very dandy of the range, jingling with silver ornaments as he stepped through the doorway. There, holding his head high, he glanced quickly over the faces, until he made sure that all was safe.

"Dude!" cried the voice of Alfred Naylor.

And a lane opened suddenly. The bride and the wedding were forgotten. There by the door their hands gripped, and they looked keenly on one another.

There was in the assemblage a newcomer to the town, a chance guest at the wedding, and he said to a lofty, grizzled trapper:

"But that's the notorious Harley, isn't it? Why isn't he apprehended? Isn't there a price on his head?"

"Son," said the trapper slowly, "money couldn't buy him − in this house."

"I don't understand!" said the tenderfoot.

"You wouldn't," said the trapper; "but him and the kid are partners. It takes a while to understand that word; some never do!"

THORNDIKE PRESS HOPES you have enjoyed this Large Print book. All our Large Print titles are designed for the easiest reading, and all our books are made to last. Other Thorndike Press Large Print books are available at your library, through selected bookstores, or directly from the publisher. For more information about current and upcoming titles, please call us, toll free, at 1-800-223-6121, or mail your name and address to:

THORNDIKE PRESS
P. O. BOX 159
THORNDIKE, MAINE 04986

There is no obligation, of course.